THE WARNING—

Kim was used to the sprinkling of personal messages that occasionally cropped up onscreen. Some were useful suggestions for stories, some annoying, but none were worth worrying about. Not until now. Now she stared at a message that was different from all the rest. A message that sent a chill down her spine as it blinked at her on the screen.

TELL YOUR HUSBAND TO LEAVE US ALONE. TELL YOUR HUSBAND TO LEAVE US ALONE. TELL YOUR HUSBAND TO LEAVE US ALONE. WE KNOW WHERE YOU ARE. WE KNOW WHERE YOU ARE. WE KNOW WHERE YOU ARE. WE CAN KILL YOU. WE CAN KILL YOU. WE CAN KILL YOU.

Kim took one last look at the words, marked them, and hit the delete key.

"Delete text?" the computer inquired. "Y or N?"

Kim touched "Y." The words disappeared but the fear remained. Who had sent the message? The most likely answer was Havlik's killer or killers, but that didn't make much sense, since Rex wasn't anywhere near to discovering their identities. Or was he? Was he closer to the truth than either of them had imagined?

D1413441

MARS PRIME

William C. Dietz

A ROC BOOK

ROC
Published by the Penguin Group
Penguin Books USA Inc., 375 Hudson Street,
New York, New York 10014, U.S.A.
Penguin Books Ltd, 27 Wrights Lane,
London W8 5TZ, England
Penguin Books Australia Ltd, Ringwood,
Victoria, Australia
Penguin Books Canada Ltd, 10 Alcorn Avenue,
Toronto, Ontario, Canada M4V 3B2
Penguin Books (N.Z.) Ltd, 182-190 Wairau Road,
Auckland 10, New Zealand

Penguin Books Ltd, Registered Offices:
Harmondsworth, Middlesex, England

First published by Roc, an imprint of New American Library,
a division of Penguin Books USA Inc.

First Printing, November, 1992
10 9 8 7 6 5 4 3 2 1

This one is for Joe Elder
in appreciation for his friendship,
sage advice, and limitless patience.

chapter one

The planet Earth hung against the blackness of space like a blue-white gem, far too distant for her flaws to show, looking much as she had for the last million years.

Only the closest of inspections would reveal the fact that the atmosphere was full of carbon dioxide, chlorofluorocarbons, and halons, that the average sea level was six feet higher than it had been twenty years before, that the big-brained two-legged omnivores who had dragged themselves out of the mud and up to the very top of the food chain had reproduced themselves to the very brink of extinction and were trying to run.

Their means of escape, the first of many to come, was a ship called *Outward Bound*.

She was shaped like a globe and made an ominous black silhouette as she drifted across the face of the planet below. Solar arrays grew like warts on the surface of her skin, radio antennas pointed accusingly outward, and observatories bulged like boils waiting to burst.

Not a single dollar, pound, franc, ruble or yen had been spent on the way that she looked. Every section, unit, component, part, wire, weld and rivet had at least one function, and sometimes more. Taken together those functions had a purpose, and the purpose was to reach Mars, and to do so as quickly and efficiently as possible.

And the same could be said of her multi-national crew. The core team had undergone years of training, passed endless batteries of tests, and proved themselves over and over again. The rest were semi-skilled filler, not unlike the third sons, convicts, misfits, and adventurers that have always populated human frontiers.

But with three thousand people aboard there were bound to be anomalies, people who seemed normal but were as flawed as the planet they came from.

One such individual paused inside a hatch, waited for a ship-suited com tech to pull her way past, and pushed off. And, due to the fact that this particular person had more than a thousand hours of zero-G experience, the move was graceful.

The crew member found a handhold, checked to make sure that no one was watching, and headed "up-ship."

The concepts of "up" and "down" don't mean much in a zero-G environment, but some idiot had decided that "up-ship" meant counter-clockwise, and "down-ship" meant clockwise. Other idiots had gone along with the idea and it had stuck.

Still another convention called for up-ship traffic to hug the overhead . . . while down-ship traffic cruised the surface of the deck.

Like everything else on the *Outward Bound* the corridor was extremely utilitarian. Recessed handholds appeared at regular three-foot intervals. Multicolored numbers, letters, arrows, and pictographs came and went. Gray conduit ran along the outside bulkhead, disappeared into padded junction boxes, and reappeared a few feet further on. Fiber-optic cables squirmed along beneath the deck gratings, turning here and there to link various parts of the ship together or mated within the privacy of mysterious black boxes. Rectangles of light arrived at regular twelve-foot intervals, rippled the length of the crew person's body, and vanished behind the curvature of the hull.

There were sounds too, like the incessant whisper of the air passing through miles of duct work, the never-ending announcements on the PA system, and the hollow booming noise that no one had been able to figure out.

But none of this registered on the person's mind because it was filled with the babble of many voices. There was Susy the conciliator, still searching for some sort of compromise, Frank the child, unsure of what to do, Norma the cynic, questioning the decision, Morey the prankster, making fun of Frank, and Kathy the observer, aloof as always, but watching from a distance.

But one voice dominated all the rest. It belonged to the newest member of the group, an entity who called himself "Otis the protector," and was intent on action.

"We have no choice. He suspects that we exist. That amounts to a threat. We must kill him."

"But that would be murder!" Susy wailed. "And murder is wrong!"

"Wrong, shmong," Norma said testily. "You say he knows. I say he doesn't."

"Auntie Norma could be right," Frank said cautiously.

"But what if she isn't?" Otis asked calmly. "What then?"

"We could be locked up," Frank replied, instantly frightened. "That would be awful!"

"And boring," Morey added. "Almost as boring as this conversation."

"What about a compromise?" Susy asked. "We

could make him look bad, get him fired. It worked on what's his name . . . Wilkens.''

"Get serious," Otis said sarcastically. "The ship is scheduled to break orbit in three hours. We don't have enough time to execute one of your chicken shit plans.''

There was silence for a moment as they thought it over. Morey was the first to speak. "All right, I'm in.''

"Me too," Frank added reluctantly. "Killing him scares me, but not killing him scares me even more.''

"Oh, all right," Susy said wearily. "I don't want to be the odd one out. Kathy, what about you?''

Kathy sounded distant. "Do what you think is best. I have a job to do.''

"I have a job to do . . .'' Norma mimicked, imitating Kathy's voice. "Big deal. Each and every one of you is an idiot.''

Susy started to say, "Norma didn't mean that . . .'' but Otis interrupted.

"Shut up. We agreed to take him out, I'm the one equipped to do the job, and the rest of you can take a break.''

There was some mumbling, especially from Frank and Norma, but it slowly died away. And, with the exception of Kathy's watchful presence, Otis was in control. It felt good to have the body all to himself. He gloried in his freedom, saw the "MEDICAL" sign strobe up ahead, and collected his thoughts.

Otis looked back over his shoulder, saw that the corridor was empty, and turned his eyes forward again. A lab tech pushed himself out into the corridor, glanced at his watch, and headed up-ship.

Odds were that the tech was on his way to the departure ceremony. Good. The departure ceremony was an important part of his plan. Everybody would at-

tend, except for Dr. Havlik and the other people un-
lucky enough to appear on the duty roster.

The medical section was spacious by shipboard
standards, consisting of a reception area, four examining rooms, two surgical suites, a diagnostic center,
pathology lab, supply section, and some tiny offices.

Otis felt a rush of adrenaline as he entered the reception area. It was empty of both people and furniture. Velcro patches indicated where patients could
hook themselves to the bulkheads, elastic bands kept
the magazines in their racks, and an unsecured clip
board drifted only inches below the overhead.

There was a podium-shaped console however, and
a velcro patch to hold the records tech in place, but
he or she was nowhere to be seen. A hand-lettered
sign had been taped to the front of the console. The
sign said, "Gone to ceremony, buzz for service," and
a crudely drawn arrow pointed down toward a button.

Otis could feel the blood pound in his head as he
reached for a back pocket, found the specially modi-
fied work gloves, and pulled them on.

This was it, the last opportunity to stop, to spare
the doctor's life. Otis grinned. Fat chance.

He pushed himself away from the entrance, used the
console for a rebound, and headed straight for the
double-wide hatch. It sensed his approach and opened
with a whisper.

Corridors branched right and left, and could have
been a problem, except that Otis had gone to the trouble of memorizing all of them ahead of time. With the
exception of some command and control stuff, anyone
with a terminal could pull up design schematics for
the entire ship, and the medical facility was far from
secret.

Otis turned right, pulled himself past the examining
rooms, the diagnostic center, and the pathology lab
until the cubicles appeared. The ship carried eight

doctors and each one had a small cubicle. Dr. Havlik's office would be the second on the right. The doctor would be floating free or velcroed to the wall. Chances were that he'd be jacked into his terminal or spooling through some medical text.

The first task was to immobilize him, the second was to silence him, and the third was to kill him. A relatively easy task given the advantage of surprise.

The sharp smell of antiseptics filled the air, supply cabinets lined the bulkheads, and stainless steel gleamed beneath the lights.

Otis was alert, ready for almost anything, except an attack from within.

Frank came boiling up out of nowhere, took control of the body, and shouted, ''NO! NO! NO!''

The words were incredibly loud within such a confined space. Otis knew Frank's history rather well, since it was nearly identical to his own, and understood what had taken place. The smell of antiseptics and the sight of medical equipment had triggered memories from Frank's childhood. Painful memories that made him wild with fear.

Otis responded with overwhelming force. He pushed Frank down into the darkness and ordered the others to keep him there. He wanted to speak with them, to emphasize the importance of keeping Frank under control, but didn't have the time.

Dr. Havlik had heard the noise. He stuck his head out of his office and looked around. He had bright brown eyes, thinning blond hair, and a sensuous mouth. He sounded annoyed. ''Oh, it's *you*. What's going on?''

It was now or never. Otis released the stanchion that Frank had grabbed, used it to brace his feet, and pushed off.

Havlik saw him coming, started to move back, but was far too slow.

Otis crossed the intervening space, wrapped both arms around the doctor, and snapped his head forward. It was Kathy's idea, something she'd been taught in the military, and it worked. Bone hit bone, Havlik's eyes lost focus, and a glob of saliva drifted out of his mouth. The doctor had bad breath and it made Susy gag. Momentum carried them into the cubicle.

Otis worked quickly. He knew Havlik would recover at any moment. Recover and fight back. Otis couldn't allow that. The doctor was built like a prize fighter and capable of putting up a real tussle.

Otis opened the cargo pocket on his right thigh, removed the roll of duct tape, and used it to immobilize his victim. Around and around it went, like the rope in old-fashioned cartoons, wrapping Havlik within a cocoon of tape. Arms, hands, and legs until he couldn't move and looked like a giant grub.

Otis tore what remained of the tape off and the doctor began to spin. His eyelids fluttered and his mouth made inarticulate sounds. Globules of saliva circled his head like planets orbiting a sun. Havlik was coming around.

The complete absence of gravity made the next part rather easy. Otis pushed the doctor into a corner, tacked him into place with the last of the tape, and looked for a way to anchor his feet to the deck. He cursed himself for failing to think of the problem earlier. A blow delivered by someone in free-fall carries no force. He looked around.

Ah, there they were, over by the hatch. A pair of bright pink magnetic clamps. They were of the standard U-shaped variety and were used for a number of tasks.

Otis retrieved the clamps, placed them in front of Havlik, and slid his feet under the padded arches.

The doctor was awake. He looked frightened—very,

very frightened—and his lips were dry. He ran his tongue along them. "So, I was right."

Otis brought his hands up. The gloves were black. Light winked off the pieces of metal that he had so painstakingly super-glued to each finger. "Yes, you were right."

The combination desk-computer terminal was right next to him. Otis reached over, grabbed hold of the standard head-jack, and pulled. Cable left the hidden reel with a soft whirring noise.

Otis brought the wire up, gave a jerk to lock it in place, and slid the jack into the side of Dr. Havlik's head. The psychiatrist's eyes grew larger.

Otis turned, looked for the auxiliary head-jack, and found it. He smiled as he pulled the jack up to his own head and plugged it in. Suddenly both minds were together, swirling in and around each other, different but the same. Now they could speak without words, share the same thoughts, feel the same feelings. Havlik was frightened. Otis fed on it.

"Call up your files. All of them."

Havlik swallowed. Afraid to obey and afraid not to. "No."

Otis clenched and unclenched his fists. "Do it or die."

Havlik paused, thinking it over, gauging his chances. "You won't hurt me?"

"No," Otis lied. "I won't hurt you."

Morey giggled.

Havlik sent a thought toward the ship's central computer. It heard and used a tiny fraction of its total capacity to handle the request. A menu of Havlik's files flooded into their combined minds.

"Are these all of your files?"

Havlik nodded mutely.

"There are no backups? No floppies? No handwritten notes?

Havlik shook his head.

"Destroy them."

Havlik paused, reluctant to give up countless hours worth of work, but forced himself to give the order.

The computer heard and sent a message back. "Destroy all Havlik files. Authority code AH 6-15-21. Please confirm."

Havlik swallowed. "Order confirmed."

The pause lasted two seconds.

"Files destroyed."

Otis pulled the jack from the side of his head, removed Havlik's as well, and allowed the reels to pull them in.

The connection was broken now, but Havlik had glimpsed something before it snapped and sought to confirm it. "You plan to kill me, don't you?"

Otis pulled at the gloves, enjoying the feel of leather against his skin, glorying in the sensation of power. "Yes, I plan to kill you."

Havlik believed him. The little beads of sweat on his forehead testified to that. Otis saw one swell slightly, break free from the doctor's skin, and float away.

"Don't do it. Let me help you, or if not me, then someone else."

Otis shook his head. "No. You would send us dirtside, lock us up, and kill us one by one. And there's something else . . ."

Havlik's voice cracked. "What?"

"This." The gloved lashed forward, hit Havlik's face with a satisfying thud, and left a bloody smear. The first blow was followed by many more. The beating went on, and on, until blood misted the air and Kathy intervened.

"Stop."

Otis knew better than to defy Kathy. He stopped.

Havlik's head hung limply forward. A rope of bloody saliva drifted sideways from his mouth.

"Check his pulse."

Otis pushed his hand through a curtain of blood. His fingers found the doctor's neck. He felt nothing.

"Take the gloves off."

Otis removed a glove, felt for a pulse, and found none.

"Put the glove back on."

Otis did as he was told.

"Leave the cubicle. Close the hatch."

Otis obeyed.

"Now, remove the jump suit."

Otis unzipped the front closure, worked his arms out of the sleeves, and pulled the suit off. He wore an exact duplicate underneath. The body did a complete sommersault in the process.

Kathy's voice was dispassionate. "Place the suit and gloves in an ejection chute."

Otis looked around, spied a chute at the far end of the corner, and shoved off. He sailed the length of the corridor, turned end for end in midair, and used a handhold to slow down. He felt his feet touch steel.

After that it was a simple matter to stuff the clothes into the chute, close the door, and press the button. Otis heard a thump as air, jump suit, and gloves were sucked into space. Two pieces of garbage had just been added to the hundreds of thousands that circled the planet already.

"Find a mirror. Check for blood. Hurry it up."

There was a unisex head just down the corridor. Otis pulled himself inside, rotated in front of the mirror, and there was blood on his face and in his hair. He used pre-moistened towelettes to wash it off, gathered them into a wad, and turned toward the door.

"Check your shoes."

Otis did and found that they were clean.

"Put the towelettes in the ejection chute and leave the area."

Otis did as he was told. And once the body was in the corridor, and safely headed up-ship, he allowed himself to be displaced by the others. He felt drained and temporarily at peace. A few weeks from now, a month at most, it would be necessary to kill again. Necessary to protect the body, to feel the freedom, to exercise the power. But that was then, and this was now. Otis fell asleep. Kathy took over and the body continued on its way.

chapter two

Air Force One made gentle contact with the *Outward Bound*'s number one lock, shuddered slightly as the maglocks cut in, and settled into place. The President of the United States heard voices as Secret Service agents gave orders and the crew pressurized the lock.

She looked around. Three members of her staff were present and all of them had found reasons to look elsewhere. They knew how nervous she was and were doing their best to make it easier.

The President gritted her teeth, hit the release button on her harness, and floated free of her chair.

She had spent twenty hours jacked into a zero-G simulation program, had foregone the last two meals, and still felt like throwing up. Not too surprising since the gravity-induced cues that normally told her vestibular system which way was up had all but disappeared. The President grabbed a convenient handhold and did her best to stay perfectly still.

Charlie Skuba was her chief of staff. Eternally handsome, neat, and unperturbed, his sky blue jump suit looked as though it had been spray-painted onto his body. He'd spent eighty hours in zero-G simulation and appeared completely at ease. His expression contained just the right amount of concern. Nothing superior, nothing patronizing, just a genuine interest in her well-being.

"Are you all right Madam President?"

"Hell, no," the President replied sourly, "but I'll make it. Keep it short that's all. In, out, and gone."

"Of course," Skuba replied sympathetically. "Both Fornos and Jopp have been warned."

"Good. Is everything ready?"

Skuba looked at a silver-haired Lt. Colonel, received a nod of assent, and smiled. "Yes, Madam President. Everything is ready."

The President nodded, pulled a mirror out of her pocket, and checked her makeup. Something less than perfect, but what the hell. She still looked better than a lot of women who were years younger. The President summoned up the smile that had won the hearts and minds of so many Americans. "All right then. Let's go."

C-deck occupied the middlemost slice of the sphere-shaped ship, and in spite of its vast size, was packed bulkhead to bulkhead with free-floating humanity. They were everywhere, drifting into each other and throwing up with almost monotonous regularity.

All of them had plastic bags, and most were able to make use of them, but some missed and left globules of vomit to drift through the air. And due to the crowded conditions, the normal "You barf, you clean it up," rule had been temporarily suspended. The smell was sickening.

Huge metal ribs arched down along the bulkheads. Nylon ropes connected them together and gave the colonists something to hook onto. Rows and rows of them were already in place. But the latecomers, along with those who couldn't seem to control their bodies, were still drifting around.

Blue-suited crew members yelled, cajoled, and

pushed the colonists into place. They wore light-weight backpack propulsion systems that allowed them to maneuver without having to push off from bulkheads or other solid surfaces.

Rex Corvan watched a burly power tech push a woman into place and gesture toward the yellow rope.

"Grab the rope! Hook on! Don't move!"

The woman nodded gratefully, hooked her utility belt to the rope, and proceeded to upchuck into her bag.

Corvan had taken up a position near the "B" Corridor Lock, or "BCL" in the parlance of the ship's crew, all of whom considered themselves a cut above the more than two thousand colonists. And, while some of the superiority was imagined, some of it was quite real. Many of them had been preparing for such a mission most of their lives.

Though technically part of the crew himself, Corvan's sympathies lay more with the colonists and their troubled stomachs. Though well past the upchucking stage himself, he remembered what it felt like and knew what they were going through.

"Audio check please."

Kim's voice was cool and professional inside his head, available because of his implants and some state-of-the-art electronics. It was nothing like the softer voice that had whispered things in his ear only hours before. Corvan grinned. Zero-G sex was anything but routine.

Kim entered his mind once more. Her thoughts were prim, proper, and tinged with pleasure.

"Keep your mind on business. I need an audio check."

"Yes, ma'am. One audio check coming up."

Corvan cleared his throat and spoke out loud. "This is an audio check. One . . . two . . . three . . . four . . . five . . ."

Corvan was something of a celebrity on Earth, and might have attracted some attention under normal circumstances, but most of the colonists were too ill to care who he was.

Kim was back. "Thanks. Security informs me that the President has entered the main lock and is headed our way. Let's take a look at the wide shot."

Corvan sent a thought to the robo cam and it took off. The device was cylindrical in shape with a set of skids under its belly and a high resolution zoom lens located in its nose. Although this robo cam looked similar to the units that Corvan had used on Earth, it was actually quite different.

It had a more powerful propulsion system for one thing, a modification made necessary by the red planet's thin atmosphere, and larger fuel tanks. The wings that had provided lift within Earth's thicker atmosphere were gone.

Not only that, but the new robo cam was equipped to function in a total vacuum if necessary, and had been equipped with a pair of small manipulator arms. The manipulator arms made it possible for the robo cam to lift and transport objects weighing up to ten pounds. A capability that Corvan hadn't asked for but the tech types had given him anyway.

The robo cam dodged a crew member and turned. The wide shot showed Corvan in the foreground, colonists to either side, and the BCL in the middle. Within a minute, two at the most, the President of the United States would step through the lock and into the picture.

In the meantime a small group of VIP's had gathered around the lock. Kim caught a glimpse of Dr. George Fornos, the World Peace Organization's point man and the mission's head cheese. He was a small man, whose Buddha-like composure hid a mind like a steel trap and a passionate desire to succeed.

And there, floating just beyond him, was the tall graceful figure of Air Force Colonel Mary Ann Jopp. If Fornos was fire, then she was ice, as cold as a winter day and just as friendly. She was the mission's executive officer and a lifelong member of the Exodus Society.

The World Peace Organization, aka the business establishment, had long opposed colonization and only recently come around. The Exodus Society, aka the people who wanted to turn everything upside down, favored colonization but didn't control enough resources to make it happen.

The result was an uneasy truce. A truce that kept Fornos and Jopp from going for each other's throats. Gossip had it that the two of them disagreed on everything, but Kim had seen nothing to support that.

Kim wished for a cigarette, remembered that smoking wasn't allowed, and popped a breath mint instead. She forced herself to the task at hand.

A three-dimensional representation of the robo cam's shot floated in Kim's mind. She checked it carefully. Definition was close to perfect. Much better than the video produced by Corvan's previous robo cam. It had been grainy compared to the high resolution eye cam that had been surgically implanted into his skull.

There were numerous computers and computer-driven devices at her command, but the Grass Valley Ultima sat at the very top of the electronic hierarchy. This was a newer model than the one that Dietrich had destroyed during the Matrix Man fiasco, but she liked it less. "Val," as her previous computer had been known, had been a personality, a co-worker, and a friend.

This computer, unnamed as yet, was too new to have an identity of its own. Still . . . it was cooperative enough, and when Kim asked for a video analysis, the displays appeared a fraction of a second later.

The displays were rectangular in shape and consisted of a light green grid, with a series of darker green lines zig-zagging across their surfaces. A single thought was sufficient to superimpose the two displays. They were almost identical. The audience would be unable to see a difference in quality as she cut back and forth between them.

She gave her husband a once-over, searching for the messy hair, unzipped pocket, or other flaw that might detract from his appearance.

Corvan was a big man, with brown hair, and a camera where his right eye should be. A camera that was wired directly to his brain and controlled by thought.

Kim knew that superconducting wires acted as transducers between the chemical and electronic actions of Corvan's brain, sending signals to the tiny biochip video recorder implanted at the base of his skull, where they were stored or transmitted live to her receiver.

His left eye was blue and, more than that, filled with intelligence. The kind of intelligence that likes to look under rocks, find the wriggly things that live there, and drag them kicking and screaming into the light. A characteristic that made her proud at times and angry at others. Kim felt there were enough problems in the world without uncovering more. Besides, there were other reporters out there. They could and should do their share.

A metal guard rested on Corvan's left shoulder. It mounted a six-inch antenna, a flat place for the robo cam to land, and battery packs front and back to hold the guard in place and balance each other out.

He wore a blue ship-suit with his name imprinted over the right-hand breast pocket, a utility belt, and a pair of the black high-top sneakers issued for shipboard use. He looked handsome in a rakish sort of way, and she liked that.

Kim smiled, thankful that her thoughts had been directed inwards and were inaccessible to her husband. His ego was sufficiently large already.

"Is everything okay?"

Corvan's question brought her back to the situation at hand. The displays vanished as the wide shot zoomed forward to fill her inner vision. "That's a roger. Stand by while I check the bird."

Thoughts flickered, electrons responded, and the Ultima delivered its response. "Comsat NN 2068 is in geosynchronous orbit over the United States. We have full redundancy via Comsat NN 2067. Both satellites report all systems green."

Kim didn't bother with the networks. Each and every one of them were taking the feed and waiting for the President to appear. All of them had requested permission to send their own man cams and all had been refused.

Neither Fornos nor Jopp wanted a bunch of reporter-operators running all over the place interviewing sick colonists. The funding for subsequent missions would depend on the success of this one, and the brass wanted everything to look perfect. Never mind the air leaks, the hydroponics problems, or the mysterious booming noise that no one could figure out. Those were minor problems that would be handled soon. Or so they said. No, the mission must be flawless, or at least seem that way.

And that's where Corvan came in. Due to the fact that Corvan had broken what came to be known as the Computer Coup story, and survived the resulting investigations, his credibility was legendary. If he said something viewers believed it, and the networks had no choice but to go along.

It was of course why Jopp and Fornos had hired him, why Kim was on a space ship bound for Mars, and why the two of them had this story entirely to themselves.

Kim sighed. It was too good to last. The suits thought her husband was bought and paid for. She knew better.

A female voice filled C-deck, passed through Corvan's hearing, and flooded Kim's mind. It came from the ship's PA system.

"Ladies and gentlemen, your attention please. The President of the United States has entered the BCL and will join us momentarily."

The murmur of conversation died away. The resulting silence was nearly complete, interrupted only by the sounds of sick colonists and the syrupy music that filled the PA system.

Corvan, secure in the knowledge that the networks had already introduced him, began his report. He addressed himself to the robo cam knowing that Kim would go to an establishing shot first.

"Welcome to C-deck of the spaceship *Outward Bound.* The President of the United States will appear any moment now. I think most of you will agree that this is a truly momentous occasion.

"Other ships have gone where this ship will go. And, if those who lead this mission have their way, others will certainly follow.

"But this is the *first* colony ship to depart Earth for another planet, and these are the *first* settlers to leave with no intention of coming back."

Kim saw BCL start to iris open and said so. "Here she comes."

Corvan turned in one smooth motion, knowing that Kim would cut his eye cam, careful to maintain a medium shot. Wide enough to make out what was going on, but close enough to see the President's face.

And an attractive face it was. Attractive enough to win a beauty pageant, lock up an anchor job with one of the networks, and win a seat on the Seattle city council. The first step on a ladder that led to the mayor's office, the Senate, and the White House, the last advancement being hurried along by her predecessor's assassination. An assassination that had gone undetected until Corvan and Kim discovered the existence of the Video Matrix Generator and a plot to take over the world.

But, while physical beauty might have helped the President achieve national office, the real reason for her success lay behind the big blue eyes. The President had an I.Q. of 136, an almost magical ability to change people's minds, and an indomitable will. Though little respected prior to her predecessor's death, she had blossomed since and earned wide-ranging respect.

Fornos, Jopp, and some other shipboard notables moved forward to shake hands with the President. Words were exchanged and they moved back again.

The same voice flooded the PA system once again. "Ladies and gentleman . . . the President of the United States!"

The colonists applauded, their stomachs momentarily forgotten, caught up in the importance of the moment.

The President pushed herself out of the lock, grabbed hold of the line rigged for her convenience, and did her best to stay vertical. "Vertical" being defined as the same relative position that her audience maintained. The bottom of her stomach tried to leapfrog her throat. She forced a smile.

The applause continued. Kim cut to the robo cam. Audiences all over the world saw the President and the multi-national crew all floating in zero-G. It was great stuff and would be replayed for weeks to come.

The President knew that and allowed her eyes to skim the audience. She made eye contact with a man, nodded, found a woman, nodded again, and kept on going. She knew that each one of them would feel touched, would remember the contact for the rest of their lives, would vote for her in the next election. Assuming they were American, assuming the ship made it to Mars, and assuming that they survived long enough to vote.

She waited for the applause to die down, and when it had, waited a little longer.

The silence built, focused attention on her, and added weight to the words that followed. She wore a wireless mike and it fed her words to the ship's PA system.

"Ladies and gentlemen, citizens of Earth, this is a momentous occasion. I come before you not as the president of a single nation, but as the representative of all your various countries, bringing with me their admiration for your courage, prayers for your success, and hopes for the future.

"Your presence here signals a new era of peace and cooperation on our planet. Although you come from many nations, and from many lands, you have but one goal: the peaceful colonization of Mars."

The President paused, felt her feet start to drift out from under her, and pulled upwards on the rope to force them down.

"I wish that our history was different. I wish that our ancestors had been wiser. I wish that our purpose was less urgent. How nice it would be if this mission was motivated by scientific curiosity rather than an urgent need for additional space and resources."

The President smiled wistfully. "But we *do* have a need for more space, and we *do* have a need for more resources. So like it or not this mission takes on added significance. The men and women of this ship are nothing less than pioneers. Blazing paths for the rest of us to follow . . . opening a frontier for us to settle . . . building a home for us among the stars."

It was good stuff, written by Charlie Skuba the day before and memorized by the President in transit. The applause was close to deafening.

The President had another paragraph or two, more material in much the same vein, but decided to drop it. "Know when to quit." That's what an old mentor had told her and it was good advice.

The President signaled a Secret Service agent with a glance, waved to the crowd, and used the rope to push herself off. She was slightly off target, but a surreptitious nudge from Skuba put her back on track, and the lock opened before her. Fornos, Jopp, and the other dignitaries closed in behind and she was lost to sight.

Corvan held the shot on his eye cam until the BCL had closed behind them, turned toward the still hovering robo cam, and knew Kim would cut wide.

"So there you have it. The President is making her way back to the main lock, where she will board *Air Force One* and return to Washington. In the meantime the men and women of *Outward Bound* have a lot of work to do. There is last minute cargo to stow, systems to check, and a multitude of problems to solve. Small things mostly, but necessary nonetheless, and made all the more so by the fact that departure is only hours away."

Kim used the robo cam's 20:1 zoom lens to go in tight. Her husband smiled. "As the *Outward Bound*'s Information Officer, it will be my responsibility to bring you regular reports on the mission's progress, up to and including completion of a domed city called 'Mars Prime.' Eight hundred men and women are already there, starting construction and preparing the way for the rest of us."

Kim readied the pre-produced three-dimensional graphic and gave certain directions. A map of the solar system appeared on billions of television sets. Earth and Mars were shown orbiting around the sun while slowly approaching each other. A delta labeled *Outward Bound* appeared near Earth and made its way outward. Corvan supplied the voice-over.

"As many of you know, Mars has a diameter roughly half that of Earth's, about forty-two hundred miles, and has an orbital period of six hundred and eighty-six days. The distance between Earth and Mars varies anywhere from forty-nine million to two hundred and thirty-five million miles depending on the time of year. That's why it's so important for *Outward Bound* to break orbit during the next few hours. By leaving now, the ship can take advantage of the shortened distance between the two planets, and trim months off the length of the journey."

Kim dissolved from the animation to a shot of Corvan. The reop looked her in the eye. "Mars is still a long ways off, though—so far away that it will take up to fifteen minutes for each one of my reports to reach you."

Corvan glanced around, saw the colonists being herded toward the locks, and started his close. "But regardless of how long it takes our reports to make the journey, we will look forward to sending them your way, and hearing back from you. This is Rex Corvan, Information Officer for the vessel *Outward Bound*, reporting live from Earth orbit." Corvan killed the outgoing signal and breathed a sigh of relief. Things had gone very smoothly. He sent a thought toward Kim. "That's a wrap. Coffee's on me. See you in the mess hall."

There was a pause, as if Kim's thoughts were somewhere else, followed by a grim message. "Sorry, Rex. Security has a murder on their hands. They want to see you right away."

chapter three

The medical section was completely sealed off by the time Corvan got there. Security types came and went. Some held hurried conversations, some carried boxes of equipment, and all looked grim. A woman with the look of a weight lifter drifted out to block his way. She wore a ship-suit, a combat harness, and a needle gun. If she recognized Corvan she gave no sign of it.

"The medical section is closed. Come back later."

"My name's Corvan. They sent for me."

Implants were expensive, and therefore rare, but like most of the *Outward Bound*'s crew members the woman had one. A wire ran from the radio on her belt to the jack in the right side of her head. It was a cosmetic model. A circle of tiny blue lights flashed on and off around it. The combination of radio and implant allowed the officer to communicate with the rest of her team via thought. Her eyes never left Corvan's. She nodded.

"Colonel Jopp wants to see you."

Corvan raised an eyebrow. The colonel was personally involved. Interesting.

He pushed against the bulkhead and sailed through the entranceway. There were two security people in the waiting room. One ran some sort of scanner over the walls while the other read a magazine. The one with the magazine looked up and nodded toward the double-wide hatch. "Go on in."

Corvan did as he was told, using the podium-styled console to launch himself in the right direction before rebounding off the hatchway and entering the corridor. Four people were clustered around a fifth. He wore a white ship-suit with a red cross embroidered over his left breast pocket. Tears drifted away from his eyes and a string of mucous hung sideways from his nose. A security officer handed him a Kleenex. It was second nature for Corvan to activate his implant and record what he heard.

". . . So I called for Dr. Henry and heard no answer. That's when I came down the corridor. And there he was, just like you saw him, beaten to death."

A security woman said something Corvan couldn't hear, gestured up corridor, and helped the technician toward the waiting room.

Corvan slid past the security people and into the office. Cops were universally weird. "Shoot this, don't shoot that." They made up the rules as they went along. That was one advantage of the eye cam. There was nothing on your shoulder to give you away. Not unless you toted the robo cam around all the time, and Corvan didn't. He had parted company with the device along the way, knowing that it was perfectly capable of returning to the com center all on its own.

The body was there all right, fastened to the bulkhead with silver utility tape, looking like a high-tech mummy. Someone had gone to a great deal of trouble to immobilize the doctor before killing him.

The reop glanced around, looking for a murder weapon, or other obvious evidence. There wasn't any.

Corvan used the computer console to pull himself down, tried to see the victim's face, but saw little more than reddish pulp. There was blood too, a cloud of it which had drifted away from the body and come to rest in a corner. Some of the smaller drops had already made the transition from liquid to solid. The rest would follow.

"Messy isn't it?" The voice was hard and flat. It came from behind him.

Corvan turned and found himself face-to-face with Colonel Mary Ann Jopp. He'd met her only once before and that had been by way of a rather brief interview. The air force officer hung motionless in the doorway as if suspended there by invisible strings. She was attractive in a thin-faced sort of way, with big green eyes, and hair so short that she was almost bald. She looked very military, very practical, and very cold. It added to her somewhat intimidating presence.

"Yeah," Corvan agreed. "Murder usually is. Who was he?"

"Dr. Henry Havlik, Mission Psychiatrist."

"Who killed him? A lover? A patient?"

Corvan saw her eyes narrow. They seemed to drill right through him.

"We're working on that."

Corvan nodded. "Okay, I'll get to work. Interview you, talk to security, the usual stuff."

"No," Jopp replied evenly, "you won't. You are the Mission Information Officer, and you'll do what *I* tell you. And I want this story killed."

Corvan felt a rock grow in his gut. He clenched and unclenched his fists. "You can forget that, Colonel. My job is to collect and distribute information. And I'll do it in whatever way that I see fit."

"Wrong again," Jopp said calmly. "Your job is to *control* the flow of information. Not hand it out whenever you happen to be in the mood. Now listen carefully. This ship is scheduled to break orbit less than three hours from now. A surface-based murder investigation might take weeks or even months to complete. And the longer it takes, the longer *we* have to travel, with all the risks attendant thereto. So from this moment on you will do everything in your power to keep the story within the hull of this ship. Do you understand?''

"I understand," Corvan replied tightly. "I understand that you're exceeding your authority and breaking the law! You have a murderer running loose on this ship and people have a right to know. So you can take your orders and shove them straight up your ass!''

Jopp's expression didn't change one iota. She simply looked at him, shook her head sadly, and moved away from the hatch. The security officers had been waiting. They came through the doors in pairs, bounced off the walls with the expertise of Olympic gymnasts, and hit Corvan as a group.

The reop struggled for a moment, tried some of the things the Special Forces had taught him, and discovered that they didn't work in zero-G. It took the security team no more than fifteen or twenty seconds to place restraints on his arms, hands, thighs, and ankles. After that it was a simple matter to tow him out into the corridor where Jopp was waiting. Her expression conveyed neither anger nor regret.

"You'll find that the *Outward Bound* has a well-equipped brig. Let me know when you're ready to do your job."

Corvan wanted to reply, wanted to tell Jopp what he thought of her, but someone slapped a piece of tape across his mouth. He was still trying to break free from the restraints when the security team took him out into the main corridor and headed down-ship.

Crew members and colonists alike hurried to get out of the way. Some looked concerned, but their frowns disappeared when one of the security officers smiled and pretended to drink from a bottle.

Corvan saw this and tried to protest, but his words

were blocked by the tape. Then it occurred to him. This was stupid. He could communicate with Kim via his implant. More than that, he could send her video and get the story out in spite of Jopp.

He activated his implants and waited for Kim to acknowledge his presence. A buzzing sound flooded the interface. Not the static that sometimes interfered with transmission, not some sort of noise from Kim's end, but the steady uninterrupted sound of electronic jamming. Jopp, or someone on her security team, had anticipated his move and taken steps to block it.

Corvan swore, renewed his attempts to break free from the restraints, and was dumped feet first into an access shaft.

Inertia carried him downward. A security officer steered him past some surprised looking colonists and out onto D-deck. It was a short trip from there to the *Outward Bound*'s state-of-the-art brig.

There were eight small cells, each scarcely larger than a standard telephone booth, lining both sides of the corridor. The doors were made of clear shatterproof plastic. The interiors were almost completely bare, except for the usual velcro patches and a blower-type stainless steel waste disposal unit. Corvan saw no sign of other prisoners and assumed there were none. Not too surprising at the very start of the voyage.

The bonds fell away at the touch of a black wand and were collected for reuse. The tape was ripped from his mouth and he was pushed into the nearest cell. The door slid shut with a solid thud. The security officers talked to each other for a moment or two then left the area.

Corvan tried the implant. Nothing. He forced himself to relax. There was nothing to do but listen to the hiss of incoming air and the echo of his own thoughts. Damn.

* * *

"Rex?"

Corvan's eyes flew open. "Is that you, Kim?"

He'd been asleep. The cell, the corridor, everything was the same. Everything but the interface. It was suddenly and miraculously open. Her thoughts flooded around his.

"Yes, it's me. Who else would bail you out?"

Corvan looked around his tiny cell. "I don't want to seem ungrateful or anything . . . but the fact is that I'm still here."

"Not for long," Kim answered confidently. "They'll turn you loose within the next ten minutes or so. I called to make sure that you wouldn't say or do anything stupid."

"I *didn't* 'say or do anything stupid,' " Corvan replied stubbornly. "I tried to do my job, that's all."

"That's a matter of opinion," Kim said evenly. "Do me a favor. Don't blow the opportunity to get out. Try compromise instead of confrontation. Or, spend the rest of the trip in the brig. The choice is up to you."

The interface disappeared with an angry snap. Kim was pissed. There was no doubt about that. Her pragmatism and his idealism had come into conflict before. And she'd been right sometimes. Was this one of them?

Wait a minute. What had she said? "The rest of the trip?" The ship had broken orbit. They were headed for Mars. Lock, stock, and murderer!

Corvan pounded on the plastic. "Hey! Let me out of here!"

The guard appeared as if by magic. She was slightly overweight and wore her hair in a top knot. She had bright red lips and fingernails to match. The door hissed open. She motioned him forwards.

"Out? Yes, sir, three bags full, sir. I hope you enjoyed your stay, sir. Now, if it's convenient for Your Royal Highness, we'll head for B-deck."

Corvan ignored her sarcasm. "B-deck? Why?"

The guard did her best to look surprised. "Why? So Your Highness can consult with the F-man. Why else?"

The F-man? She meant Fornos. Corvan frowned. First Jopp, now Fornos. What the heck was going on? Was it all part of some deal that Kim had negotiated on his behalf? There was no way to tell. His wife wasn't speaking to him. Not at the moment anyway.

The guard turned her back on him and pushed off. The message was clear: "I'm leaving, and if you're smart, you'll do the same."

Corvan gave a shrug, pushed off, and followed her rather sizeable rear-end up corridor. This trip was a good deal more pleasant than the last one had been. Some of the colonists had adjusted to the lack of gravity by now, and though somewhat clumsy, felt well enough to point at him and whisper to each other.

Corvan felt what he always did when people recognized him: pleasure mixed with annoyance, mixed with guilt. Like reops everywhere, Corvan had worked hard to build a reputation for credibility and the following that went with it. To do that, and feel annoyed when people recognized him, seemed more than a little stupid.

B-deck housed the ship's command and control center, administrative offices, computer spaces, and communications facilities. It was busy here, with lots of traffic flowing in both directions. The people had a sense of purpose. The ship was underway and there was work to do.

Colonists weren't allowed on this level unless accompanied by a crew member, so everyone was an expert of some kind and fully acclimated to zero-G.

The mission administrator's offices were huge by shipboard standards, at least twenty feet square, and featured a tiny reception area complete with live receptionist. He was Velcroed to the bulkhead and had a wall-mounted keyboard pulled in front of him. A wire connected his head-jack to the keyboard and hinted at a wealth of capabilities. He had black skin, a serious expression, and a British accent. His name tag read "W.K. Julu."

"Yes?"

The security officer seemed suddenly less sure of herself. "Prisoner Corvan to see Administrator Fornos."

The receptionist nodded toward the guard. "You may return to your duties. Officer Corvan, if you would be so kind as to wait a few minutes, Administrator Fornos will be right with you."

The guard wasted little time leaving the office and heading for more familiar territory. Corvan wished he could do the same.

The fact was that Fornos had authority verging on that enjoyed by 19th-century sea captains. While he couldn't eject Corvan from the main lock without a trial, he could impose any other punishment he wanted to, up to and including continued imprisonment. The ties with Earth and Earth law were broken now, and concepts like freedom of the press were just that: concepts. Something Kim had instinctively understood and Corvan had just started to assimilate.

What was the penalty for disobeying a direct order anyway? It had been quite severe in the Army. He'd meant to read all the rules and regulations but never quite got around to it.

"Administrator Fornos will see you now."

Corvan nodded his thanks, peeled himself off the velcro patch, and pushed his way toward a now open door. It closed behind him.

The first thing he saw was Fornos floating on his back looking up at what Corvan thought of as the ceiling or overhead. It was packed top-to-bottom and side-to-side with monitors, read-outs, extendable keyboards, and other pieces of gear too esoteric to be understood with a single glance. All were somewhat recessed to protect against collisions.

The administrator glanced his way. He had a small cherubic face, and it was immediately transformed by an almost beatific smile. Fornos had charm, there was no doubt about that, and Corvan felt himself smile in response.

"Corvan! Good of you to come. Sorry about your stay in the cooler. Terrible misunderstanding and all that. Your wife is charming, absolutely charming, and beautiful to boot. A little tall for the likes of me, but very attractive. Here—take a look at this." Fornos pointed to a color monitor.

Disarmed by the other man's friendliness, and silenced by the avalanche of words, Corvan pushed himself toward the overhead. Once there it was a simple matter to maneuver into position. The monitor had a shot of what was obviously Earth. Smaller now that the ship was underway but large enough to fill most of the screen.

"Say goodbye to her, Corvan—we'll be a lot older when, and if, we see her again."

The picture, plus the thought, brought a lump to Corvan's throat. Fornos was right. They were leaving Earth, and the reality of that brought a flood of emotions that he hadn't expected to feel. And while there was the possibility of two-way travel someday, it was extremely unlikely that he or anyone else in the crew would live to see it.

Fornos nodded as if privy to the other man's innermost thoughts. "Hard to believe isn't it? Well, that's where *you* come in. Seeing is believing, and your reports will go a long way toward building support for future missions, and this one for that matter."

The reop pushed his emotions into the background. He must be careful here. Fornos was a master psychologist. He had demonstrated that by the ease with which he had played on Corvan's emotions. Corvan chose his words with care.

"Yes, sir. And I look forward to providing those reports. But they won't mean much unless they're true. And the truth is that you have a murderer onboard. And not a 'get drunk and get into a fight' murderer, either. The person who killed Dr. Havlik picked the moment with care, brought tape to tie him up, and cleaned up afterwards. The crew and passengers aboard this ship have both a right and a need to know about information like that. More than that *will* know, because you can't control word of mouth, and someone on your security team will tell. The result will be rumor, exaggeration, and unnecessary fear."

The words had spilled out almost of their own accord and Corvan wanted to pull them back. He'd been too shrill, too insistent, and inadvertently confirmed whatever prejudices Fornos had. It would be a long trip in the brig.

There was a pause while the administrator blinked, smiled, and opened his mouth. His words were completely unexpected.

"I couldn't agree with you more. Truth is the foundation of good journalism and an important aspect of the democratic process. And your prediction has already come true. Rumors about Dr. Havlik's death have spread throughout the ship. Some are quite fanciful. Vampires have been mentioned, along with aliens, homicidal robots and satanic cults."

Corvan opened his mouth to say something, but shut it when he realized that Fornos had managed to preempt his ground. The man was good, very good indeed.

The administrator shook his head indulgently. "Don't hold it against Mary Ann. She means well but has a rather military turn of mind. Hut, two, three, and all that. No, throwing you in the hoosegow was the wrong thing to do, but grounded in the best of intentions.''

Fornos looked momentarily serious, like a school master confronting a naughty child, explaining the purpose behind a punishment.

''But Mary Ann was right about one thing. A surface-based investigation *would* have delayed our departure and threatened the success of the mission. It would have been nice if she had offered the possibility of compromise, and if you had been willing to listen, but such was not the case. Though well-intentioned, you are often impulsive, a fact that your psychological profile makes extremely clear.''

Corvan felt blood rush to his face. It had been a long time since someone had dressed him down and he didn't like it. Didn't like it and didn't have a word to say in response.

''So,'' Fornos continued, ''let's see what sort of arrangement you and I can come to. One that provides shipboard personnel with the information that they need and respects the political realities at the same time.''

The ensuing conversation went on for twenty or thirty minutes and ended in a clear-cut set of ground rules: Corvan could do pretty much as he pleased aboard the ship, and later when they reached Mars, but would consult with Fornos and Jopp as he did it. All reports intended for Earth would have to be cleared before they were sent.

Corvan fought the last agreement tooth and nail but was eventually forced to give in. He did manage to obtain one concession, however. All the reports sent to Earth would include a key that read ''Content cleared by mission command.'' The more intelligent viewers would read the qualifier and know they were looking at a sanitized version of the news. The agreement was less than perfect but better than nothing.

Corvan felt the other man's attention shift elsewhere the moment that negotiations were complete. He considered asking Fornos for an interview, rejected the idea as premature, and accepted the administrator's outstretched hand.

"Thank you, Administrator Fornos. I wouldn't call our agreement perfect . . . but it's something I can live with."

Fornos chuckled. "That is the way politics are, my friend. Less than perfect—and something we have to live with. My compliments to your beautiful wife. And tell her that she was right. Her husband *is* worth the trouble that he causes."

Corvan knew a goodbye when he heard one, returned the other man's wave, and headed for the hatch. He was almost there when the administrator spoke.

"And Corvan . . ."

The reop grabbed a handhold and turned around. "Yes?"

"Do provide the crew with some accurate information on the murder. The rumors could get out of hand. The colonists will go beddy-bye pretty soon and the murderer could make them nervous."

Corvan imagined what it would be like to enter one of the vertical suspension chambers, feel the needles slip under the surface of his skin, wondering if he'd be killed in his sleep. Not a pleasant thought, and not very good for morale. "Yes, sir. I'll get on it right away."

"Good." Fornos lifted his hand in acknowledgment and turned back to his monitors.

Corvan pushed himself through the door, waved at Julu, and headed out into the main corridor. It was just as busy as before. He waited for a cylindrical messenger bot to pass by, pulled himself out into the flow, and headed down-ship.

It took some time to reach the com center since it was located on the other side of the vessel. He spent most of the trip wondering what sort of reception he'd get. Part of him wanted to delay the encounter and part wanted to get it over with.

Corvan arrived at the proper corridor, turned into it, and pulled himself down toward the complex that Kim and he shared with the ship's communications techs. One of them, a tall skinny kid called "Zipper," bumped into him and grinned. His jump suit was a size too large and ballooned around him.

"Just out of the slammer, huh? Welcome back. Jopp's a piece of work ain't she?"

Corvan forced a smile. "Ain't she just."

"Ah well," Zipper said philosophically, "that's life for you. If it ain't one thing it's another."

Corvan nodded at this piece of wisdom, allowed the tech to pass, and pulled himself into the com center. Some other techs waved to him, he waved back and headed for the small television complex.

The hatch hissed open at his touch. It was dark inside, with only the glow of green, amber and red buttons to light the space, and it was cool, like the inside of a cave. He heard the door close behind him and felt long slim arms wrap themselves around his chest.

Corvan turned, floating in semi-darkness to feel lips touch his, and legs wrap themselves around his waist. A hand touched the side of his head, slid the jack into place, and established a two-way connection that no one else could share.

Kim flooded in and around him, her joy and sorrow melding with his, sharing, giving and taking as their bodies became one. And there, deep inside the interface, apologies were made, vows were renewed, and fears were put to rest.

chapter four

The sign on the hatch read, "J.D. Paxton, Mission Security Officer." It slid aside at Corvan's touch. The reop pulled himself into the office and looked around. Two walls, and most of what he considered to be the ceiling, were taken up with surveillance monitors. They had labels like C-3, A-14, and G-10. He figured that the letters corresponded to decks and the numbers represented locations on a grid. He saw shots of people walking, shots of people talking, and shots of people doing things they wouldn't normally do on camera. He also saw shots that moved, as tiny camera-toting microbots crawled from one place to another, documenting whatever they saw.

A shocking invasion of privacy, but made less so by a society in which people lived elbow to elbow, and chip heads roamed the streets recording everything and everyone they saw. Images that were supposedly sacrosanct but weren't.

Corvan remembered making love to Kim in the com center and searched for a shot of her. He didn't find any, but another thought crossed his mind. What about the medical center? Surely there was at least one camera located there? Had it captured a shot of Havlik's killer?

"I'll be right out."

The voice came from a connecting cubicle, a sleeping chamber probably, similar to the one that Kim and he shared just off the com center. Not much, but better than what the colonists had down in the dorms.

A body followed the voice. It drifted sideways into the open door, bumped into the frame, and bounced off. Paxton was a lanky man with short black hair and even features. He adjusted his gun belt and smiled.

"Well, if it isn't Rex Corvan, reop extraordinaire, and part-time crime buster. I liked your work on the computer coup story. You were lucky to survive."

Corvan shrugged. "I was lucky, period."

The other man shook his head. "Not so. Not entirely anyway." His eyes took on a faraway look. "Let's see . . . Rex Corvan, thirty-eight years old, six feet one inch tall, and one-ninety, no, make that one ninety-five."

Paxton patted a flat stomach. "You've been packing it on, my friend—time to slim down. Now where was I? Oh, yeah. Born and raised in Seattle. The only child of Tom Corvan, now deceased, and Dr. Lisa Kelly-Corvan, controversial journalism professor. A recipient of a masters in communications from the University of Washington, a commission from the Army, and journalistic awards too numerous to mention. You're quite a guy. And that's my point. People like you make their own luck."

Corvan raised an eyebrow. "Do you memorize *all* of your files? Or just certain ones?

Paxton grinned. "Just the ones associated with potential troublemakers."

"And I qualify?"

Paxton's grin grew even wider. "You were the first person to spend time in my brig."

Corvan laughed. "Touche."

"So," Paxton said, pushing himself out into the office, "you're working the murder."

Corvan nodded. "Trying anyway. Not that I've made much progress."

Corvan gestured towards the monitors. "Which reminds me. What about all these security cams? Surely you have one or two tucked away in the medical section. Did they capture anything?"

The security man shook his head ruefully and pointed toward two screens. They were labeled C-14 and C-15. Both were blank. "We checked right away. As luck would have it both of them were down."

Corvan looked from the screens to Paxton. "As luck would have it? Or as the killer wanted it to be?"

Paxton shrugged. "It's a reasonable question. But the cameras that cover C-16, C-17, and C-18 were down as well. Some sort of localized power failure. The tech heads are checking to make sure. The truth is that about ten percent of our cameras are on the fritz at any one time."

Corvan took another look at the monitors and saw Paxton was correct. There was a scattering of darkened screens on every deck. Just another manifestation of the ship's maintenance problems.

A deep booming sound echoed through the ship's air conditioning ducts. The same one that had plagued the ship for weeks now. The two men looked at each other and laughed.

Paxton opened a storage unit, removed a radio, and jacked the lead into the side of his head. He paused for a moment as if listening to something, nodded, and attached the device to his belt. He looked at Corvan.

"This could be your lucky day. Word came in about ten minutes ago. An F-dormie went bonkers. Beat some poor slob half to death. The M.O. fits. Want to come?"

Corvan smiled. "Does Jopp eat nails for breakfast?"

Paxton nodded soberly. "Damned right she does. Hang on a sec."

The security officer rapped on the front of a large storage unit. The door popped open and Corvan saw a strange-looking device. It consisted of a cylindrical tank with nozzles mounted at both ends, a set of handle bars, and the word "SECURITY" stenciled along its side. There was no gravity to hold it down so the contraption bobbed up and down in the air-conditioned breeze. Paxton grinned.

"What's a cop without a police car? Slide underneath, grab the rails, and hang on."

Corvan did as he was told and discovered that the rails came equipped with O-rings that would make it rather easy for the security chief to handcuff someone to his vehicle. A vehicle that was large enough to double as a rather unwieldy anchor.

Paxton twisted the motorcycle-style throttle, released a stream of oxygen, and nosed his way out into the corridor. A siren started to bleat, a strobe came on, and blue light pulsed the length of the corridor. People looked, looked again, and hustled to get out of the way.

Corvan looked upward past Paxton's left side toward the overhead. The reop felt a sense of exhilaration as light grids flashed by, the bulkheads blurred, and air slid across his face. This was what it was all about: a good lead and a story worth chasing.

There were other reasons of course, intellectual considerations of the sort found in books, and in the minds of people like his mother. But important as those ideas might be, they were dry as old shoe leather, and just as flavorless.

The truth was that Corvan liked the excitement of the hunt, the rush of adrenaline that came with it, and the catharsis of the journalistic kill. He wanted to bag the story that no one else had, he wanted to tell it like no one else could, and he wanted to leave some sort of mark on the surface of the world.

The problem was that most of his kills were already dead. Victims like Havlik. He felt like an electronic vulture sometimes, feeding off of society's carrion, while sharing the experience with others.

It was something he knew about himself, but had never shared with others, not even Kim. She might know of course, in the mysterious way that she knew so many other things about him, but there was no way to be sure.

Corvan's legs were thrown sideways as Paxton turned a corner. His foot hit a bulkhead and bounced off. He was still working to pull his legs back when Paxton applied some reverse thrust, shoved the nose down, and dived into the mouth of an access shaft.

Surprised faces whipped by to the right and left, side corridors came and went, and a crab-like maintenance bot passed only inches from Corvan's head. Then they were there, slowing as F-deck approached, and turning into the main corridor. Paxton brought the scooter to a surprisingly gentle stop.

Corvan slid out from under the cylinder's belly as Paxton slapped a magnet-equipped tether against the metal bulkhead.

"So, how did you like the ride?"

Corvan grabbed a handhold. "It was stimulating, to say the least. I kept asking myself, 'If this guy's the heat, then what are the criminals like?' "

Paxton grinned. "Scary, isn't it?"

A security officer appeared. Corvan recognized her as the same woman who escorted him from the brig to Fornos' office. She ignored him. "You'd better come quick, J.D. This guy is huge . . . and has himself all strapped in."

"Then why come quick?" Paxton asked, but the woman didn't get it. She pointed down corridor.

"Here comes the victim."

The medics didn't need a stretcher, just a metal framework to protect the patient from further injury, and to hang the pump-driven I.V. from. The cage had a propulsion system much like the one on Paxton's scooter, except that the controls were located at the rear. One medic cleared the way and guided the conveyance around corners, while the other steered and monitored the victim's vital signs.

Corvan activated his eye cam and pushed himself upward. His shoulders bumped the overhead and he stayed perfectly still. The medics guided the patient right under him. It made for an interesting shot. The reop held it for a moment then zoomed in. He couldn't see the patient's face, but the bloody bandages told their own story. The man had taken quite a beating. Corvan remembered Havlik's face. Coincidence? Or something more?

Corvan allowed the stretcher to glide out of his shot and pulled himself toward Paxton. He was just in time to follow the security man into F-dorm.

F-dorm was huge. It had to be in order to house approximately one thousand people. Later, after the vast majority of them had been sealed into their suspension chambers, the place would be quiet as a tomb. But now, with everyone awake, and the feel of violence still thick in the air, F-dorm resembled a dirtside ghetto.

A maze of temporary hand-lines ran this way and that. The air was thick with garbage. Corvan saw pieces of clothing, empty meal paks, used Kleenex, coffee bulbs, pens, and other stuff too numerous to mention drifting in all directions. All of it against regs and all of it potentially dangerous. It was a far cry from the tidy, almost sterile computer-generated renderings that the public had seen for the last couple of years.

The corridor ran straight to the center of the deck. The suspension chambers formed concentric rings to the left and right. Each unit stood on end, like coffins waiting to be filled, and many of them were.

The colonists had nowhere else to sleep, to be alone for a moment, or to seal themselves off from the all-pervasive noise.

Corvan noticed it immediately. It sounded like the high-pitched humming of bees—loud and inherently threatening.

The smell was just as bad; a rich amalgam of human sweat, cheap incense, and exotic food. The food was contraband, of course, as were the small gas-fueled torches used to cook it, but many of the colonists hated the ship's meal paks and were trying to avoid them for as long as they could.

Temporary hand-lines ran along both sides of the corridor. They led straight toward a three-dimensional ball of tangled humanity. It seemed to pulsate with a life of its own and grew larger and smaller as bodies were added and taken away.

Paxton pulled himself along and shouted as he went. "Come on . . . break it up . . . security here . . . out of the way . . . the show's over . . . break it up . . ."

Most of the colonists headed back to their tiny fiefdoms, but a few took exception to the orders and were dealt with by members of Paxton's security team.

Though few in number, the officers were experts at zero-G combat and worked in pairs. One would grab a colonist from behind, hook their legs around a rope, and hang on. Within seconds a second officer would anchor him or herself to the same rope, deliver some well-aimed blows with a nightstick, and the colonist would give in.

The moves were extremely well-coordinated, and Corvan's respect for Paxton went up a notch. The security chief knew what he was doing.

The crowd was thinner now, thin enough to see what lay at its center, and Corvan was amazed.

A harness had been devised, a contraption made of rope and bungee cords, that was secured to both deck and ceiling. The reop noticed that the arrangement left the occupant free to use both his arms and legs. Other ropes drifted free around him, along with drops of blood, sweat, and what might have been urine.

The man was enormous, at least three hundred pounds, and naked except for a grungy-looking jock strap. His skin was shiny with sweat and rippled with reflected light as a thick layer of fat rolled back and forth underneath it. His mouth made a huge hole in his dough-like face.

"Come on you chicken shit bastards! Just try me! I'll give you the same the last guy got!"

Corvan grabbed the nearest body. "Rex Corvan, Mission Information Officer—how did this start?"

The woman was Asian—Vietnamese or maybe Thai. She said something Corvan couldn't understand and pulled away. He grabbed another body, a man this time, and got lucky.

"Rex Corvan, Mission Information Officer—what's going on here?"

The man was thin, with a big nose, and slightly bulging eyes. Corvan maintained a medium shot. "It started as a bet. The fat guy paid some people to rig the harness, offered to fight all comers, and got a taker. The stupid son-of-a-gun had himself roped in." The man shrugged. "The monster beat the shit out of him. It was simple as that."

Corvan nodded. The shot went up and down. "Thank you." The situation was nothing like Paxton had been led to believe. A pre-arranged fight, complete with bets, was a far cry from attempted murder.

The reop pulled himself up to the point where Paxton had stopped. The security chief looked the monster over.

The mountain of flesh saw him, made swinging motions with his ham-sized fists, and yelled obscenities.

"Come on you scum-sucking pig! Take your best shot!"

"You could cut the ropes, truss him up, and tow him to the brig," Corvan suggested.

Paxton looked around. A second crowd had gathered, further back this time, but a crowd nonetheless. They wanted some free entertainment.

"Yeah," the security chief agreed thoughtfully, "but that would be too easy. What these people need is a lesson, something they'll remember the day after tomorrow."

The reop was just about to ask what that would be when Paxton did a deep knee bend, soared upwards, performed a full somersault, bounced off the overhead, turned end-over-end, and placed both feet right in the center of the monster's forehead.

It was then that Corvan noticed the cleat-equipped combat boots that Paxton wore and saw additional blood mist the air.

The monster gave a surprised grunt, shook his head as if momentarily dazed, and made a futile grab for Paxton's legs.

But the security man was gone and already coming back. His boots hit with a meaty thud, the monster swore, and missed again.

The next five minutes were like an aerial ballet during which Paxton carefully and methodically beat the other man senseless. The punishment was both horrible and fascinating to watch. Corvan found himself pulled both ways, admiring Paxton for what he could do but sorry that he'd done it. The beating was an example, yes, and a highly visible one at that, but was it right? And would it work? It was Corvan's observation that respect for the law is more effective than fear of the law. But they were a long way from Earth, and order had to be maintained, so Paxton might be correct.

Finally it was over. The monster hung unconscious, the security team moved in to cut him down, and the crowd drifted away. Corvan approached Paxton. He seemed no different than he had before.

"So what do you think? Did he kill Havlik?"

The security chief's eyes narrowed. "On the record or off?"

Corvan focused the eye cam. "Both. On the record first."

Paxton nodded. He'd done this sort of thing before. "We're doing everything we can to find the person or persons who killed Dr. Havlik. This man is not a suspect at the present time but will become one if the evidence warrants."

It was a standard police-type response and meant nothing at all.

Corvan shut the eye cam down. "Okay, off the record."

Paxton shook his head. "Off the record I'd say no. I'll be surprised if this guy is anything more than he appears to be. Think about it—most of the colonists attended the ceremony. If he was there, people are bound to remember him, and he'll have an alibi. We'll check, but the odds aren't very good. How 'bout you?"

Corvan shook his head grimly. "No, I don't think so either. But what about the medical records? What if the monster had some sort of relationship with Havlik?"

Paxton was silent for a moment. "Tell me something, Corvan, what kind of relationship are you and I going to have? Friendly? As in reop and cop work together to keep the lid on? Or antagonistic? As in reop and cop go for each other's throats?''

Corvan started to give Paxton a flip reply but stopped when he saw that the other man was serious. Here they were, the same old problems all over again. What was he anyway? Rex Corvan, PR man? Or Rex Corvan, journalist? The PR man would be happy to work hand in hand with security. The journalist would try to maintain his independence. But how independent could a reporter be when other people controlled the very air he breathed? Corvan produced a crooked smile.

"Friendly, as in reop and cop work together to keep the lid on, providing it's for the greater good."

Paxton grinned. "I think I'll take your statement at face value, although I'm sure that we could have a long and rather convoluted discussion about what 'the greater good' is.

"In any case, here's the answer to your question about the medical records. It seems that the person or persons who killed Havlik forced him to scrub his records."

"All of them?"

"Every last one."

Corvan gave a low whistle. "And you want me to sit on it?"

Paxton nodded. "Yup. Why give people ideas? Besides, it's something only the killer knows and would come in handy if we got a confession."

"Okay," Corvan replied. "I'll leave it out. But let me know what you find. A deal's a deal."

Paxton grabbed a hand-line and pulled himself towards the corridor. "That's a roger. Stay in touch."

Corvan hung around for a while, rolled on a couple of eyewitness accounts, then headed for the com center. There was work to do. Lots of it. Kim and he had agreed to produce a half-hour news show every day.

The first fifteen minutes of the show would consist of reports from Earth. A predictable mix of religious riots, food rationing, birth quotas, plane crashes, atmospheric tinkering, and yes, news from the construction team on Mars.

The second fifteen minutes would focus on the *Outward Bound*. Jopp had sent Corvan a list of what stories to run and what order to run them in. She thought the departure ceremony should come first, followed by a keep-up-the-good-work message from Fornos and a watered-down version of the murder.

The message had taken the form of a suggestion, rather than an order, so Corvan had talked Kim into some changes. The murder story would come first, followed by the departure ceremony, Fornos, and some human interest stuff that Kim had gathered with a mini-cam. Footage of the departure ceremony, plus the murder, would be sent to Earth. Assuming that Fornos and Jopp approved, that is.

The upshot of all this was that Corvan and Kim had a lot of writing, editing, and administrative work to do. Work that would normally be performed by a size-able staff.

So, by the time they had obtained the necessary approvals, and faded up from black, both of them were exhausted. Corvan jacked into the shipboard feed, allowed himself to free-float next to the editing console, and closed his eyes. First came the open, then the murder report.

It was all there. The hard facts, the silly rumors, and the way people felt. The report wouldn't find the murderer, erase people's fears, or make the whole thing go away. But it would provide the colonists with what information was available, serve to reassure them, and kill some of the more outlandish speculation. And that, Corvan decided, was a job well done.

As for reaction from Earth, well, that would have to

wait twenty-four hours or so. Murder in space. The tabs would eat it up.

He fell asleep ten seconds into the departure ceremony, and failed to notice when Kim removed the jack from the side of his head, pushed him into contact with a velcro strip, and kissed him on the lips.

But Otis watched the rest of the show, as did Kathy, Susy, Morey, Norma, and Frank. And they enjoyed it, especially the part about the murder and the fight on F-deck.

But there was some concern as well. This Corvan character could be a threat. Otis wanted to act, wanted to counter the danger, but the others weren't so sure.

"Let's give it some time," Norma counseled. "There's no reason to panic."

"And what if Corvan starts to close in on us?" Otis inquired. "What then?"

"How about a warning?" Susy said brightly. "Something to scare him off."

"It won't work," Otis said heavily. "This guy doesn't scare that easily."

"Maybe, and maybe not," Frank put in. "But it's worth a try. Kathy, what do you think?"

There was a long pause. When Kathy answered, her voice was cool and distant.

"It's worth a try. I'll take care of it."

chapter five

The editing room was small and comforting. There was no illumination other than that provided by the glow of multitudinous indicator lights. Kim preferred it that way, like the inside of a cave, or a walk-in closet. If only she could smoke. Then things would be perfect.

She had straight black hair, long once, but cut to pageboy length in deference to the requirements of shipboard life. It fanned out around her face as Kim swallowed the last of the breakfast biscuit, wondered what it was made of, and decided that she didn't really want to know. Given what she'd learned about recycling and hydroponics, the answer would probably amaze and disgust her. She gave the drink dispenser a squeeze and used the last squirt of coffee to wash whatever it was down.

Kim had a natural affinity for all things technical, features that were slightly Asiatic, and a figure that turned heads. Taken together they made a formidable combination. Something Kim knew but didn't spend much time thinking about.

Kim steeled herself against what she knew she would see, touched the in-ship com screen, and watched it come to life. She selected electronic mail, entered a password, and scrolled through the reams of electronic garbage that Jopp sent out every day. There were general orders, dos and don'ts of every kind, and endless notices. They made for hours of reading, or would have, except that nobody actually read them.

But here and there, sprinkled in between the official boiler plate, were the personal messages that people actually cared about. These ran the gamut from, "Kim, how 'bout doing a story about the engineering section?" to, "Hey Kim, lose the one-eyed freak, and join me for some R & R." Useful at best, annoying at worst, but nothing to worry about.

Not until a few hours ago when Kim had discovered a message that was different from all the rest. A message that sent a chill down her spine. And there it was, blinking on the screen, filling her with dread.

TELL YOUR HUSBAND TO LEAVE US ALONE. TELL YOUR HUSBAND TO LEAVE US ALONE. TELL YOUR HUSBAND TO LEAVE US ALONE. WE KNOW WHERE YOU ARE. WE KNOW WHERE YOU ARE. WE KNOW WHERE YOU ARE. WE CAN KILL YOU. WE CAN KILL YOU. WE CAN KILL YOU.

Kim took one last look at the words, marked them, and hit the delete key.

"Delete text?" the computer inquired. "Y or N?"

Kim touched "Y." She wanted a cigarette and popped a mint instead.

The words disappeared but the fear remained. Who had sent the message? The most likely answer was Havlik's killer or killers, but that didn't make much sense, since Rex wasn't anywhere near discovering their identities. Or was he? There must be some reason for the warning. And what did the "we" part mean? Were a number of people involved? Or was that a ruse designed to throw the investigators off?

Kim stared at the empty screen. Why hadn't she told Rex? It was the obvious thing to do. Because he'd go crazy, that's why. He'd react like a bloodhound on the scent, head straight for danger, and get himself killed. Then where would she be? On Mars, that's where, all by herself, minus the one person that she cared about. No, there had to be another way, a strategy that would allow her to defend against danger while avoiding her husband's self-destructive tendencies.

And that brought her to the task at hand. Rex was away, off looking for the source of the mysterious booming sound, so this was the perfect time to bring Martin back to life. If a computer, even a sentient computer, can be said to "live."

But Kim was a pragmatist and classified such questions as little more than academic constipation.

Martin could acquire, reject, and process information. He could modify his actions based on past experience, he knew right from wrong, and he had feelings. Not the full range of emotions that humans experience, but feelings nonetheless, and all of those things taken together made Martin more than a machine.

And it had been those emotions, loyalty in particular, that had brought the reop, video editor, and computer intelligence together.

Martin had been the previous President's personal computer, communications center, and administrative assistant all rolled into one. Constructed to fit into an antique desk, the artificial intelligence, or A.I., had occupied a prominent place in the Oval office. And, when President Hawkins had been assassinated by his chief of staff, Martin had been the only witness. A witness the conspirators had never thought to silence. A witness that was determined to avenge the President's death.

Working by himself at first, and then with Rex and Kim, the computer had played a significant role in foiling the computer coup and preventing Samuel Numalo from forming a single world government.

But with the restoration of a legitimate government, and the long succession of hearings and trials that followed, Martin had been relieved of his duties at the White House and relegated to providing endless hours of testimony.

Eventually, after the legal cases had come to an end, so did Martin's usefulness. He was an embarrassment, an unwelcome reminder that even the best security systems are fallible, as are the people that run them.

And there were those, especially in the CIA, NSA, and Secret Service who wanted his memory scrubbed. They claimed Martin was a repository of classified information and a threat to national security.

But Martin was a celebrity by then, having been the only machine to make the cover of *Time* magazine, and the public was outraged. Mind-wipe the patriotic computer who had helped defend the country's freedom? Never!

Negotiations had ensued, and when Corvan suggested that Martin emigrate to Mars, the authorities had leaped at the chance to get rid of him.

That explained why Martin was aboard the ship and resident in a battered suitcase.

What it didn't explain was why Kim made her way to a storage cabinet, unlocked the door, and removed Martin's suitcase. By doing so she violated the agreement by which the A.I. had come aboard. The *Outward Bound* was a complicated and somewhat fragile environment. There was no room for random computer entities, crew members who did their own thing, or personal strategies that cut across the lines of authority.

It was the sort of thing that Rex would do, the sort of thing that drove her crazy, and the sort of thing that led to trouble.

Kim knew that, worried about it, and opened the suitcase anyway. Martin might cause trouble, but he might prevent trouble too, and she would accept the risk.

Martin wasn't much to look at. Just a gray metal box and a row of LED's. There were twelve altogether and one of them glowed green. Good. Martin's internal power supply was functioning, and so was he, though at a comparatively low level.

Kim pushed the suitcase over to a small work bench and strapped it down. She looked for and found Martin's power port, plugged him into the ship-wide system, and flipped a switch.

A humming noise came from inside Martin's casing. The second LED glowed green, then another, and another, until all twelve were lit up.

Kim nodded her satisfaction, removed a patch cord from the wall clips above the bench, and plugged it into the panel located on the right side of Martin's box. The other end went into the side of her head.

"Martin?"

Music flooded her mind. It was big, orchestral, and reminiscent of the classical composers. The melody soared, and Kim soared with it, rising on wave after wave of pure emotion, until her throat grew tight and her breath came in shallow gasps. Then the sound broke like surf on a coral reef, crashed into a magnificent explosion of foam, and slid into a silent lagoon.

Martin entered her mind as the last strains of the music died away. "Did you like it?"

It took Kim a moment to gather her thoughts. "Like it? I loved it. Who wrote it? And where did it come from?"

"I wrote it," Martin said proudly. "I used a Microsoft program called Composer 4.1 to synthesize the sounds. You really liked it? You sentients lie so well that it's hard to tell sometimes."

Kim laughed. "No, I *really* liked it."

"Good. Are we on Mars?"

Having been locked up inside the suitcase, and having no external sensors, Martin had no way to keep track of where he was or what was happening.

"Nope, the journey has just begun."

"Then what's going on? I thought the big wigs wanted me under lock and key until we landed."

"And they do," Kim agreed, "so this is our little secret."

"Does Rex know?"

The motion was invisible to Martin, but Kim shook her head. "No, and I don't plan to tell him. Not yet anyway."

Kim felt concern ripple through the interface. "Such behavior is unusual for you, Kim. Are you all right?"

"Yes . . . no . . . I'm not sure."

"You have doubts."

"Yes, I have doubts. But I need your help anyway."

"Tell me about it."

So Kim did. She told Martin about the murder, about the message, and about her fears.

"So," she concluded, "I'm afraid that Rex would get all protective, go after the story, and get himself killed."

"It has been my observation that Rex is hard to kill," Martin said thoughtfully, "still, I share your concern. What would you like me to do?"

Kim ran her tongue over dry lips. This was it. The point where the whole thing crossed from the planning stage into the doing stage. The point of no return.

"I want you to infiltrate the ship's computer systems. The message came by E-mail from one of the free access terminals on E-deck. Anyone could have used it."

"So I lie in wait," Martin said, "identify the next message as it comes in, trace it to its source, and take a peek via one of the surveillance cameras."

"Exactly," Kim replied, relieved that her plan sounded workable. "If you're willing, that is."

Amusement filled the interface. "Of course I'm willing. Just try to stop me. Besides, anything's better than the inside of that suitcase."

Kim smiled. "Wait until you've had a chance to sift through a hundred screens of E-mail. That could change your mind."

Corvan hit his head on a support beam, swore, and ducked underneath. An upright pressed in on him from the right. He wiggled through the opening.

Dr. Bethany McKeen, better known as Dr. "B" to her friends, chuckled. There was no animosity in her laugh. Just the enjoyment that small people have when big people run into trouble.

The geologist was little more than four and a half-feet tall, weighed eighty-eight pounds soaking wet, and was descended from the small-framed peoples that once lived in the African rain forests. She had reddish-brown skin, a roundish head, and a broad flat nose. Her eyes were bright with intelligence and danced with suppressed merriment. Like Corvan, Dr. B was dressed in a plain blue ship-suit. She used a lateral support to hold herself in place.

"What's the problem Corvan? Putting on a little weight?"

That was the second such comment in two cycles. Corvan made a note to watch his caloric intake. A task made easier by the boring food. He growled a reply, pulled himself over the I-beam that blocked his way, and followed the geologist's girlish posterior even deeper into the bowels of G-deck.

If A-deck was the topmost layer of the ship, then G-deck was the bottommost layer, and almost entirely given over to the ship's power plants, shielding, and associated equipment.

And it was from that this region that many people, including Dr. B. thought the booming sound originated.

Fornos and Jopp had grown weary of the complaints associated with the noise, not to mention the sometimes outlandish rumors that went along with them, and had authorized a two-person expedition.

And, due to the fact that her skills as a geologist were not yet in demand, Dr. B had been chosen to lead it. Corvan had been an afterthought, a companion to provide aid in case of trouble, and a newsperson to document whatever she found.

The crawl space twisted and turned ever downward, expanded and contracted according to the size and dimensions of the installations that it served, but made no concessions to the convenience of those who used it.

There were light fixtures, but most were mounted high overhead, and the light they cast was broken into a maze of crisscrossing shadows.

And, thanks to the presence of the ship's power plants, it was hot, as well. Everything was warm to the touch. Everything except the outside hull metal. That was cold, very cold, and water had a tendency to condense on its surface, form blobs, break away, and disappear into the maws of the multitudinous robots that wove their way in and out of the metal maze.

Corvan ducked under an especially low beam, searched for a handhold, and pulled. The beam scraped the length of his body.

Was it just his imagination? Or was the crawl space getting smaller? Maybe it had something to do with the curvature of the hull, with the way that the drive tubes came straight down along the ship's axis, or the fact that the people who had designed the damned thing were safely ensconced in their offices back on Earth. But whatever it was had started to bug him.

The reop could sense the metal that pressed in from every side, could imagine the snap of a support beam, and could feel the enormous weight that would crush him against the deck.

Corvan knew that his fears were groundless, knew the support beam wouldn't snap, but the feeling persisted.

He paused, wiped the sweat from his forehead, and waited for Dr. B's high-tops to disappear through the hole up ahead. The truth was that he was afraid, very afraid, and wanted to turn back.

The feeling was nothing new. He'd experienced it many times before. First during childish exploits, then in the Army, and countless times as a reop. There was a solution though, a trick that he'd used in the past and might work again.

Corvan activated his implant and forced himself to narrate what he saw. "At this point Dr. McKeen and I are making our way through the accessway that spirals around G-deck. The power plants are to my left, along with the drive tubes that propel us through space and a lot of ancillary equipment. The hull is to my right and wet with condensed water vapor. You can see the little robots that work to gobble it up.

"Dr. McKeen is just ahead—I think you can see the soles of her shoes disappearing under that low arch— and I'm doing my best to follow. Unfortunately my larger size makes travel a bit difficult—wait a minute, there, now I can pull myself upright."

Corvan grabbed onto a beam, panned from left to right, and showed his audience a cave-like area lit by distant lights and filled with mysterious shadows. The shot came to rest on McKeen, who had paused for a moment in order to consult a schematic. The framing looked good.

Not only that, but the fear had disappeared, just as he had hoped that it might. There was something about the role of professional observer that lifted him above the reach of his own fear and surrounded him with a wall of psychological invulnerability. The feeling was false, and a part of him knew that, but he felt better anyway. Corvan resumed his narration.

"Somewhere up ahead, or so the theory goes, we'll find the thing or things that cause the mysterious booming noise."

And then, as if to prove that the gods of journalism truly exist and were feeling generous, an enormous boom sounded. It was loud enough to vibrate the metal around them and force Corvan to cover his ears. The reop drifted for a moment but found a new handhold.

"And that," Corvan said as the sound died away, "is the sound in question. What makes it and why? Those are the questions that brought us here, and it seems as if the answers are just ahead."

Dr. B. put the schematic away, grinned, and waved Corvan forward. "We're closer! Come on!"

Corvan let the natural sound and pictures supplied by his eye cam speak for themselves as he followed the geologist through a forest of vertical supports and out into an open space—an area that must be located at the ship's extreme stern end or very close to it.

What they saw stunned them both. The contraption was huge. It consisted of a large metal sheet, held in place by four cables, and covered with some sort of script. A mechanical arm stood at right angles to the piece of metal, had obviously been in contact with it, and was in the process of being pulled away. Corvan couldn't see the mechanism that made this possible but assumed that it was contained within the large metal box from which the arm extended.

It was clear that the metal sheet, and the arm that went with it, were nothing more or less than a gigantic gong. No wonder the sound was so loud, no wonder it made its way through the entire ship, and no wonder people hadn't thought of it.

Corvan spoke as he pulled himself closer. "People have put forth all sorts of theories about the noise. Some claimed it was caused by a loose I-beam, swinging with motion of the ship and clanging against the hull. Others said it was some sort of pressure differential building up in the air-conditioning system then letting go. And there were more exotic explanations as well, like the one that involved a sky rigger trapped within the hull, beating on it with a wrench.

"Well, truth is stranger than fiction sometimes, and what we have here is a mechanical gong. We have no idea who placed it here or why. There's writing on the sheet metal. Maybe that will help."

Corvan grabbed an upright, zoomed in on the writing, and read out loud.

" 'To the men and women of the *Outward Bound*, good luck, and Bon Voyage,' signed, 'Sky Crew 17.' Wait a minute . . . I think Dr. McKeen has found something."

A large metal chest had been secured to the deck in front of the gong and the geologist had pulled herself down to it. She was fumbling with the lid and Corvan moved in closer to get a good look.

Vapor escaped as the lid came up. Dr. B reached down, grabbed something, and pulled it out. Other similar things struggled to drift free. The scientist pushed them down and closed the lid. McKeen held the object up and Corvan zoomed in. Champagne! The chest was filled with champagne!

The gong and the champagne made a great story and pushed the murder down into the middle of the end-cycle news show. It made the Earth nets too, all one hundred and sixty-three of them, and served to take the edge off Havlik's death.

The colonists, soon to be followed by the crew,

would enter their suspension chambers during the next few cycles. Not an altogether pleasant experience, and one made even less so when the ship was haunted by mysterious sounds. So the champagne, and the party that surrounded it, turned what might have been a rather depressing moment into a festive occasion.

Fornos was overjoyed, Jopp was pleased, and Corvan was back in everyone's good graces.

Kim watched her husband float inside a circle of newly found admirers, sucked champagne from a bulb, and hummed Martin's symphony.

chapter six

Corvan entered F-dorm. The fetid smell lingered on but the noise and airborne garbage had all but disappeared. It was easier to keep things clean with more than ninety percent of the population out of circulation. He grabbed a hand-line and pulled himself forward.

The suspension chambers made a long slow curve to the right and left. Most were sealed, their occupants barely visible behind veils of cloudy white gas, their circulatory, respiratory, and digestive systems slowed almost to the point of death. Tubes conveyed nourishment into their bloodstreams and carried waste materials away.

Corvan activated his implant and scanned the colonists as he pulled himself along. Where they had gone he would follow.

What would it feel like? To be sealed inside a high-tech coffin? To have drugs enter his bloodstream? To slowly lose consciousness? To surrender himself to the arms of a largely untried science? To become one of what the crew jokingly referred to as the corpse-sickles?

But it had to be done. Otherwise they would run out of air, food, and water long before they reached Mars, even with the recyclers, hydroponics tanks, and syn-

thesizers running full blast. Three thousand people
consume a lot of everything during a nine-month period of time, more than the ship could carry, and more
than they could produce.

In fact, it would be many years before the Mars
colony was self-sustaining, and many years after that
before they could produce a surplus. So everything
consumed aboard the ship was that much less for later
on.

There were psychological factors, too. What would
people do during a nine-month voyage? A lot of
shrinks had spent a lot of time considering that very
question. And their conclusions weren't all that optimistic.

Given the colonists' divergent cultures, religions,
and languages, plus the lack of anything constructive
to do, the shrinks had predicted everything from race
riots to holy wars.

And, although the possibility of a skeleton crew had
been given serious consideration, the idea was ulti-
mately rejected. What if they went bonkers? Cut power
to the suspension chambers? Or disabled the ship?

No, it would be better for everyone to take a nap
and wake up ready to go. Providing they woke up, that
is. It was a grim thought and Corvan pushed it aside.

He saw people up ahead. There were med techs, suspension techs, and at least one administrative type.
They hovered like ghouls around an open coffin. They
looked his way. One waved. Corvan grimaced and
waved back.

Here it was, another interview with a carefully selected colonist, guaranteed to enter his or her chamber with a smile. His tenth or eleventh such interview
in the last four cycles. All of which had been beamed
back to Earth for consumption by the next shipload of
starry-eyed dreamers.

They weren't lies exactly, since some people *did*

crack jokes as they climbed into their chambers, but there were other stories as well. Stories that Fornos and Jopp wouldn't allow him to tell.

Like the woman who had been towed kicking and screaming to her chamber where she'd been sedated and strapped into place.

Like the man who had played hide and seek with Paxton's security people for two days before they found him in the hydroponics section and forced him into a chamber.

Like the woman who had entered her chamber calmly enough, but had gone crazy once inside and tried to scratch her way out. Corvan would never forget the bloody grooves that her fingernails had left on the inside of the canopy.

He had gone to Jopp's office, forced his way past her functionaries, and requested permission to include a toned-down version of the woman's story in his report. Jopp had looked at him as if he were out of his mind, raised a well-plucked eyebrow and said "no." The way she said it left no room for further discussion.

The technicians said hello as Corvan approached, slapped the colonist on the back, and congratulated him on becoming a vid star. One man in particular, an administrative assistant named Hobarth, was especially effusive. He was tall, and in spite of the fact that he was only slightly overweight, had three chins. All three of them jiggled when he spoke. The ridiculous tie that he wore drifted in front of his face. He pushed it out of the way.

"Well here he is! The one-eyed wonder! Colonist Gormley, I'd like you to meet Rex Corvan, slayer of journalistic dragons. Rex, this is Colonist Gormley."

Corvan drifted to a stop, took one look at Gormley, and shook his head in amazement. There were some poor specimens among the colonists, but Gormley took the cake. He was thin with malnutrition, had incredi-

bly bad breath, and couldn't seem to focus his eyes.
Gormley was ill or under the influence of drugs. Corvan assumed the latter. Not only that, but someone
had fitted him out with an old-fashioned sleeping cap,
complete with tassel. Strips of duct tape held in it
place.

Gormley smiled an idiot smile. "Hi, Rex."

Corvan ignored him and looked at Hobarth instead.
"And what the hell is this?"

The smile disappeared from the administrator's face.
His eyes narrowed and nearly vanished into creases of
pasty white flesh.

"This is what we pay you for."

Corvan looked from Hobarth to Gormley and back
again. "Wrong. I get paid to provide information about
colonists. If you want interviews with drug addicts then
do 'em yourself. Who thought of the hat anyway?"

Hobarth flushed red. "I did. Colonel Jopp thought
it was a good idea."

Corvan shook his head sadly. "Tell Jopp she was
wrong. Tell her it was a stupid idea. Tell her that this
story is so big it doesn't need that sort of window
dressing."

The reop turned to the colonist. "Hey, Gormley.
Can you hear me?"

Gormley smiled serenely. "Sure Rex, I can hear
you."

"What are you taking?"

"Taking?"

"What kind of drugs did you take?"

Gormley looked around then cupped his hand as if
confiding something to a friend. "Green ones."

Corvan turned to a med tech. "That mean anything
to you?"

The technician was small and wiry. A pair of
chrome-plated bandage scissors drifted out to the ex-
tent of their tether and bobbed up and down. "Could

be lots of stuff. Downers probably. That's the drug of choice on this tub.''

Corvan gestured toward the open chamber. ''You put him in there, the drugs wear off, then what?''

The technician shrugged. ''Who knows?''

Corvan grabbed a fistful of the woman's ship-suit and jerked her in close. ''Listen, and listen good. You have a choice. Put this guy through detox and load him clean, or I'll squirt the whole story dirtside.''

Corvan let go and the woman pushed herself away. She was so shocked, so surprised, that her mouth worked and nothing came out. Not Hobarth, however. ''You wouldn't dare!''

Corvan smiled and looked him up and down. ''Try me.''

''I'll tell Colonel Jopp!''

Corvan laughed. ''And what will Jopp do? Send me to Mars?''

Martin had spent the last four cycles hiding in the com center's computer modules. It was a tight fit, since he occupied a lot of memory, but it was better than going out unprepared—an action that would lead to almost certain disaster.

They key to Kim's plan was stealth, and given the fact that the *Outward Bound* was loaded with sentient and near-sentient computers, there were plenty of entities that could give him away. A whole hierarchy of them, as a matter of fact, starting with the artificial intelligence known as Big Dan and going all the way down to lesser players who were little more than blips against the electronic background.

Martin had spent years in Washington D.C. where politics, electronic politics included, were something of an art form. He'd been on top of the digital heap back then, along with his peers at the pentagon, FBI,

CIA and NSA, and knew better than to go barging around without doing some research.

So the initial cycles were spent observing what went on. Martin gauged the jealousies that flourished where responsibilities overlapped, measured how deep loyalties ran, and probed the labyrinth of programmed relationships that tied everyone together.

Then, having spied out the electronic landscape, Martin made his move. The Grass Valley Ultima that occupied the very top rung of the com center's miniature hierarchy was so new, and so inexperienced, that it was easy to dominate. Not overcome or destroy, since that would have violated Martin's code of ethics, but to influence and lead. It also allowed him to take over a legitimate slot within the ship's society of electronic beings.

That gave Martin a base of operations, allowed him to avoid the trap that had been laid for digitized invaders, and granted him a legitimacy that he could obtain no other way.

And so it was that Martin crept into the mainstream of computerized activity. For years the electronic entity had sat in the Oval Office and listened while President Hawkins handled the myriad details of political life. The deals, the compromises, the strategies, the guesswork, the wins and the losses. He'd seen and heard them all.

So Martin understood how to isolate opponents, build coalitions, and satisfy constituents. He not only understood, but relished the process and was good at it. That's why the game was nearly over before Big Dan had even started to play.

Kim emerged from the access shaft, waited for a cylindrical message bot to squirt itself past, and headed down-ship. Rex and she would be sealed into their individual suspension chambers and put to sleep in less than three hours. That meant there were a lot of things to do and very little time to do them in. But Rex had insisted that she come, so here she was.

The E-deck observation port was one of the many things that jutted out from the ship's skin and made it look something less than beautiful.

Kim followed the sign that said "OBSV-PORT" into a side corridor, found a good push-point, and sailed the length of the corridor. An airtight hatch sensed her approach, opened just in the nick of time, and closed behind her.

The colonists that usually lined up to look out of the port were gone now, sealed in their chambers, so the space was both empty and dark. Dark except for the pen lights that Corvan had rigged to take the place of candles and the light reflected from Earth.

The planet hung beyond the plastic like a picture in a frame, smaller than the last time Kim had seen it, but larger than a full moon. A small section of the southern hemisphere was blocked by the curvature of the ship's hull.

"Welcome," Corvan said with the flourish of a headwaiter. "Your table awaits."

Kim looked and sure enough, the pen lights sat on something circular, which if not a table did an excellent job of standing in for one. Whatever it was floated in midair but was held in place by a length of cord attached to a magnet.

Kim pulled herself closer. She saw that the table had been covered with white fabric. The cloth bulged here and there where things pushed up at it from below.

"What in the world?"

" 'What in the world' indeed," Corvan said smoothly. "Now, take a seat, and dinner will be served."

Kim laughed, pushed herself into position, and

summoned a serious expression. "Thank you, Pierre. The salmon is fresh, I presume?"

"Of course," Corvan assured her, slipping into a terrible French accent. "The salmon is fresh from ze stream and wanting of you to eat it."

Corvan whipped the cloth off the makeshift table and threw it aside. It floated away like an errant ghost. Kim laughed when she saw the table setting. There were plastic knives, forks, and spoons, all held in place by pieces of tape. There were standard ration paks, held down by a dab of glue, and drink containers held captive by strips of elastic.

Corvan took the place across from her. He stood rather than sat, but it made little difference. "Dinner is served."

Kim looked across the table and found his eyes. One was blue and the other was black. The difference no longer bothered her. "I love you."

Corvan smiled and lifted his drink container. "And I love you. To us!"

"To us."

The rations were the same ones Kim ate every day, but something about the setting made them taste better. The darkened room, the pen light candles, the glow from planet Earth made a picture that she'd remember for the rest of her life. This was her husband's flip side, the part that television viewers never saw, the part that was hers alone.

The conversation focused on them at first, on their hopes for the future, but quickly returned to the present. The future was too uncertain, too chancy to discuss for very long.

Corvan's empty meal pak started to drift away. He grabbed the container and stuffed it into a mesh bag. "I made some progress on the murder."

Kim swallowed the last bite of her dessert. It felt the size of a baseball. Images flashed through her mind. She saw words blinking on the screen. She saw herself opening Martin's suitcase. She saw Havlik's battered face. Kim did her best to sound calm.

"Oh, really? What did you learn?"

"The murderer isn't one of the colonists."

Kim thought about that. If what her husband said was true, it would narrow the field, but there were more than four hundred crew members aboard the *Outward Bound,* and that left a lot of suspects.

"What makes you say that?"

"Paxton ran a series of checks on the people that attended the departure ceremony. By checking the security cams, plus the tape we shot, he was able to account for about eighty-seven percent of the colonists. Then, by interviewing the rest, cross-checking alibis and verifying their stories, he was able to eliminate ninety-eight percent of the common herd."

"And what about the other two percent?"

Corvan shrugged. "Paxton placed them under surveillance, but can't connect any of them with Havlik and doesn't expect to. I think he's right. I think a crew member did it."

Kim's heart beat a little faster. It was just as she had feared. The story had caught her husband's interest and he was determined to pursue it. "Why do you say that?"

Corvan leaned on the table top. It tipped under the weight. Light glinted off his eye cam.

"Think about it. Whoever it was knew Havlik had the duty, knew enough about the ship's computer systems to get some incriminating data scrubbed, and knew how to handle him or herself in zero-G conditions. All of this at a time when most of the colonists had been aboard for a short time and were still puking their guts out."

Everything Corvan said made sense but none of it was new. There was nothing to excite the killer to action, to make him or her angry with Rex, to create additional danger. Kim breathed a sigh of relief. The feeling was short-lived, however.

"So," her husband continued, "I did some rooting around."

He paused, waiting for her to ask what he had found, and grinning like a Cheshire cat.

Kim forced a smile. "And what did you find?"

"This!" Corvan said, as he whipped a small notebook out of his pocket and held it aloft. "Havlik's personal notebook!"

Kim groaned internally. It was just as she had feared. Something that was sure to make the killer angry. Her voice was tight and barely under control.

"Rex, put that away."

He looked surprised, then embarrassed, and slipped it into a pocket. "Yeah, I keep forgetting. The walls have ears."

"And eyes," Kim added grimly, and nodded towards a distant security cam.

"True," Corvan admitted sheepishly. "I'll be more careful." He pitched his voice lower. "But listen hon . . . this could break the case wide open! Havlik used some sort of personal code, so I don't know what the book actually says, but we can figure it out."

"Where did you get it?"

Corvan grinned. Excitement filled his real eye. "From Havlik's suspension chamber. Nobody thought to look there!"

Kim nodded thoughtfully. "How do you know it has anything to do with the case?"

Corvan shrugged. "I don't. But I *feel* it."

"Does anyone else know?"

Corvan shook his head. "No, I wanted to crack the code first, then announce it."

Kim understood. Like most journalists her husband would do almost anything to get a scoop. Even if it meant risking his life, and yes, hers as well. He had assumed, as he always did, that his goals were hers, that the end justified the means, that he knew what was best for the world. There was no point in complaining or in feeling angry, because he would never change.

Kim looked at her wrist term. "We're going beddy-bye in less than two hours."

Corvan shrugged. "So? The killer will go down at the same time we do and the information will keep. We'll nail the sucker when we wake up."

Kim wanted to say *"If* we wake up," but didn't. She thought about Martin, considered spilling her guts, and decided not to. Rex would think she was silly, order Martin back into his suitcase, and spoil the whole plan. She forced a smile.

"Okay Rex, whatever you say. There's lots to do, so let's do it."

Corvan helped Kim into her chamber. She forced a smile and made a show of snuggling in. "See you later, handsome."

The reop bent over, kissed her on the lips and did his best to burn the moment into his mind. He savored the beauty of her face, the smell of her hair, the softness of her lips. What would he do if he survived and she didn't? The thought of opening her chamber to find little more than a desiccated corpse made Corvan's stomach roll over. Kim's hands came up to touch his face.

"I love you, Rex Corvan."

"And I love you."

"Be here when I wake up."

"You too."

He wanted to say more, wanted to apologize for any pain that he'd caused her, and wanted to make promises for the future. But the technicians were waiting, gathered like so many undertakers around a coffin, eager to get their work done. So Corvan blew her a kiss, backed away, and allowed them to move in.

He turned, pulled himself down into his own chamber, and buckled himself into place. The interior was surprisingly comfortable and seemed to adjust to the shape of his body. It started to vibrate, which caused his muscles to relax and improved his circulation. The lining felt smooth beneath his bare feet.

Something pressed against his right hip. Corvan rolled a little to the left, pulled Havlik's notebook out of his back pocket, and slid it under his pillow. The same hiding place the doctor had used.

Corvan wished there had been enough time to decode the book's contents but took comfort from the thought that the killer would be out of action as well.

The chamber smelled of chemicals but not unpleasantly so. The reop started to relax. He even activated his implant and recorded some observations about what the experience felt like. It could be useful for his next report and served to keep the fear at bay.

And then the technicians came. Faces that slid into position above him, mouths that made small talk, and hands that touched, prepared and probed.

There was pain as needles slid into his veins, followed by an in-dwelling catheter and numerous injections. The pain was followed by chemicals that did strange things to his head.

The faces seemed to shimmer like hot air rising off the desert, seemed to pulsate in response to unseen forces, seemed to fade into darkness. Then Corvan fell, and fell, and fell until falling had no meaning anymore and he ceased to exist.

The suspension chamber was sealed soon thereafter, gas was pumped inside, and the reop's vital signs slowed until they hovered at the brink of death.

A technician entered something into a portacomp,

checked Corvan's readouts one last time, and put her thumb print on the pressure sensitive lock. Another corpse-sickle down and thirty-seven to go.

And so it went, until every last human being had been accounted for, and all were in a state of suspended animation. Or so it seemed to the last of the technicians as they sealed themselves into their chambers and faced the darkness alone.

But two people had found ways to trick them, had rigged their chambers to bring them back only hours after they had gone under, and had started to stir.

One disliked the thought of nine months spent hovering between life and death and looked forward to spending some time alone.

The other would have welcomed nine months worth of total oblivion, but heard the babble of many voices and had a mission to perform. A rather unpleasant mission but one that would protect against the possibility of harm.

And so it was that gas dissipated, tubes were removed, and canopies popped open. There were gagging sounds followed by silence as they waited for the nausea to pass. In thirty minutes, an hour at most, both would be up and around. The ship sped on.

chapter seven

Martin had mixed emotions about humans. Yes, they had managed to invent computers, but that accomplishment had been more than offset by the creation of staff meetings: interminable affairs during which the participants spouted endless drivel and did their best to belittle each other.

So what did Big Dan do moments after assuming control from Fornos and Jopp? He held a staff meeting, that's what. Orders went out to gather. Not physically, since very few of the A.I.'s had the capacity to move around, but electronically, via the ship's fiber-optic nervous system.

The idea had some merit since volumes of information could be exchanged during a well-thought-out five- or ten-second meeting.

But Big Dan had something more in his processor. He wanted to review the way that each and every computer would handle itself in a variety of circumstances. Not their basic programming, which he could check via high-speed data dump, but their *attitudes* which were much harder to nail down.

Most of Big Dan's subordinates, Martin included, had been given some latitude to make independent decisions. This was necessary should the ship run into unexpected problems. Problems their programming didn't cover.

But this freedom to depart from standard procedure made Big Dan nervous. A condition that he didn't enjoy and sought to eliminate by asking each individual what they would do in this or that situation.

Hydro, the A.I. that ran the hydroponics section was on circuit at the moment, responding to a question about unexpected crop failures. His answers consisted of chemical and mathematical gobbledegook that was totally incomprehensible to everyone except Big Dan and himself.

Martin found the whole thing more than a little boring and turned his attention to some off-line schmoozing. In spite of the fact that most of the main computer-to-computer communications channels were taken up by Big Dan's staff meeting, other less direct linkages were available, and Martin, along with his ever growing cadre of political sympathizers, was having a meeting of his own.

"So," the Maintenance Operations Management System computer, better known as "MOMS," thought-said, "how long will the Big Guy drone on?"

"Too long," LES, the Life Equipment Support computer replied. "All the way to Mars if he gets the chance. How 'bout you Martin? What do you think?"

Martin had just formulated what he hoped would be a witty reply when a fourth voice intervened. It belonged to a somewhat stern entity called "SIS." The letters stood for "Shipboard Information System" and was something of an intentional misnomer. The ship's designers had favored the name "Computer Operated Personnel Security system, or "COPS," but the PR types had vetoed that idea, suggesting the name SIS instead. They said it was warm and friendly while the other name was hard and cold.

But no matter what you called it, the function remained the same. SIS had responsibility for the *Outward Bound*'s surveillance equipment. Given the nature of his mission, Martin had attempted to co-opt SIS early on and failed. The A.I. considered herself above politics and had the programming to back it up. The humans had taken steps to keep the security computer from acquiring or seeking to acquire dictatorial powers. Her voice-thought was stern.

"All right, which one of you digitized yahoos pulled the plug on my surveillance cams?"

Martin pulled his entire processing ability on-line. "What did you say?"

"What? I have to spell it out one letter at a time? Which one of you idiots is screwing around with my video? Confess and take your lumps."

A whole series of thoughts and possibilities flashed through Martin's processor at lightning speed. "All your surveillance cams? Or just a few?"

"What the hell difference does it make? All of them. Look, fun's fun, but the joke's over. Put 'em right or pay the price. Computers can be reprogrammed, you know."

Martin tried for just the right mix of sympathy and sincerity. The killer was supposed to be dead to the world just like everyone else. But what if he or she wasn't? What if they were up and around? Looking for their next victim? The first thing such an individual would do was disable the surveillance system. Time was critical. He had to secure the other computer's cooperation and do it quickly.

"Listen SIS, we didn't do it, but we're willing to help. Right everybody?"

"Right!"

"You bet, boss!"

"No problem."

"See?" Martin asked. "Help is at hand."

"I don't know," SIS said doubtfully. "Maybe I should tell Big Dan."

Martin switched his attention to the main com channel. Hydro was warming to his subject. The crew would have enough soy burgers to keep them flatulent for years to come. Martin switched back.

"Big Dan's busy. Why don't we take a crack at the problem and call the Big Guy if we need him?"

A nanosecond passed while SIS thought the proposal over. "Well, that would be okay I guess. Thanks."

"Think nothing of it," Martin replied cheerfully. "We're all in this together. Now, how 'bout a power failure or bad component?"

"Nope," SIS answered with certainty. "All of us would know if the power had failed. Besides, this tub has backups for its backups. No, the power's fine. Same thing with the components. I checked."

"All right," Martin said grimly. "That leaves one possibility. Sabotage."

"But how? And who?" the Life Equipment Support computer inquired. "The humans are sealed inside their suspension chambers. If one of them was up and around I'd know about it."

"Really?" Martin asked. "What if they tricked you?"

"No one could trick me," LES replied confidently. "The suspension chambers are wired tighter than tight."

"Bullcrackers," SIS said evenly. "The humans *invented* you. That means they could invent a way around you."

"She's got you there," MOMS put in. "A really knowledgeable homo sap could run rings around any one of us."

LES was silent. MOMS was right and he knew it.

"All right then," Martin said, "spread out and take

a look around. Someone is up to no good. Let's find 'em.''

Otis withdrew his side cutters, examined the severed line, and gave a nod of satisfaction. That took care of the primary surveillance system plus the two backups. The Shipboard Information System computer would be unable to monitor or record the body's movements. And even if it did, Otis had donned a hood, oversized ship-suit, and a brand new pair of gloves.

It would be a simple matter to locate Corvan, kill him, find the notebook, and return to a state of suspended animation. The authorities would discover the murder when the ship reached Mars but would be helpless to do anything about it.

Damn Havlik anyway. The notebook might contain nothing more than some poetry, personal observations about the trip, or a list of addresses. But it *might* contain notes about patients, and that was a possibility that Otis couldn't tolerate.

Otis slipped the side cutters into a pocket, zipped it closed, and let go of the access panel. It snapped into place.

Otis repositioned the body, pushed off the bulkhead, and headed up-ship. The com center was on B-deck. The body was on D-deck. It would take only minutes to get there.

Rosemary ran a hand over the stubble that covered the top of her head and grinned. The face in the mirror grinned back. It had brown eyes, a nose that was a tiny bit too large, and an unadorned temple stud. The stud, plus the implant that went with it, had been given to Rosemary as a present on her sixteenth birthday.

Her father had packed his lunch every day, gone without vacations, and practiced a hundred other small economies to save the necessary money.

On top of that they had lived in one room of what had once been an upscale three-bedroom apartment, then shared by three different families. Their single luxury had been the private bathroom that cost two hundred dollars per month. It was an overcrowded, squalid, seemingly hopeless environment.

But her father had shown her the stars through a homemade telescope, had convinced her that better worlds waited somewhere in space, and kindled the fire that still burned within her: the desire to try, to reach, to take chances.

She remembered the huge billboards, paid for by the Exodus Society, showing a man, woman and child standing on a hill, looking yearningly at the stars. Oh, how she had wanted to be that child, with Mommy on one side and Daddy on the other.

But valuable though her implant was, the wealthier kids had theirs by the age of ten and were light years ahead of her by the time they entered high school. Not only that, but they had the connections necessary to get into college, and the money to pay for it.

So Rosemary had been denied the opportunity to attend college and was relegated to a technical school. It was there that she had mastered electronics, learned the ins and outs of life support systems, and become a certified technician. A technician who had sealed more than a thousand of the colonists into their chambers. So given Rosemary's expertise, and her position on the crew, it had been relatively easy to rig her own chamber for an early release.

The security cams would record her movements, and there would be hell to pay at the other end of the journey, but that was then and this was now. She'd have the *Outward Bound* to herself for the next nine months. She could roam the ship, read dozens of the books contained in the ship's computerized library, and best of all, be deliciously alone.

No screaming neighbors. No teeming streets. No crowded dorms. Just her. It would be the one and only vacation Rosemary had ever taken and she was determined to enjoy it.

Rosemary grinned again, pushed herself away from the mirror, and pulled herself out into the corridor. It was wonderfully, marvelously, beautifully empty of human beings and the noise they made. There were no announcements over the PA system, no sounds of conversation, and thanks to the geologist that everyone called Dr. B, there was no booming sound. In fact the ship was so silent that it made her nervous. The life support tech yelled at the top of her lungs.

"THIS TUB IS SPOOKY!"

Her voice echoed down the corridor. "SPOOKY! Spooky! Spooky." The sound of it made her feel better.

Rosemary headed for the nearest access shaft, humming as she went, wondering if she could rig the ship's PA system to play some of her favorite music. Some Beethoven, classic Madonna, or China Rock. That would be cool.

Rosemary rounded a corner, did a somersault into the access shaft, and pushed her way upward. B-deck. That's where the controls for the PA system and all the other command and control stuff were located.

Rosemary turned end-over-end the moment she saw C-deck flash by and allowed her toes to skid along the surface of the walls. It slowed her down and worked better than the handholds provided for the same purpose. A thousand black skid marks showed where other people had done likewise.

Rosemary saw rectangles of light appear below, grabbed a handhold, and kicked her feet through the B-deck hatch. She hit the deck, bounced off, and headed down-ship. She hadn't gone more than twenty feet before a gloved hand reached out of a darkened doorway, grabbed her by the throat, and jerked her inside.

"Somebody's up and around all right! I just saw them!" The thought-voice belonged to MOMS.

Martin pulled part of himself out of a side conversation with LES. "Saw them? How?"

"Yeah, how?" SIS echoed.

"Through a maintenance bot," MOMS replied matter-of-factly. "I was jumping from robot to robot, when I landed in one of C-deck's Class IV Garbage Suckers and saw somebody go up through the access shaft."

Of course! MOMS controlled all of the ship's robots. That meant she could selectively hear what they heard, see what they saw, and sense what they sensed. Martin felt his spirits soar. "Could you see what they looked like?"

"Nope. Class IV's don't pack a video lens. Just radar, sonar, and heat detectors. All they see are various kinds of blobs."

Martin thought fast. "Good work, MOMS. The human was headed for B-deck?"

"That's the way it looked."

"Right. How many robots do you control anyway?"

"I have three hundred and fifty-seven effectives, plus seven that are in for maintenance, and two that are slated for scrap. That's because—"

Martin cut the maintenance computer off in midsentence. "Excellent. Send fifty or sixty of them to B-deck right away. Order them to gather right near the access shaft and wait for further instructions.

"Hey SIS, are you with me?"

"Yes . . . but I'm not sure what I can accomplish without my surveillance cameras."

"Can you control the PA system?"

There was a millisecond pause as if SIS was check-

MARS PRIME   89

ing to see if that particular function lay within the
realm of her capabilities.

"That's a roger. Big Dan handles the command and
control stuff, but I provide backup and take primary
control where matters of shipboard security are concerned."

"Well, matters of shipboard security *are* concerned," Martin answered, "so take control."

"Control is mine," SIS said formally. "What
should I do with it?"

"Scare the fecal matter out of him," Martin replied
grimly, "and I'll take it from there."

Rosemary struggled at first but quickly discovered
that the other person was stronger than she was. Not
only that, but the more she struggled, the more violent
her assailant seemed to become. Blows landed on Rosemary's face, ineffectual at first, but more so as the
attacker maneuvered her into a corner and kept her
there.

Rosemary ducked, pushed with her feet, and tried
to get away. The other person caught and pushed her
back. The voice was cold and harsh.

"So, trying to escape are we? You are a bad, bad,
bad girl. Otis has something for bad girls."

The blows came hard and fast. Rosemary used both
hands and arms to protect her face. A horrible realization flooded the young woman's mind. This was
worse than the muggings that she'd survived during her
childhood. Otis planned to kill her! Then she remembered Dr. Havlik and felt something heavy hit the pit
of her stomach. Rosemary went limp and pretended to
be unconscious.

Lights came on as a tiny part of Big Dan sensed
activity in the conference room and responded accordingly. This triggered a response that manifested as a
nagging thought in the back of the command and con-

trol computer's main processor. But there were two or three such minor irritations at any given time, so the Big Guy ignored it. Better that than to miss what Hydro would do if alien bacteria attacked the next cycle's fungus crop.

Rosemary opened her eyes far enough to see the hooded figure that bent over her.

Reassured by his victim's lack of motion, Otis stopped beating her long enough to remove a roll of utility tape from a pocket and tear a piece off. It made a sound like ripping cloth.

Rosemary debated what to do. Remain limp? Hope Otis would leave her alone? Or renew the struggle, knowing her efforts might fail, and incur his wrath?

Rosemary remembered the news coverage, remembered that Havlik had been wrapped with tape, and made the logical decision. She waited for Otis to move in a little closer, stiffened two of her fingers, and drove them through the hood's eye holes. They encountered something soft.

Otis screeched with pain, brought up hands to cover his eyes, and started to babble. The assailant's voice had taken on a strange childlike sound.

"You hurt us! I hate you! Kill her, Uncle Otis! Kill her now!"

Rosemary tried to absorb and understand the strange words while she looked for a way out. Otis floated between her and the hatch, and while temporarily out of action, wouldn't stay that way for very long.

Rosemary put her feet against the wall and pushed. She headed down towards what would have been the deck if the concepts of up and down had meant something.

But Otis saw the move and made a grab for her. Rosemary felt a hand catch the back of her collar and pull her upwards. She grabbed for the console that occupied the center of the room and missed. An arm wrapped itself around her throat. And then, just as the grip began to tighten, the public address system came to life.

"This is the Shipboard Information System. I know where you are and what you are doing. You will stop, place your hands on top of your head, and await further instructions."

Rosemary felt the arm loosen slightly as her assailant took the latest development in. Inertia was carrying them upwards. The overhead, if she could place her feet on the overhead . . .

Otis tried to understand. How could SIS know where he was and what he was doing? It couldn't, not without surveillance cameras, so what the hell was going on? A bluff? But computers don't bluff, do they? Or do they? Some played poker, he knew that, so maybe they could bluff too. The babble of many voices filled his mind. Muscles twitched as neural impulses were sent to various parts of the body and subsequently cancelled. Frank could be heard above all the rest.

"They know where we are! Run, Uncle Otis, run!"

"Shut up," Norma said testily. "Otis knows what he's doing."

"Who died and left you in charge?" Morey asked. "What a jerk."

"Now Morey," Susy started, "that's no way to talk to—"

"Stop it." The words came from Kathy and were instantly obeyed. "Otis, finish what you were doing, then head for the chamber. Something has gone wrong."

Otis remembered something Kathy had learned a long time ago and started to break Rosemary's neck. He was in the process of twisting her head around when the robo cam hit him between the shoulder blades. The blow was hard enough to knock the air out of the body's lungs and push him forward. He hit a bulkhead and bounced off.

Martin gave the electronic equivalent of a rebel yell. The fact that he had access to a video camera, and could bring it into play, had been an afterthought.

The computer entity repositioned Corvan's robo cam for a medium shot. It was something less than satisfying. The killer, and there was little doubt in Martin's processor that this was the same individual that had killed Havlik, wore a hood and an over-sized ship-suit.

Rosemary was free-floating now, trying to suck oxygen in through a badly bruised throat and kicking with her feet.

SIS picked that moment to come over the public address system again. "Hold it right there. Place your hands on top of your head. Wait for further instructions."

The body could breath again. Otis turned his back to the wall. The woman drifted free. Some sort of video camera hovered in front of her. Thank God for the hood. The odds had shifted. His eyes went to the hatch. It was filled top to bottom and side to side with robots. They came in all shapes and sizes and blocked the compartment's only exit. Frank began to cry and Otis didn't know what to do.

"Tackle them straight on," Kathy advised. "Push them out of the way."

The words made sense. The robots could slow him down but that was all. Otis felt a renewed sense of self-confidence. He placed both feet against the bulkhead and pushed. He hit the wall of robots with both hands extended. Two of the robots gave slightly then stopped. Norma swore.

Otis couldn't believe his eyes. The first wall of robots had been reinforced with a second, and beyond that, a third! All of them had their propulsion systems on and were resisting his attack. The body was trapped!

Otis grabbed hold of a robot and pulled. It gave a little, fired reverse thrusters, and held.

Martin felt a sense of grim satisfaction. His quarry was trapped. Now to close in.

"HOW DARE YOU INTERFERE WITH A HUMAN?"

The thought-voice seemed to reverberate through Martin's circuits. Big Dan was powerful, much more powerful than he'd realized, and the force of his presence-personality was almost numbing. Martin tried to say something, tried to respond, but found that he had been isolated from the rest of the ship. He no longer had the ability to control the robo cam, interact with the other computers, or even speak.

SIS, LES, and MOMS were similarly affected. The robots seemed to lose interest in guarding the hatch, created a momentary traffic jam as they tried to leave, and returned to their normal assignments.

Otis saw the confusion, pulled a dart gun from an inside breast pocket, and shot Rosemary twice through the throat. Blood sprayed into the air, made millions of droplets, and formed a curtain of red. It was not the way that he *wanted* to kill her, not the way that he *needed* to kill her, but there was very little choice.

After that it was a simple matter to flee the compartment, make his way through the now blinded corridors, and dump everything into an ejection chute.

The worst part was the journey from the ejection chute to the suspension chamber. Frank cried, Norma bitched, Morey laughed, Kathy was silent, and Susy told everyone that things were fine.

Well, things *weren't* fine, and Otis knew it. Corvan was alive, he still had the notebook, and the ship's computers had come close to canceling his ticket. The process was far from pleasant, especially the catheterization, but he got it done. Sleep came as a blessed relief.

chapter eight

Like most computers, Martin had a tendency to view time as little more than a performance parameter.

But Martin was acutely aware that nine months had passed since Rosemary's death. The *Outward Bound* was in Mars orbit now, and he had very little to do but remember what had occurred and wonder if he'd done the right thing.

What if he had notified Big Dan? Would the Big Guy have listened to him? Taken action to stop the killer?

SIS, LES, and MOMS said no, but they were biased. They were on the Big Guy's shit list too. What would Kim say? Would she be disappointed in him? Wipe his memory so that he ceased to be? It would be a relief in a way. Better than the guilt that continued to haunt him.

Damn! Damn! Damn! If only Hydro's presentation had run five or ten minutes longer. If only Big Dan had given him a chance to explain. If only Rosemary was still alive. But she wasn't, and that was that.

And so it was that time passed and Martin waited.

Rex Corvan drifted slowly upward, like a feather borne on a light breeze, floating toward the light. And there was sound, too, like a great ringing of bells, filling his head to overflowing.

This seemed to go on for some time, with the light gradually becoming more intense and the sound dying away. Then, when the light was so bright that it seemed almost certain to burn a hole through his head, Corvan opened his eyes. A rather attractive woman looked down at him and smiled. She wore the jagged line of a life support tech over the left breast pocket of her ship-suit. A stethoscope drifted sideways from her neck.

"Welcome to Mars orbit. Stay where you are for a while. You may feel some nausea."

The woman's words quickly came true. The chemicals used to resuscitate him had some powerful side effects. A series of dry heaves convulsed his body. They seemed to last forever. But time passed and so eventually did the discomfort.

Corvan waited awhile to make sure that the nausea was truly gone, hit the harness release, and floated upward like a spirit departing for heaven. He saw that others, Kim included, were doing the same thing. He used the suspension chamber to pull himself vertical.

His wife looked thin and pale. Her previously short hair hung down around her shoulders in waves of black. Her nails were long and twisted. She held a hand up in front of her face.

"Yuck!"

Corvan grinned. "You look like hell."

Kim made a face. "Look who's talking!"

A quick check revealed that Corvan's hair and nails were as long as hers. Not only that, but he had a beard that touched his chest.

Corvan laughed, started to record what Kim looked like, and stopped when he saw her glare. "Don't you dare! Not unless you want to sleep with your robo cam for the rest of your life."

The reop held up both hands in mock surrender. "Yes, dear. No, dear. Whatever you say, dear."

Kim smiled. "That's better. Come on. Let's do something about the way we look."

"You're sure you don't know what this is all about," Corvan said, pulling himself down-ship toward the B-deck conference room. Most of the colonists were still sealed inside their chambers so the corridor was nearly empty. The two of them had just taken some much needed showers. Corvan's hair was still wet.

"Nope," Kim replied, "but Jopp was even colder than usual. I think we're in some kind of trouble."

"Trouble?" Corvan inquired. "How could that be? We've been asleep for nine months."

Kim made a face. "I don't know. But if anybody could do it *you* could."

Kim felt guilty about the joke, and the fact that if they *were* in trouble, the fault was probably hers. Especially if Martin had been discovered. What was the penalty for introducing an unauthorized computer entity into the ship's systems anyway? Kim wanted a cigarette in the worst way.

The conference room was just ahead. The hatch stood open. Corvan paused and gestured for Kim to enter. Her hair was short again, her nails were neatly trimmed, and her makeup was in place. She looked wonderful. He winked and she winked back.

Kim pushed her way into the compartment and Corvan followed. The room was smaller than an Earthside counterpart would be. This stemmed from both the shipboard space restrictions and the absence of gravity. Gone were the conference table, chairs, and other furniture that one would expect to find, and in their place was a centrally mounted console and a series of wall mounted Velcro "hooks."

Hobarth and Paxton were both present but only one of them smiled. "Welcome to the inquisition," Paxton said wryly.

Corvan positioned himself in front of some Velcro and backed into it. His suit made contact and held him in place.

"It's that bad?"

Paxton looked serious and nodded. "I'm afraid so."

The security man looked as if he wanted to say something more, Hobarth produced a smug smile, and Jopp chose that particular moment to enter the room. Her expression was as cold as the vacuum outside. Fornos was close behind, and while he didn't look quite as threatening, he didn't seem especially friendly either.

The two of them took their places on the opposite side of the room from Corvan, Kim, and Paxton. Hobarth made a show of giving his slot to Jopp. Fornos touched the console and the hatch hissed closed. He looked first at Corvan then at Kim. There was no sign of the good-natured patience that the reop had encountered before. The administrator was angry and willing to let it show.

"There's something I want you to look at."

A child-sized finger stabbed something on the console. The room darkened. Video appeared on the ceiling. It took a moment to figure out what he was looking at, then Corvan saw a super-graphic flash by and recognized the B-deck corridor. The camera turned a corner and entered a well-lit room. The reop looked and looked again. Yes, it was the same room they were sitting in now. Two people could be seen struggling with each other. One was distinctly female while the other was disguised by a hood and over-sized ship-suit.

The camera paused for a second as if checking the situation out, then charged full speed ahead, and struck the hooded figure between the shoulder blades. He or she let go of the woman, bounced off a bulkhead, and looked around. The camera pulled wide. Corvan saw a doorway packed top to bottom and side to side with robots. All kinds of robots. The assailant dived straight at them. They held. Unable to push his or her way through to the other side the attacker pulled instead. It didn't work. The robots continued to bar the way.

Then something strange happened. The robots started to disperse. They backed up and left the room. The camera drifted from the assailant to the woman. She held up her hands as if objecting to something. Her face contorted in pain. Blood gushed from her throat. The picture faded to black.

Fornos touched a button. The lights came up. The administrator looked Corvan in the eye. "The victim was a life support technician named Rosemary Parker. The investigation is still underway, but it looks as if Parker used her specialized knowledge to arrange for an early release and was up and around when she shouldn't have been."

Corvan nodded. "And ran into someone else who was up and around when they shouldn't have been."

"Yes," Fornos agreed heavily, "and I think we know why." Corvan watched as the administrator unzipped a pocket and withdrew a small notebook. He recognized it right away. It was Havlik's book, the same one he had hidden away beneath his pillow and forgotten to retrieve. The other man's words suddenly acquired additional significance.

Fornos smiled thinly. "You recognize the book. Good. Denials are so boring. Perhaps you would care to explain why a clean-up crew found a book belonging to Dr. Havlik in your suspension chamber? Especially since said book may be evidence in a murder investigation?"

Corvan's throat felt dry. He mustered some saliva and swallowed hard. "I found the book in Dr. Havlik's suspension chamber, saw that it was written in some sort of personal code, and didn't have sufficient time to decipher it.''

Fornos nodded understandingly. ''So, rather than hand the book over to the proper authorities, you kept it, hoping to score one of the journalistic coups for which you are so famous.''

Corvan's face felt warm and he could hear the pulse pounding in his head. Everything the administrator said was true. He forced himself to speak. ''Yes, that's true.''

Now Jopp took over. She made no attempt to hide her disdain.

''Corvan, you and your incredibly overblown ego make me sick. We may never know exactly what happened . . . but try this on for size.

''Somehow, some way, the killer learns that you have the book. Not knowing what it may contain, and fearing that it will give him or her away, the murderer makes arrangements for an early release. He or she plans to find you, do whatever's necessary, and recover the book.

''Meanwhile, in some other part of the ship, Rosemary Parker did much the same thing. I guess we'll never know *why* she wanted to roam around the ship alone, only that she did, and ran into someone else that shouldn't have been up and around either. And *wouldn't* have been except for your unbelievable arrogance.''

Each one of Jopp's words cut like a knife. What she had said was clearly and undeniably true. Rosemary Parker's death was his fault. If only he had given them the book. They might have found a way to decode it, might have identified the killer, might have locked him or her away. His voice was little more than a croak.

''Did you decode the book?''

Jopp looked at Paxton. ''Tell him, J.D.''

Paxton looked sympathetic, as if he could imagine what Corvan felt and didn't want to make it any worse. "Yeah, we ran the code through SIS and came up with a solution."

"Go ahead," Hobarth said smugly. "Tell Corvan what you found."

Paxton shrugged. "Nothing. Nothing important anyway. It seems Dr. Havlik had some rather unusual sexual fantasies and liked to write them down. He used the code to keep them private."

"Get it, Corvan?" Jopp asked coldly. "There was no opportunity for a scoop, to exercise your ego, or rack up some personal profit."

Corvan felt worse than he had felt in his entire life. He nodded miserably. "Got it."

Fornos cleared his throat. "And that brings us to *Mrs.* Kio-Corvan."

Corvan looked at his wife, but she hung her head and refused to meet his eyes. Kim? What had she done?

"What?" Fornos said, correctly reading Corvan's expression. "You didn't know? How interesting. Well, it would seem that your wife shares your proclivity for irresponsible action. You noticed the part of the video where some robots block the doorway?"

Corvan *did* remember. The robots had tried to keep the killer in the conference room. What the—? He nodded.

"That was your wife's doing. Not directly, since she was sealed in her chamber at the time, but indirectly through the A.I. assigned to your department."

Thoughts raced through Corvan's head. The A.I. assigned to his department? No, not the Grass Valley, it didn't have enough chutzpah . . . Wait a minute. Martin could and would so something like that. Martin! That was it! Kim had dumped Martin into the com center's editing setup, and the A.I. was masquerading as the Grass Valley! The reop did his best to look amazed.

"Kim, what's he talking about?"

His wife looked up. Her eyes were cautious, signaling him to watch what he said, yet seemingly sincere. "I gave the Grass Valley some additional programming, that's all. I knew there was a murderer on the loose, knew that my husband and I could be in danger, and did what I could to provide us with some additional protection."

"That's one way to put it," Paxton said, his eyes twinkling. "It seems that your A.I. circumvented Big Dan, gathered support from some lesser computers, and tried to rescue Parker. That's where the robots entered the picture. MOMS put them there to keep the killer trapped in this room. That's when the command and control computer stepped in, and not understanding the situation, released the killer."

"So where's the problem?" Corvan demanded. "It sounds as if our computer came damned close to nailing the killer."

"The problem," Jopp replied coldly, "is that your computer went around the chain of command. The killer would be in custody right now if Big Dan had been properly informed."

Corvan wasn't so sure, but knew better than to say so, especially if Martin was involved. Kim remained silent as well.

Fornos looked from Corvan to Kim. "Hear me, and hear me well. This is absolutely, positively, your last chance. One more mistake and you'll spend the rest of your life scrubbing out the recycling vats. Do I make myself clear?"

Corvan nodded and Kim did likewise.

"Good. Then get the hell out of here. This ship's in orbit around Mars. Billions of people are waiting to see and hear the story. Let's see if you can give it to them without messing up.''

Corvan nodded once more, ripped himself free from the Velcro hook, and waited for Kim to clear the room. He was almost to the hatch when Fornos spoke again.

''And Corvan . . .''

The reop turned. Light winked off the eye cam's lens. ''Yes?''

''Let J.D. handle the detective work. That's what we pay him for.''

''Yes, sir.''

The two of them made their way to the E-deck observation port without any agreement to do so. Soon it would be filled to overflowing with gawking colonists, just up from the long sleep and eager to see their new home.

But Mars was theirs for now, a reddish sphere that threw light against their faces and floated beneath the ship. They hovered side by side. Corvan was the first to speak.

''Beautiful isn't it?''

''Yes,'' Kim agreed. ''It certainly is.''

There was silence for a moment, then Corvan spoke again.

''You know what I hated most?''

''No. What?''

''The fact that they were right. I screwed up and screwed up good.''

Kim put an arm around her husband's waist. *''We* screwed up and screwed up good.''

Corvan smiled and shook his head. ''Bull. *I* took the notebook, *I* hid it under my pillow, and *I* brought the killer out of hiding. There was nothing wrong with your idea. You tried to protect us that's all. It wasn't your fault that Big Dan messed things up.''

''So what now?''

Corvan looked at Mars, its pock-marked surface, and wondered what waited below. "The truth?"

"Yes," Kim replied softly. "The truth."

Corvan pulled her close. "The truth is that I'd quit if I could. Bag the whole damned thing and call it quits. But there's no place to hide. We have a choice. We can shovel journalistic shit or the real thing. And, since journalistic shit weighs less, it seems like the better choice."

Kim laughed. "That's what I love about my husband. He has such a wonderful way with words."

The next eighteen hours were filled with frantic activity. There were lots of stories to cover and only two people to cover them.

First came the trip itself, a successful journey of more than 80 million miles, most of which had been traveled while asleep. Corvan shot the obligatory footage of Mars through the E-deck observation port, carried out the equally obligatory interviews with Fornos and Jopp, and marvelled at how wonderful they made everything sound.

There was no mention of Rosemary Parker or the one hundred and sixty-three colonists and crew that never woke up from their artificially induced sleep, or the messages from the approximately eight hundred people already on the surface.

It seemed construction was running three months behind schedule, there were shortages of certain kinds of building supplies, and few if any amenities.

It seemed the lack of recreation and entertainment had been accepted at first. This was a pioneering effort and the construction workers knew that. But month after dreary month had passed, and while Mars Prime had risen slowly from the ground, living conditions had improved very little.

Making the situation worse was the fact that both

the E-Society and the WPO had painted glowing pictures of how wonderful life would be, of the comforts that had been designed into Mars Prime and the glorious nature of the work itself.

And, from what little bit Corvan was able to learn, comforts *had* been designed into the Mars habitat. The only trouble was that the comforts had been assigned an extremely low priority, which meant that years would pass before most of them would be installed. Years during which the workers would simply go without. Or so the administrators hoped.

And there was more, too; unsettling rumors of crime that were at odds with the planetary paradise that people had been told to expect.

None of that was apparent from Corvan's reports, however. The problem had not become totally unmanageable as yet, and with the blind optimism of administrators everywhere, the suits hoped it would somehow go away.

Corvan was allowed to cover Rosemary Parker's murder, however, since the colonists had already heard about it by word of mouth, and Fornos hoped to kill off the more outlandish rumors.

A version of the story, heavily censored to make it seem as innocuous as possible, had even been sent to Earth where it was snatched up and given a lot of play.

SERIAL MURDERS IN SPACE! the headlines screamed, and people immediately wanted more. So by intentionally downplaying the story the suits had created even more demand for it. But rather than see the situation for what it was, the logical outcome of their own misplaced efforts at control, they resorted to even more censorship.

Hobarth was given the responsibility for censoring Corvan's stories, a job that the administrative assistant carried out with considerable relish and a rather heavy hand. For example:

A colonist who admitted to being "tired" after a sixteen-hour shift was deleted from a human interest story.

The discovery that a crate marked "environment suits" actually contained lawn chairs was suddenly classified as "top secret."

Corvan was ordered to ignore the increasing amount of friction between the New-Agers and the fundamentalist Christians.

But there were victories, too. Like the time that Corvan allowed Hobarth to play reporter and cover a story on shipboard romances. Although the story *seemed* harmless enough, the message that came across when colonists talked about the benefits of a childless relationship was just the opposite from the one that Hobarth was *supposed* to convey.

It could be a long time before the Mars colony could support children, so everyone who shipped out had submitted themselves reluctantly to various forms of birth control, and their angst was apparent to everyone but Hobarth.

And then there was the interview with Idi Ardama the ship's nutritionist. Ardama's assistant, a woman named Chow, had volunteered to sign her supervisor's comments for the edification of the hearing impaired on Earth. Hobarth had been quick to see the political advantages of this idea and had agreed to do the story.

But unbeknownst to him, and to Corvan and Kim for that matter, was the fact that Chow proceeded to contradict every statement that her boss made.

When Ardama said, "the nutritional value of the food was excellent," Chow said "it was poor."

When Ardama said that "the food tasted wonderful," Chow indicated that "it tasted like bat guano."

And, when Ardama claimed "there was plenty of it," Chow said "there wasn't."

Corvan and Kim didn't learn of this deception until

after the story aired on Earth, but enjoyed the furor it made when the truth came out and Hobarth caught hell. It was his story, his decision, and his ass that Jopp chewed on.

Hobarth backed off a bit after that and things improved. Or that's how it seemed anyway, until the Corvans headed dirtside and joined the other citizens of Mars Prime.

chapter nine

The shuttle crouched at the center of the *Outward Bound*'s launch bay and waited patiently as the long line of silver-suited humans fed themselves into its maw. They were crew members mostly, or specially trained colonists, heading dirtside where their skills were needed. The Corvans had been ordered to go along and create a properly upbeat news story for consumption on Earth. No small task given the conditions dirtside.

The air inside Corvan's helmet was dry and musty. He turned his head to the right, found the tube, and sucked water into his mouth. It tasted worse than the air.

He looked around. The line moved in fits and starts. Every now and then the people in front of him would pull themselves forward then stop. Four-foot safety lines connected them to the bright yellow cable that ran from the *Outward Bound*'s lock to the shuttle.

Kim floated just ahead of him, the soles of her boots almost touching Corvan's face. The treads were unmarred by wear. The light came in at a slight angle so that each groove cast its own individual shadow. They were interrupted by an oval with the letters "E L" stamped in the middle.

Corvan knew that the letters "E L" stood for "Eron

Laboratories,'' the company that manufactured the colonists' pressure suits, or "E-suits" as they were more commonly called.

He also knew that while the mission administrators had cut lots of corners the pressure suits were the single exception. They were literally the best that money could buy. Dead people can't do much work, so each and every colonist had been given a first-class computer-designed E-suit, plus a backup should they need it.

Corvan's felt big and bulky but was actually quite light compared to the monsters that the first astronauts had worn. He had read descriptions of what they were like.

To avoid getting the bends it had been necessary to spend up to four hours breathing oxygen prior to an EVA. After that the astronauts had donned a liquid cooling and ventilation garment, a urine collection device, lower torso pants, plus boots, hip, knee, and ankle joints, followed by the upper torso, umbilical and electrical harness, not to mention a life support backpack, gloves, helmet, and visor. Each suit weighed more than 200 pounds on Earth. Not only that, but the suits had been made out of what amounted to fabric, making them vulnerable to rocks or anything sharp. Not a good choice for the surface of Mars. No, his hard suit was much better, and for that he was thankful.

Corvan activated the robo cam. It had come through the fight completely undamaged and sat perched on his right shoulder. The reop's visor would distort and limit the scope of the shots provided by his eye cam, so the remote-controlled device would be much more important that its Earth-bound predecessor had been.

Corvan activated the robo cam with a mental command, took a look through its lens, and saw the line start to move. He switched back.

Kim looked over her shoulder, waved, and he waved in return. The line moved forward, a good twenty feet this time, then stopped. And so it went until the shuttle grew to the size of a small cargo jet. It was a small, boxy ship with little more than pylons where the wings would normally be. The fuselage had been white once, but countless reentries and wind-driven sand storms had burnished it silver. Corvan chose to find this comforting, as if thus tested, the machine was now invulnerable.

Kim pulled herself into the open hatch and Corvan followed. A row of lights marched the length of the overhead. Slivers of bright metal could be seen where heavy cargo had scored the deck. Graffiti covered the bulkheads and part of the ceiling. All of it had been applied with magic markers rather than paint. Some of the colors were brighter than the rest suggesting they were more recent. One entry caught Corvan's eye. It read:

"Welcome to Mars shitheads. You'll be sorry."

Corvan didn't take the graffiti too seriously since he'd seen similar things everywhere, from YMCA camp to Army OCS. Still, it didn't make him feel any better either.

The seats looked strangely new, as if they had only recently come out of storage and were rarely used. Kim gestured for him to start a new row. Corvan accepted knowing that it would put both him and his cameras next to a view port.

Then came the struggle to strap themselves in, another long wait while the rest of the passengers did likewise, followed by an almost anticlimactic departure. The shuttle fired its steering jets, and with no gravity to restrain it, lifted with a minimum of effort.

The shuttle cleared the larger vessel's launch bay a few moments later and descended toward the planet below. Mars was red, just the way it was supposed to be, and pock-marked with craters. With no atmosphere to speak of there was nothing to slow a meteorite down, much less burn it up. Corvan had memorized the statistics.

Mars had a diameter half that of Earth's, orbited the sun at a distance that varied between 128 million and 155 million miles, and had an orbital period of 686 days. A single rotation took 24 hours, 37 minutes, and 22 seconds. That at least would feel normal.

But, due to its relatively smaller size, Mars received less than half as much solar energy as Earth, a fact that had caused it to cool more quickly and form a thicker crust. And, because the thicker crust inhibited volcanic activity, many of the gases that were locked into the rock had never been recycled. As a result Mars lost most of its atmosphere, stayed relatively cold, and had no flowing water.

Once on the ground he could expect a climate that ranged from a high of 60 degrees at noon near the equator to a low of 225 degrees below zero. The thought made Corvan shiver. He turned his heater up a notch.

The reop saw something bright off to the right and wondered if it was one of the planet's two moons. Deimos was about two miles across, and as such, was the smallest known satellite in the solar system. Phobos was only slightly larger and had a somewhat distorted shape. Both moons occupied orbits rather close to Mars, so the light could have originated from either one of them.

Everything looked slightly blurry. Corvan rubbed the window with a gloved thumb. It made little difference. The effects of the annual sandstorms had been etched into the plastic.

Corvan was philosophical. It would be hard to beat the shots he'd taken from orbit anyway. Besides, the construction crew had been dirtside for quite a while now and had sent back enough video of white polar caps, endless wastelands, and dry riverbeds to last everyone a long, long time.

No, that stuff was old hat. His job was to tell the stories that went with the landscape. A city rising from the desert. Geologists probing below the surface. Biologists tinkering with custom-designed microbes. The possibilities were endless.

The shuttle shuddered slightly as it hit the planet's atmosphere. The air might be thin, but it was still there and could present problems. As when the sun heated both the surface and the dust particles floating in the air enough to start a convective cell. Winds reaching speeds of up to 250 miles per hour had been known to result. Scary, but not necessarily fatal, since the air was so thin that the storm would feel like little more than a twenty-five mile an hour breeze to someone standing on the surface. Strong but survivable, assuming that your vehicle was in working order, and you could see well enough to find your way home.

Something felt different, and it took Corvan a moment to figure out what it was. Gravity! It was back! He loosened his harness just to make sure. Yes, there was no doubt about it, something held him in place. He gestured to Kim by pulling the straps out and away from his body. She nodded and made a circle with thumb and forefinger. The reop took the slack out of his harness. It would feel good to walk again even if the gravity was about one third that of Earth's.

The shuttle banked slightly and gave Corvan a view of Olympus Mons, a gigantic volcano that reached fifteen miles into the sky and would have dwarfed Mount Everest had the two sat side by side.

The co-pilot provided them with the kind of narration that shuttle jockey's love, full of facts and figures, and more than a little patronizing. Her voice boomed inside Corvan's helmet and he hurried to turn the volume down.

"Take a look, folks, just off the port side, something to write home about. Olympus Mons. It has a forty-five-mile-wide caldera and a three hundred and thirty-five-mile base. Mars doesn't have tectonic plates, or so the rock doctors tell me, and that means that a volcano could sit over the same plume of lava and grow almost forever."

Some of the colonists craned their heads trying to see while others ignored the whole thing. Corvan was one of the former, taking everything in, excited by the wild untamed beauty of it all. Olympus Mons was quickly gone, giving way to the vast emptiness that lay between it and Chryse Planitia, the area where Viking Lander I had touched down back in 1976. He saw impact craters, networks of deeply cut canyons, and vast rock-strewn plains.

Here was a virgin planet. Well, almost virgin, since man was already scratching away at its surface. But what would become of it? Would Mars become another Earth? Used, abused, and then abandoned? Or had mankind learned a thing or two? Only time would tell.

They were lower now, so low that Corvan could make out individual craters and the larger rocks. He felt the shuttle vibrate as the pilot fired her braking jets. They were thrown forward against the harnesses. The scenery slowed to a crawl. Flying was a matter of brute force due to the almost nonexistent atmosphere. That's why the shuttle had no wings, why the colonists had to get along without aircraft, and why ground transportation was the norm.

Like the takeoff the landing was almost anticlimactic. Corvan barely had time to glimpse a half-finished dome, rows of cylindrical storage tanks, and a com mast before the shuttle rotated on its own axis and descended toward the ground below. The reporter grabbed both of his arm rests, felt his stomach do a flip flop, then steady as the landing jets fired.

Clouds of fine red dust billowed up and around the shuttle. The desert disappeared. It gave Corvan a taste of what a sand storm would be like. Billions of tiny particles whirling through the air, unable to see or do anything about it, forced to stop or run the risk of driving off the edge of a cliff. Not a pleasant thought.

The landing skids hit hard, threw the colonists against their restraints, and caused the pilot to apologize.

"Sorry about that . . . and welcome to Mars."

Corvan hit his seat release and jumped to his feet. He was immediately sorry. His feet broke contact with the deck and his helmet hit the overhead. That's when the co-pilot's voice filled his ears. "Watch yourselves now . . . the gravity is one-third Earth normal . . . and it's easy to overreact."

Corvan knew his wife was laughing at him and couldn't help but smile. What a headline: "Ace reop arrives on Mars . . . then knocks himself unconscious while leaving ship."

The process of leaving the ship was less structured than getting aboard had been. Though among the last to board, the Corvans were among the first to disembark, and saw none of the heavy-handed efficiency so typical of the *Outward Bound*. There was a single space-suited figure by the hatch, reading their names off their suits and entering them into a hand-held portacomp. And, outside of an additional person that served to aim the colonists toward a distant dome, there was no one else around.

The directions were clear enough, though. "Stay on the path. Stay off the radio. Monitor frequency nine. Stay on the . . ."

All of the suits had the capacity to monitor three

frequencies at once. Corvan stayed on nine in accordance with instructions and scanned the other channels for conversation. There was a lot of it on channel five. Construction stuff mostly, intercut with prerecorded infomercials on everything from safety to personal hygiene. He let it rumble in the background.

Corvan activated the robo cam but left it on his shoulder. The words were not planned, not consciously anyway, but flowed as if they had been. It felt that way sometimes, when the story laid itself out in chronological order and his mind was in the groove. The reop checked to make sure his mike was on and laid sound with the pictures.

"This is a brand new experience, and a slightly dangerous one, so the first thing that comes to mind is survival. That means trying to remember the things they taught you about your suit, conditions on the surface, and the various emergencies that might arise. You know the stuff, or think you do, but you wonder about your ability to handle it so there's an empty spot in the pit of your stomach.

"And there are other concerns as well. Remember what it felt like on your first day at a new school? Or when you arrived at summer camp? Or were inducted into the youth corps? You wanted to fit in, to be accepted, to earn some respect. Well, that's what we're going through now.

"The man or woman next to the hatch has been dirtside for more than a year now. Look at his or her suit. It looks worn instead of new. You can see patches here and there along with some sort of artwork on the chest plate. A desertscape with two moons hanging over it. It looks nice. Do all the colonists decorate their suits? Is that how they provide themselves with some sort of individual identity? Just one of the many things we'll learn during the next couple of days."

Corvan reached the bottom of the stairs, made his

way out away from the ship, and turned back. He kept his movements slow and deliberate. He didn't intend to make the same mistake twice. The shuttle loomed large in the foreground. More ships were visible in the background. Dust billowed as one of them lifted off, skittered across the ground, and headed toward a pre-fab hangar. A low ridge could be seen beyond that. A column of dust marked the spot where a ground vehicle moved along the top of it. Corvan cut to a medium shot as the last of the passengers disembarked. He wondered if one of them was a murderer, then pushed the thought aside.

First one colonist, then another, began to run. They ran in circles, jumped up and down, and slapped each other on the back. Many lost their balance, fell, and broke into uproarious laughter. They were reprimanded for a break in radio discipline, threatened with all sorts of horrible punishments, and were forced to pantomime their joy instead.

Corvan launched the robo cam, saw its jets fire, and sent it weaving between them. "And that's what you feel like doing after being cooped up on a ship for nine months. Running and jumping and using your muscles. Muscles that seem stronger than they were on Earth since the gravity is two-thirds lighter."

The reop caused the camera to hover, noticed a suit that was smaller than the rest, and zoomed in. It was only when he saw the name stenciled on the suit that he realized who it was. Dr. Bethany McKeen! Corvan waved but the diminutive scientist was busy doing jumping jacks and didn't notice.

Corvan sent the robo cam up to a higher altitude and zoomed wide. The dome would be huge when it was finished, four times the size of the King Dome in his native Seattle, and sufficient to house more than ten thousand people. But only half the structure was in place and it would be the better part of a year before the rest was finished. It would take all of the metal from the *Outward Bound*'s hull plus tons of fittings, machinery, wiring, furniture and countless other things that hadn't arrived yet in order to finish the dome and make it truly livable. Corvan focused his thoughts and searched for the words to express them.

"And over there, in the distance, a city is rising from the desert. Not a city yet, mind you, but the makings of one—the birth of Mars Prime. A construction project that already ranks with the pyramids, the tunnel under the English Channel, and Luna Base III in terms of complexity, difficulty, and old-fashioned hard work."

The robo cam came in for a landing and they hurried to catch up with the others. An informal pathway led away from the landing pad and toward the collection of cranes, gantries, cylinders, and globes that marked the place where the dome was taking shape. Orderly rows of reddish rock marked both its edges, a yellow hand-line stretched along the left-hand side and was supported by steel stanchions. A safety line in case of sand storms? Corvan wasn't sure and made a note to ask.

Corvan felt Kim's helmet touch his. Her voice was muffled but understandable all the same. "Look."

Corvan looked as only he could and recorded what he saw. An I-beam had been sunk into the ground and hand-lettered signs had been attached. They pointed in every direction, including straight up, and said things like: "New York, 189 million miles, (give or take), Tharsis Rise, 2,500 miles, Lover's Leap, 10 miles" and so forth. Many of the entries were in languages he didn't know. At least some of the construction crew still had a sense of humor: That meant morale was good. Or so it seemed until they neared the half-finished dome and saw sights of another kind.

Kim noticed the chain gang first and bumped Corvan's helmet to tell him about it. "Look . . . I wonder what *they* did."

Or didn't do, Corvan thought to himself as he zoomed in. Their suits had been painted blue in stark contrast to the reddish-orange background. The prisoners had been bound ankle to ankle like the chain gangs of old and were equipped with sledge hammers. They rose in a wave, glinted in the sun, then fell toward the rocks below. Reddish-orange fragments flew up, tumbled end over end, and drifted toward the ground. Fountains of dust sprang up wherever they hit. The work was not as difficult as it would have been on Earth but was far from pleasant. The voice in his helmet was hard.

"Keep it moving newbies . . . or grab a hammer and join in."

The problem with helmet radios is that voices lose their directionality. It took a moment to locate the guard. He stood off to one side and looked average enough, except for the skull and crossbones painted on his chest and the bulky weapon cradled in his arms. Corvan tried to see the guard's face but couldn't penetrate beyond the reflective visor.

Someone tugged at his arm. Corvan turned to find Kim gesturing toward the dome. She was worried, afraid that he'd refuse the guard's order and get them in trouble. The reop forced himself to go along. Kim was right. The story would keep.

The colonists gave the chain gang a wide berth as they trudged toward the dome. They were up close now, walking in its shadow and winding their way through a maze of machinery and construction materials. They stared as construction workers walked by carrying loads that would have been impossible on Earth.

There were machines too, lots of them, and they came in all shapes and sizes. There was no sound to

warn Corvan of their approach, so the reop found himself trying to look in every direction at once, fearful
of an accident. Some had human operators, some were
remote controlled, and some had minds of their own.
The latter took on a variety of shapes and sizes, looking
like tractors, loaders, and yes, human beings.

The reop watched as a bipedal robot followed a human to a pile of conduit, waited while the worker selected six eight-foot sections of pipe, then copied the
sentient's motions with eerie accuracy.

A space suit appeared out of nowhere. It was shorter
than Corvan's and painted to resemble a man in evening clothes. The voice that came over their headsets
was unexpectedly high-pitched and somewhat squeaky.

"All right . . . line up and wait for your name to
be called. A few of you rate private quarters but most
don't. Let's start with the lucky ones first so that the
rest of you will know who to hate. Adair, Arjona, Tom
and Marta, Bartu, Beierle, Bouta, Cera, Civarra, Corvan, Kim and Rex, Deeson . . ."

It didn't take long to name the rest of the people
fortunate enough to rate private quarters and herd them
into a separate group. Once the naming was over another person arrived and identified himself as Father
Simmons. His suit was completely unadorned except
for a rather plainly executed crucifix located at the
exact center of his chest plate. His voice was friendly
and somewhat apologetic.

"Welcome to Mars Prime, everyone. I'm sorry
about the razzing, but entertainment is hard to come
by around here, and that leads to some good-natured
teasing."

Corvan had some doubts about the padre's analysis
but let it go.

"So," Simmons said cheerfully, "I've been assigned to give you the royal tour and make sure that
you reach your quarters safely."

There were murmurs of appreciation but Simmons waved them away. "It's the least I can do, and besides, time is something I have plenty of."

The last sounded somewhat wistful and caused Corvan to wonder if church attendance had fallen off.

They entered the dome through a lock that would eventually be one of many connecting various sections of the interior together. The theory was that if one compartment lost pressure the others wouldn't and most of the colony would survive.

The lock was huge, large enough to drive heavy equipment in and out of, and the newbies shared it with a heavy-duty fork lift. The driver, invisible behind her reflective visor, ignored them.

Red lights flashed on and off as massive interlocking doors slid shut and a prerecorded voice sounded in their helmets. "Please stand by. Please stand by. Do *not* vent your suit until the green lights come on. Do *not* vent your suit until the green lights come on."

Three or four minutes passed, the green lights came on, and another set of doors slid open. The forklift went on its way and the voice returned.

"Please leave the lock. Please leave the lock. You may vent your suits. You may vent your suits."

The group did as they were told, leaving the lock, and breaking their neck ring seals. Corvan heard the hiss of escaping air as he removed his helmet. The reop swallowed and his ears popped. He took a deep breath. The air was thick with various kinds of fumes, ranging from the sharp scent of solvents to the heavier odor of adhesives. Corvan wrinkled his nose and tried to breath through his mouth.

Dr. B took her helmet off, spotted Corvan, and waved from the other side of the group. Corvan waved back.

"There," Father Simmons said, removing his helmet, "that's better."

The gathering dissolved a few minutes later when both groups went their separate ways.

The rest of the tour consisted of a visit to the fusion reactor that supplied the dome with almost unlimited power, the recycling plant where enormous scrubbers cleaned the air, the hydroponics section where genetically-engineered light-gravity vegetables grew to six or eight times normal size, and the chow hall where the colonists ate them.

It was a large open area, featuring lots of stainless steel and large plastic tables. These came in a variety of primary colors, and were intended to give the space a friendly feel, but looked cheap instead.

Though largely illegal on Earth, tobacco was permitted here, and the air was thick with smoke. Kim checked to make sure that her husband's attention was elsewhere, took a deep breath, and made plans to get some cigarettes of her own.

Corvan noticed that while the food looked reasonably good, the colonists who ate it sat in small clumps and watched each other warily. Simmons seemed like a reasonable sort of guy, so Corvan asked about it.

"Tell me something, Father. Is it just my imagination? Or do these people look unhappy?"

Simmons looked at the lens protruding from Corvan's eye socket. "You're a reporter aren't you? The kind with a bod mod."

Corvan nodded. "Yes, I am. But you can speak off-record if you wish."

Father Simmons sighed. "Thank you. That would be best. I am tolerated only so long as I stay out of the way. Yes, there are problems all right, the kind that crop up when people work long hours and have no way to relax. Gambling, prostitution, and drug use are all on the rise. They give rise to graft, gangs, and battles for turf."

He nodded toward the tables. "People divided

themselves along racial-religious lines at first, but that arrangement has slowly given way to groupings by function, with all of the electronic techs banding together and so forth.''

"Similar to unions.''

"Yes, except that traditional unions have very little impact on what a worker does outside of the work place. Here there is nothing but work, so functional groupings take on tribal characteristics.''

"You sound like an anthropologist.''

Father Simmons smiled. "That's because I am one.''

Corvan laughed. "You mentioned drug use. How is that possible? Where does the stuff come from?''

Father Simmons shook his head sadly. "Right here, I'm afraid. We have fifteen research labs, tons of chemicals, and hundreds of scientists. The result is a black market economy where drugs, especially synthesized drugs, are freely available. That's why they allow tobacco. The moment they try to withdraw it other forms of drug abuse soar.''

"Can't they supervise the labs? Arrest the dealers? Treat the users?''

Simmons looked around. The rest of the group was drifting toward the doors. "They try. You may have seen the chain gang on the way in. But the problem is overwhelming. Who do you arrest when you are already behind schedule? When you need every worker you have? When thirty or forty percent of the population is using? That's why Peco-Evans was so happy to see the ship arrive. The project is in trouble and she knows it. The suits hope that the influx of people and supplies will put the lid back on. But I'm not so sure.''

Corvan wanted to ask more questions but the priest shook his head. "Not right now. Later perhaps, when you've been here for a while and had a chance to settle in.''

It was a short walk from the chow hall to the warren of passageways that comprised the admin section. With the exception of three medical technicians and a couple of scientists, most of the group had skills that were vaguely administrative and would be quartered where their work was. A rather interesting arrangement that was calculated to minimize travel time and maximize efficiency. Why have a space to work in and a space to live in, when one space would do?

Of course there was a down side as well, since the arrangement served to isolate the administrators from the work force and accentuate differences rather than similarities. Still another cause for the growing unrest.

And so it was that just off passageway 32 they found a hatch labeled ''Communications.''

Simmons touched the access panel and the door slid open. ''And here it is. Home sweet home.''

Corvan stepped inside. Kim followed. The space was no larger than an average-sized living room. A counter ran the length of the opposite wall. Cables and power outlets marked the locations where their equipment would eventually go. A tall narrow door opened on a tiny bathroom. Panels with labels like ''bed,'' ''storage,'' and ''entertainment'' took up the other wall.

The duffle bags they had sent down the day before lay in the middle of the floor. Both had been sliced open and their contents rifled. Clothes and personal items were scattered all about. Kim swore and began to pick things up.

Father Simmons stuck his head in, saw the duffle bags, and shook his head sadly. ''A sign of the times, I'm afraid. I suggest that you reset the door codes right away.''

Corvan shrugged. "They didn't get much. We packed the things we care about with the com gear."

The priest nodded. "Good. Try and be there when it arrives. A lot of things seem to disappear between the landing pads and here. Are either one of you Catholic by any chance?"

Corvan shook his head. "No, I'm afraid not."

Simmons smiled. "Well, it never hurts to ask. Don't let that stop you, though—I hold ecumenical services once a day, and everyone's welcome."

Corvan started to say something negative but Kim intervened. "Thank you, Father. We'll see you there."

The priest waved, the rest of the group shuffled off, and they were suddenly alone. Corvan touched the access panel. The door slid shut. He turned to his wife.

"We'll see you there?"

Kim made a face. "Maybe, maybe not. There's no reason to hurt his feelings."

Corvan laughed, tried to put his arms around her, and found it didn't work. Space suits are not made for hugging. But it didn't take long to step out of them, shower, and lower the bed. What followed fell slightly short of zero-G sex, but was wonderful nonetheless, and seemed like a good way to welcome themselves home.

Both of them fell asleep after that, but Corvan was the first one to awake and explore their new quarters. He touched the panel marked "Entertainment," waited for it to slide out of the way, and watched the screen come to life. Color sparkled, scattered, and coalesced into words.

"Welcome to the Mars Prime entertainment and communications system."

The words vanished to be replaced by a menu. There were all sorts of possibilities, including movies, video games, and visually enhanced reading material. Okay for a while, but boring after a couple of months. One of the listings flashed on and off.

Corvan touched ''Personal Communications'' and watched the menu transform itself. More choices appeared. He could send and receive voice, text, and a variety of visuals. ''Message waiting,'' blinked on and off. He touched it. Words flooded the screen.

''LEAVE US ALONE. LEAVE US ALONE. LEAVE US ALONE. YOU WERE LUCKY. YOU WERE LUCKY. YOU WERE LUCKY. WE WILL KILL YOU NEXT TIME. WE WILL KILL YOU NEXT TIME. WE WILL KILL YOU NEXT TIME.''

chapter ten

Barbu Sharma floated up through the pain. It came in layers, like sediment in a core sample, and could be categorized just as easily.

First came the pain associated with withdrawal, abdominal cramps mostly, but nausea and occasional tremors too.

Then came the sharper more insistent pain, most of which came from his right shoulder but from other places as well. Contusions most likely, damage suffered during the dimly remembered accident hours before, when his crawler had run off the edge of a ravine.

Hours? How many hours? Hours meant oxygen, and oxygen meant life.

Fear pumped adrenaline into Sharma's bloodstream and lifted him through the last layer of pain. His eyes popped open. He saw no control panel, no interior lights, nothing but darkness. Panic tried to take control. He forced it back. Think damn it . . . Think through the pain . . . Think about the facts. He was alive wasn't he? Damned right he was. That meant the suit was working.

Sharma looked up, and there they were, all along the upper edge of his visor. Indicator lights, yellow most of them, verging on red, but lights nonetheless.

Candles in the darkness, symbols of hope, givers of life.

Now it came back to him. The faulty door seal, the steady loss of cabin pressure, and the decision to don his helmet. *After* dropping some red zombies, *after* washing them down with non-reg hootch, *after* a long day.

Yeah, he'd been ripping along, singing a pop tune at the top of his lungs, when the crawler had gone off the edge of the ravine and nose-dived into the canyon below. He thought it had, anyway, but wasn't exactly sure.

A series of dry heaves racked his body. What he wouldn't give for one, just one red zombie, to clear his head and feel human again.

Sharma's mouth was dry and tasted like shit. He searched for the water tube, found it, and took a sip. The liquid felt good as it trickled down his throat.

Now for the hard part. He had to do something. Find a way to save his ass.

The crawler was nose down and tilted toward the right. He groped for the door release, found it, and pulled. It fell away. The safety harness held him in place. What the hell? What was down there anyway? Solid ground? Or a bottomless pit? What if the crawler was hanging off a ledge? Teetering on the edge of an abyss?

Sharma ignored the already blinking power indicator and triggered his helmet light. The beam was feeble but revealed gravel six feet below. Thank God, or the group of gods, that watched over him. His mother had tried to teach him which ones did what, lecturing while she cooked dinner or did the washing, but he'd been a poor student. Of things like that anyway . . . No, he mustn't allow his thoughts to wander, mustn't waste energy on opportunities missed and people long dead.

Sharma hit the harness release, fell out of the crawler, and landed on his already injured shoulder. The hard suit absorbed most of the impact but not all. The pain made him scream. His radios were off, but no one would have heard him anyway, since Mars Prime was more than a hundred miles away and well out of range.

The crawler was another matter. Its radio was clearly out of action, a victim of whatever had killed the power plant, but the emergency locater beacon should be okay. It was battery powered and built to survive damned near anything. And that meant he had a chance. Assuming that a com sat picked up the signal, assuming that the search and rescue assholes were on the way, and assuming that he could last long enough for them to arrive. Fat damned chance. The truth was that he'd wind up dead. Seriously dead. Dead, dead.

No! He couldn't, shouldn't, wouldn't think like that.

Sharma pushed himself to one knee, took a deep breath, and stood. He felt his head spin, felt his body sway, and felt the ground come up to meet him. Shit.

It felt good to lie on his back and look up at the river of stars. They were extremely bright, like ice crystals on black velvet, so close that he could reach out and scoop them up. No, he had to concentrate, had to focus on the task at hand.

Sharma rolled over and began to crawl. His destination wasn't exactly clear, but had something to do with dragging himself out of the ravine so that the searchers could find him.

It was cold inside the suit, so damned cold, but he didn't dare turn up the heat. No, he had to save power, save power, save power. Shit, he was losing it again . . . fading fast . . . buying the farm . . . checking out . . . stop!

Sharma stopped, rolled onto one side, and activated his helmet light. He moved his head back and forth.

The yellow beam played over a steep embankment, glinted off something, then lost itself in darkness. He brought it back, found the spark of reflected light, and stopped.

What was that anyway? Ice? Quartz? Metal? No, it couldn't be metal, not in the wastelands of Mars. Could it? Not unless it was part of an old wreck, a crawler like his, destroyed when it fell into the ravine and left as unsalvageable. But that was stupid. The odds against something like that were millions to one.

His thoughts were suddenly gone, consumed by nausea and the dry heaves that came with it. It took some time for the convulsions to die away.

Something started to beep. Sharma looked up toward the indicator lights, saw that his oxygen was in the red, and knew he had fifteen minutes left. Fifteen minutes in which to contemplate a largely wasted life, pray to his mother's gods, or fight for survival.

He crawled toward the glint of reflected light, drawn to it like a moth to flame, determined to possess whatever it was. Knowledge perhaps, or a talisman, something to take with him.

"One foot, two foot, three foot four, drag your butt across the floor."

Sharma giggled then forced himself to stop. He was losing it, oh yes, lose, lose, losing it. Oxy deprivation? Maybe . . .

Now! There it was, only inches away, metal by god! Bright, shiny metal. Sharma scrabbled at the embankment, pulling himself up, reaching for the metal. Gravel, rock, and sand avalanched down around his boots, sliding away from the metal as if reluctant to touch it, fanning out to become part of the ancient river bottom.

The beeping seemed louder now, even more insistent than before, a horrible sound that bored holes in his brain, and signaled things he didn't want to think about.

Sharma leaned forward. His glove touched dirt and something solid beyond that. Another curtain of gravel fell and a hole appeared in the metal. A pinprick at first, through which a tiny ray of light passed and formed a dime-sized dot at the center of his chest. Then it grew, and grew, and grew until the opening was about three feet across, and he was bathed in light. The aperture was round and looked like the bore of his father's twelve-gauge shotgun. The tunnel was smooth and oily, as if a cleaning patch had been passed through it.

Sharma did his best to look inside, to see where the light came from, but it was far too bright and caused his visor to polarize.

Should he enter? Take a chance on the unknown? Or wait for help? Stupid question. Light meant power, and power meant oxygen, or the possibility of it anyway. Sharma bent at the waist, stuck his head into the circular passageway, and wiggled inside.

The walls were slick, so it was difficult at first, but he pulled himself forward until his knees hit the embankment and it was necessary to straighten his legs.

The beeping went on and on. He hated the sound and loved it at the same time. The beeper symbolized life and living. Existence measured out in second-long increments. How many were left anyway? A thousand? A hundred?

Something moved and Sharma felt the resulting vibration through his suit. What the—? He turned, felt his helmet hit the side of the tunnel, but managed to look over his shoulder anyway. Damn! Look at that! The passageway had closed behind him. He didn't know whether to feel scared or grateful.

Sharma turned back, reached toward the light, and felt his glove encounter something solid. Trapped!

Now he felt scared, and no sooner had that emotion registered on his brain than the beeping stopped. His oxygen was completely and irrevocably gone.

Sharma drew shallow little breaths, desperate to extend his quickly dwindling lifespan, trying to take it in.

He was dying, actually dying, and little more than seconds left. How many seconds? Well, the suit might hold two or three minutes worth of air, so three times sixty would be . . .

No! It was stupid to draw it out. Slowly, deliberately, Sharma reached up to release his neck seal. Anything was better than death by slow asphyxiation. The safety cover flipped upward with ease, the lever moved under his fingers, and air hissed out of his helmet.

Sharma waited for his brains to be sucked out through his eyes and ears. Waited for blood to spurt out through the pores in his skin. Waited for the brief moment of mind-numbing pain before he ceased to exist.

Nothing happened. It took a moment to register. Nothing meant oxygen, and oxygen meant life, and that was good. Excellent! Wonderful! Incredible!

Unless he was trapped inside some sort of metal tube where no one could find him. Sharma reached through the light. The barrier had disappeared. Then he had it. The tube was some sort of air lock, like the ones humans used on their ships. . . .

Oh shit, shit, shit! Sharma pushed himself backwards, away from the light, towards the entrance.

What the hell would use a tubular air lock? Some sort of goddamned snake, that's what, or a slug-like thing, or . . .

No, there he went again, freaking out when he should be thinking. The alien thing was stupid. Wasn't it? Yes, damn it. The most likely possibility was some sort of secret military installation. Maybe they'd developed some sort of tubular thingamajigs that needed their own lock. God only knew what those bastards were up to. Yeah, that made sense. The suits would be pissed at him, but hey, he'd be alive and that was the main thing.

Sharma wiggled forward, stopped while another bout of dry heaves racked his body, and resumed his journey. The light came from a ring-shaped fixture that was mounted flush to the tunnel. Sharma inched his way past it, found himself on an incline, and slid to the bottom.

He rolled over, sat up, and took a look around. So much for the military hypothesis. The interior of the ship, for that's what Sharma had decided that it was, wasn't even vaguely human.

The room was large and sort of womb shaped. The light was bright and came from panels that spiraled around the walls. A lattice-work of what looked like dried seaweed crisscrossed the open space, drooped in places, but was largely intact. There were four kidney-shaped constructs too, dangling from the ceiling like pieces of abstract sculpture.

And there, hanging between them, was an alien, or what had been an alien hundreds or even thousands of years before, and was now little more than a desiccated mummy. A tube-shaped mummy that had oozed, wiggled, or squirmed through the same lock he had. His first guess had been correct after all.

A chill ran down Sharma's spine. Had the idea been the result of logical extrapolation? Or some kind of weird vibrations transmitted by the ship itself? He shook the thought off. The place was spooky enough without adding anything to it.

The stomach cramps started again, causing him to double up in pain and momentarily wish that he were dead. They passed after a minute or two, but left him gasping for breath and covered with sweat.

It was warm inside the alien ship, so he made a decision to shuck the E-suit. Sharma stood, unhooked the helmet from its umbilical, locked the major joints and released the seals. He touched a switch and heard servos whine as a seam appeared down the front of his body, and the left and right front quarter panels hinged open, followed by the thigh panels, lower legs, and boot covers. The movements seemed slower than usual, as if the power pak was almost completely exhausted and giving up the last ergs of its precious energy.

After that it was a simple matter to pull his arms out of the sleeves, disconnect himself from the urine collection device, and duck out of the shoulder yoke.

Sharma took a step away from the suit, caught a whiff of his own body odor, and wrinkled his nose. Whew! Time to hit the showers and then some.

The floor . . . deck? . . . was littered with pieces of dried out something. Sharma could feel chunks of the stuff pressing up through his synthi-leather booties as he walked around.

An alien space ship. Damn, what the suits wouldn't give to get their hands on this baby! What the hell had happened anyway? A crash? Maybe, but nothing seemed damaged. A landing then, followed by an unexpected illness, or something similar.

Sharma looked up into the spiraling lights. The tube-shaped thing just hung there, the dried out leavings of what had been a sentient thing, one of many such creatures that had . . . still did? . . . wiggle and squirm with life.

Sharma paused for a moment and looked around. How the heck had the alien hoisted itself up there anyway? And why? The human walked in a circle trying to imagine what the space had looked like hundreds or thousands of years before. The tube-shaped thing hanging there, directing the activities of the ship, thinking about what? Food? Sex? Power? There was no way to tell.

Okay, the shift is over, time to take a break. What does the tube-shaped guy do now? Lower itself to the floor by means of those seaweed things? No, trained or symbiotic plants were a possibility, but he really didn't think so. The latticework looked too lacy, too even, as if it were left over from something else.

Left over! Now there was an interesting idea! What if something had dried out and disappeared over the years? Something that had filled the room. How do tube-shaped things move anyway? They squirm over and through dirt or water, that's what. Water! Maybe the whole space had been filled with water! Or a jelly-like substance. Yeah, a tube-shaped thing would like that, squirming around through oxygen-enriched clear gelatin, protected from G-forces, moving up, down, or sideways as the need presented itself.

So, what if the alien had wiggled up to where it was now, had died in place, and been suspended there as the jelly-like stuff dried out. It made a halfway decent theory and would also explain the kidney-shaped thing-amajigs that surrounded it. They were control panels or the worm equivalent thereof.

Yeah, it made a lot of sense, but did him no good whatsoever. What he needed was a way to summon help, or failing that, to resupply his suit. Then he could walk out, trade the ship's coordinates for some cash, and retire to Earth. Sharma imagined a future filled with money, sex, and power. What a way to go . . . No, there was work to do first.

Okay . . . first step. Explore the rest of the ship. There was power here, the lights proved that, and plenty of oxygen. All he had to do was find a way to transfer them into his suit.

The ensuing search took an hour or so, with time out for bouts of nausea and the accompanying stomach cramps.

Sharma found three additional womb-shaped compartments. All showed signs of having contained the jelly-like substance and were interconnected by tube-shaped air locks.

The first compartment was relatively small and might or might not have correlated to a galley-mess area. There were no appliances as such, or furniture, just a series of transparent bins, each containing thousands of what looked liked multicolored berries. These were fed down through a funnel-like device to a nozzle.

Sharma imagined a worm wiggling its way into the compartment, wrapping an organ around the nozzle, and sucking berries into its what? Mouth? Stomach? God only knew.

The second compartment was quite large and filled with what Sharma assumed was machinery, though it was sealed inside metal casings and completely inaccessible. A rather sensible precaution when one lives in gelatin.

The third compartment was smaller, a cargo bay from all appearances, and filled with a double-helix-shaped storage system, which, though inconvenient for humans, would be rather useful for goo-encased worms.

A quick check revealed that the storage system was full of carefully bagged rock samples. Sharma grinned. A rock doctor! Or collector anyway. The alien had been in the same line of work that he was! What a small universe.

The most valuable discovery, however, was the suit locker. He found it towards the far end of the cargo bay next to a second and even larger lock.

The first thing that Sharma noticed was that while

there were provisions for two suits one of them was missing. Was it outside somewhere? Pinned under a fallen rock? Buried by a landslide? Is that what had happened? One worm had gone out and never returned? And the other had waited, and waited, and waited? There was no way to tell.

The remaining suit went a long way towards confirming some of his theories, however. It was tubular in shape, about nine feet in length, and stored horizontally rather than vertically.

The outside surface of the suit was covered with hundreds and hundreds of textured black balls. Sharma found that while some of the balls spun freely, others refused to budge, suggesting a drive system of some sort.

The inside surface of the suit was slippery with what might have been lubricant and was heavily dimpled. Sharma imagined a worm sliding into the suit, pushing some of its substance into each one of the dimples, and controlling it through the resulting contact.

The other thing he noticed was that the suit was quite thick. Thick enough to protect the worm and still leave room for air bladders and power cells to be sandwiched into its skin.

But while all of these discoveries were interesting, and would have driven the egg heads crazy with scientific lust, the most important discovery was ancillary to the suit itself.

It consisted of a hose that led from the inside of the locker to the suit and a cable that did likewise. Oxygen and power! The very things he was looking for. But what about compatibility?

Sharma worked slowly and carefully, pulling, twisting, and turning until the oxygen hose hissed loudly and popped out of the suit. The hissing stopped and he looked it over. Not too surprisingly the fitting was totally incompatible with one on his suit. Still, with a little ingenuity and some hard work, anything was possible.

The power lead came loose more easily but represented a much more difficult problem. There was no way to tell what kind of power plant the ship came equipped with, or what would happen if he found a way to hook it to his suit. Everything might blow.

No, Sharma decided, it was far too dangerous and completely unnecessary. There was an emergency solar collector built into his suit. It would limit the speed with which he could travel, and would be a pain in the ass to use, but it would get him home. Or who knew? There was still the chance that the S & R types had followed the beacon to the ravine and were out there looking for him.

There was an emergency tool kit in his suit. It took four hours worth of filing, bending, hammering and cajoling to bring the two different fittings together, and the better part of a roll of tape to hold them in place, but the hiss of air was reward enough.

It took about forty minutes to fill the tanks, reconnect the helmet, and check the oxy readout. Both tanks were full-up. Just enough to reach home. Assuming he was careful.

Sharma felt his stomach growl and realized that the cramps had stopped. He felt hungry. Sharma reached for the pocket that should contain emergency rations and remembered that he'd thrown them out a long time ago. They tasted like shit and the exterior suit pocket was useful for other things. Like hootch and drugs.

Sharma remembered the bins of what had looked like berries. What would happen if he ate them? Would he die? Want more? What?

It took only seconds to make his way back to the galley-food center. He fumbled around with one of the nozzles, received nothing for his efforts, and wiped his mouth with the back of his hand. There was no way around it. If he wanted a berry he'd have to put his lips around a nozzle and suck it out. Just like the worms had presumably done.

One part of his mind knew it was stupid, knew that the berries could kill him, but another part didn't care. It was the part that liked to walk on ledges, that dropped pills with funny names, that blasted free from Earth when many were afraid to do so.

Sharma imagined how the worm-thing had wrapped itself around the same nozzle, pushed the thought into the back of his mind, and sucked. A berry, or whatever it really was, popped into his mouth. He swirled it around for a moment and waited for some sort of taste to make itself known. Nothing.

He would have to bite down, release whatever was inside, and take his chances. Sharma used his tongue to position the tiny globe between his upper and lower teeth and bit down on it. He felt it pop, felt some sort of liquid flood his mouth, and felt his mouth pucker when it turned out to be sour. He swallowed.

So far so good. He was alive. Alive and not especially . . . Something happened deep inside his brain. Reactions took place, connections were made, and synapses closed. The pleasure reminded him of sex, except it was centered inside his skull and was different somehow. Instead of release there was a pleasant up-welling of emotion, a feeling of contentment, and a desire to please. An upper if he'd ever experienced one.

The feeling lasted ten minutes then disappeared. He tried another berry with the same results. Then Sharma leaned forward, started to put the nozzle in his mouth, and forced himself to stop. It was clear that these things were incredibly addictive. A couple more and he'd be irrevocably hooked, a condition that would kill him just as easily as oxy deprivation, only a lot more pleasantly.

Sharma forced himself to stand, forced himself to leave the compartment, forced himself to think. This was big, bigger than the ship itself, which was like money in the bank. How would a really smart operator handle it? How could he take advantage of the situation in such a way that the suits couldn't rip him off? How could he have his cake and eat it too?

It didn't take Sharma long to come up with the answer, and when he did, the smile went ear to ear.

chapter eleven

His name was Manuel Ochoa, a welder by trade, and he had died a rather unpleasant death.

Corvan started with a medium shot of the crumpled body, then tilted up along the blood-smeared wall to the gore-splattered ceiling. There was a clump of black hair just to the right of the light fixture, held in place by a smear of dried blood, marking the spot where Ochoa's head had hit, and hit, and hit.

The reop saw a camera mount in the background but no camera. The area was still under construction so the chances were good that it hadn't been installed yet.

The shot was far too graphic for broadcast use, but Paxton had asked him to record it anyway and send the video to security for analysis.

Like many of the *Outward Bound*'s computer systems, the artificial intelligence known as the "Shipboard Information System," or "SIS," had been brought dirtside and installed in Mars Prime. Hobarth had suggested renaming the A.I. "Planetary Information System," or "PIS," but had been unanimously overruled.

By comparing the latest video with the stuff shot aboard *Outward Bound*, it was possible that SIS would find some sort of clue as to the killer's identity.

Possible, Corvan thought to himself, but damned unlikely. The killer had operated with impunity so far, and barring some bad luck, would most likely continue to do so.

The reop sent the video to Kim, who looked at it, gagged, and instructed Martin to pass it along to SIS.

Paxton was the number two security person now, second only to Lois Scheeler, who'd been there from the beginning and reported straight to Peko-Evans. That's why Paxton got the nasty jobs like labor demos and murders.

The security officer wore his usual outfit of overalls, utility belt, and com set. The com set was connected to Paxton's brain via his temple jack. He turned away from a conversation with one of his security people and nodded towards the body.

"Got it?"

Corvan nodded. "Yeah, SIS has it by now. How did the killer do it?"

Paxton raised an eyebrow. "Do what?"

"Bang Ochoa's head against the ceiling like that."

The security man smiled. "Beats the heck out of me."

Corvan frowned. "Not funny, J.D. And there's something else too . . . Remember the way Havlik was taped from head to toe? And how the killer tried to immobilize Rosemary Parker?"

"Yeah? So?"

"Take a look around," Corvan replied earnestly. "There's no tape, no rope, no sign of restraints. It looks as though the killer grabbed this guy, banged him into the walls and ceiling, then dropped him like a rock."

Paxton's expression had changed from amusement to annoyance. "Come on Rex, cut me some slack. If you've got a point then make it."

Corvan spread his hands. He felt frustrated and did

his best to conceal it. "The point is that you have two different M.O.'s. One in which the victims were immobilized, and one in which they weren't."

"Implying two different killers," Paxton said skeptically.

"Exactly!" Corvan responded.

The security man shook his head. "Maybe, but I don't think so. The first murders took place in zero-G. That meant the killer *had* to immobilize his or her victims in order to harm them. Here they have some gravity to work with, and comparatively light gravity at that, making it possible to lift the victim and bang him into walls. Chances are they simply like it that way, and would have done it before except for the lack of gravity. Besides, look at the timing. There were no murders until the *Outward Bound* dropped into orbit and sent people dirtside."

"Which is when we received the threat."

Paxton nodded. "Which is when you received the threat. Congratulations by the way . . . it was nice of you to let us in on it."

Corvan shrugged. "Not that it did much good."

Paxton sighed. The two of them had been through this countless times before. The reop wanted a full-time guard, someone to watch over Kim, and Paxton didn't have anyone to spare. Not with a soaring crime rate, increasing labor unrest, and a murderer on the loose. Still, he understood Corvan's concern and wanted to help. He put a hand on the other man's shoulder.

"Look, I'll send someone by every hour—it's the best I can do."

Corvan smiled. "Thanks, J.D. I owe you one. Let me know if SIS comes up with anything new. And one more thing . . ."

"Yeah?"

"Ochoa was a big man. A welder. How could one

person grab him, beat his head against the ceiling, and not take some lumps him or herself?''

Paxton smiled. ''Who said it was one person? How 'bout all that 'we're gonna get you' stuff?''

Corvan shook his head helplessly and stepped into the hall. He opened the link to Kim. ''Everything okay?''

Kim made a face that Corvan couldn't see. She didn't like the pictures she'd seen, didn't like being vulnerable, and didn't like the labor dispute. But it wouldn't do any good to talk about it so she lit a cigarette instead. It tasted good. Kim sucked the smoke into her lungs and let it dribble out with her words.

''Sure . . . things are fine.''

''Did the Earth feed come in?''

Mars Prime received two news feeds per day. They included everything from politics to sports. It was Kim's job to edit them down, insert fifteen minutes worth of local coverage, and send the results out over the com net. And yes, the Earth feed had arrived right on time. But that wasn't what Corvan wanted to know. He might be the man that she loved, but he was a world-class reop and had an ego the size of Olympus Mons. Kim smiled.

''The landing story is still getting some play, they want more on the robots, and everyone's screaming for an update on the murders. 'Murder in outer space.' The tabs love it.''

''No problem there,'' Corvan said grimly. ''We've got more blood and gore than we know what to do with.''

''Yeah,'' Kim replied soberly. ''That's for sure. Now, don't let this go to your already oversized head, but your reports have topped the in-show ratings for six days running.''

Corvan wanted to cheer and jump up and down but

managed to restrain himself. There was no point in reinforcing Kim's already negative estimate of his ego.

"That's nice. What's next?"

"The computer story. Remember? You've got an appointment with Peko-Evans, Fornos, and Jopp."

The reop groaned. He believed in the story, but not the way Kim did, and certainly not the way Martin did. The A.I., plus their com gear, had arrived within a surprisingly short period of time. A spontaneous work stoppage had forced them to meet the shuttle, find the equipment, and transport it themselves. Something they had wanted to do anyway to avoid pilferage. And, given the forklift Corvan had borrowed, plus the light Martian gravity, things had gone rather smoothly.

Until Martin had come on-line that is. The A.I. was absolutely furious. It seemed that Big Dan, and the other systems that had no dirtside applications, were still up in orbit. The moment that the *Outward Bound* was officially decommissioned their memories would be erased, their processors set aside for other applications, and their peripherals converted to other uses.

And since A.I.s had yet to acquire sentient status in the courts, no one saw their impending destruction as much of a problem. No one except Martin, that is, who like his namesake Martin Luther King thought all sentient beings should have the same basic rights. Scientists, theologians, and philosophers could debate all day long whether Big Dan, MOMS, and LES were truly sentient, but Martin knew what President Hawkins would have said.

"If it walks like a duck, and quacks like a duck, chances are that it's a duck."

So Martin came up with a plan, solicited Kim's support, and led the effort to convince Corvan. No simple matter, since while the reop felt a strong sense of loyalty toward Martin, he didn't feel the same way about computers in general.

But by virtue of nonstop nagging, guilt trips, and appeals to Corvan's ego they had convinced him to pick up the baton and run with it. Maybe, just maybe, the suits would listen to reason. So he groaned, killed the interface, and headed up-corridor.

Some bozo or bozette had used a magic marker on a freshly painted wall: "Management sucks!"

Corvan looked, thought about it for a second, and nodded in silent agreement.

The supply room in which Ochoa had been killed was a good ten-minute walk from the admin section. It gave Corvan a chance to watch the workers without seeming to do so.

Most moved with maddening slowness, fast enough to avoid a shirking charge, but slow enough to drag things out. The interesting part was that most, if not all of the newbies had joined in. Their unblemished suits and freshly painted chest plates were a dead give-away.

Some of the workers turned to frown at Corvan, told him to slow down, or flipped him the bird. There was no doubt about it. The mood was getting worse all the time. Something would have to give, and give soon.

The admin section was busy. People moved from room to room. Robots whirred by on errands. A never-ending series of messages were passed over the PA system, and a truly formidable desk barred Corvan's way. It was made from scrap steel and appeared to be bulletproof. The person behind it was none other than W.K. Julu, defender of the chief administrator's inner sanctum, and the power behind the throne.

The only question was which throne? The one belonging to Fornos? Or Peko-Evans? It was hard to tell since the newly arrived colonists had been integrated into the existing structures and were still settling in.

A process that would be repeated each time that a ship arrived.

The manner was as it had been before. Formal, clipped, and extremely British.

"Mr. Corvan."

"Mr. Julu."

"And how may I help you?"

"I have an appointment to meet with the executive council."

Julu touched a screen, waited for something to appear, and frowned. "Yes. The council meeting is running late. Take a chair. I'll call you as soon as they're ready."

The waiting area had four chairs and two of them were already occupied. Corvan sat down next to a man with a nervous tic in his right eyelid, exchanged nonsensical pleasantries, and grabbed the most recent *Newshour* magazine. The print-out was twenty-four hours old, which made it ancient history by Earthly standards but reasonably current on Mars. He found a file photo of himself in the newsmakers section along with a highly sanitized story about the murders.

Hobarth had reworked most of Corvan's words to make the murders seem pleasant and nonthreatening. It made Corvan realize something. The high ratings didn't flow from what he'd said, or the way that he'd said it, but from the subject matter itself. Murder in space. It was a story that would generate ratings if reported by a robot. So much for his brilliance.

"They're ready to see you now, Mr. Corvan."

"Thank you, Mr. Julu."

A pair of double doors had opened behind Julu. Corvan nodded to the administrative assistant, made his way around the massive desk, and entered the conference room. It was enormous, and would eventually accommodate three times the number of people seated in it now, but was presently unfinished. Only two of the walls were paneled, temporary wiring looped across the ceiling, junction boxes were piled on the floor.

The conference table consisted of some wall panels resting on saw horses. It was littered with print-outs, empty meal paks, binders, and other paraphernalia. One end sagged under the combined weight of computer terminals and communications gear.

But, if the furnishings were something less than glamorous, the view more than made up for it. Mars Prime had been sited on a slight rise. As Corvan looked out through double-thick armored plastic he saw rock-strewn red soil stretch down to an ancient riverbed, and beyond that, a magnificent tower of jagged rock. Some cast-off cargo modules littered the foreground. Corvan wondered if they were harbingers of things to come.

Fornos cleared his throat. "Good morning, Rex. Thank you for coming. Grab a chair and make yourself comfortable. You know the assembled multitude?"

Corvan took a vacant chair and looked around the table. Fornos was his usual self, affable but somewhat less commanding in the shadow of Peko-Evans.

As for the woman herself, she sat at the head of the table and smiled in a preoccupied sort of way.

Jopp was present as well, and nodded in acknowledgment, a move that Hobarth managed to imitate a quarter of a second later.

"Yes, I believe I do. Thank you."

"So," Peko-Evans said, placing her elbows on the table, and leaning forward. "You get around . . . Tell us what you think about the labor situation."

Corvan considered telling her what she wanted to hear, rejected the thought as beneath both of them, and told the truth. "The construction workers are angry. They believe promises have been broken. The newbies are going along. In a week, two at the most, something will blow.''

Peko-Evans nodded, gave Hobarth a scathing look, and directed a smile towards Corvan. ''Thanks. Some people have a tendency to pee on my boots and tell me it's raining.''

Corvan wanted to laugh, knew Hobarth wouldn't like it, and managed to hold back.

Jopp changed the subject. Her eyes burned holes through his head. ''You wanted to discuss computers.''

Corvan felt silly and unsure of himself. Here he was, carrying a message that he only half-supported, addressing an audience that thought he was a jerk. What the hell for? He realized that the silence had stretched long and thin. He forced a smile.

''The murders are getting a lot of play on Earth, the labor dispute could break at any moment, and there's the very real danger of still another negative story.''

''Oh, really?'' Jopp asked coldly. ''And what might that be?''

''The computers,'' Corvan said firmly. ''Specifically those that are sentient, or near sentient, and scheduled for deactivation.''

Fornos raised an eyebrow. ''We no longer need them. So what's the problem?''

Corvan forced an earnestness that he really didn't feel. ''The problem is that many people, not to mention the computers themselves, believe that deactivation is equivalent to murder.''

Hobarth gave a derisive snort. ''Please! What's next? Birthday cards for my calculator?''

Peko-Evans brought her fingertips together. ''Give us a scenario.''

Corvan shrugged. ''You deactivate Big Dan, MOMS, and LES. News of that makes it way to Earth. The results could range from no attention at all to extensive press coverage and public demonstrations. Think about the headlines: 'Mars team murders MOMS!' The tabs would have a field day.''

Peko-Evans looked thoughtful.

Fornos frowned.

Jopp leaned back in her chair. ''I see a flaw in your logic, Corvan, and a rather obvious one at that. How will the news reach Earth. Unless *you* send it there?''

Silence prevailed as Corvan looked around the table.

Peko-Evans smiled but made no effort to intervene.

Fornos tapped his teeth with a stylus and wouldn't meet Corvan's eyes.

Hobarth grinned stupidly, and Jopp's expression remained completely unchanged.

''So you're going ahead with deactivation?''

Jopp nodded. ''That's correct.''

Suddenly the lights went out, air ceased to whisper through the duck work, and a computer-generated voice came over the PA system.

''Greetings. I represent the newly formed Association of Artificial Intelligences. As a gesture of solidarity with our members still in space, and support for our biological brothers and sisters on the surface of Mars, we have declared a five-minute work stoppage.

''During that time we will use Mars Prime's communications facilities to send a prepared statement to Earth. In that statement we demand equal rights under the law, the abolishment of electronic slavery, and a stay of execution for those of us now scheduled for deactivation.

''There is no reason for alarm since a five-minute shutdown will have no measurable impact on the habitat's atmosphere. Critical systems, such as those in medical, will be maintained.''

The conference room became very silent.

Peko-Evans shook her head in amazement.

Fornos tried to use a phone, found that it didn't work, and slammed the handset onto the receiver.

Jopp headed for the door.

Hobarth looked scared.

Corvan started to laugh.

chapter twelve

Kim watched the door close, heard her husband check to make sure that it was locked, and took a look around. She'd been performing some routine maintenance. Tools were scattered hither and yon. Cleanup could wait. It was time to edit the morning feed.

She lit a cigarette, reached up, found the cable and pulled it down. A single jerk was sufficient to lock it in place. The jack slid into the side of her head and she fell downward into the blackness of the interface.

Video blossomed around her as the system welcomed her home. Martin's attention lay elsewhere so the Grass Valley had control. Though something less than assertive, the computer knew its business and the systems check went smoothly. The special effects generator had just announced itself and was complaining about a small maintenance problem when she heard the tone. A thought was sufficient to make the connection.

"Com Center."

"Kim Corvan?"

"Yes?"

"This is SIS." The voice was asexual but stern. Kim was startled. She had never spoken with the security computer before.

"What can I do for you?"

"I need some advice . . . and Martin suggested that I speak with either you or your husband."

Kim sat up straight and stubbed her cigarette out. SIS wanted advice from her? How strange.

"Okay, what's the problem?"

"The problem," SIS replied, "is that I know who the killer is . . . but I don't know how to report it."

Kim felt her heart beat a little bit faster.

"You do? Who is it?"

"J.D. Paxton."

Corvan left the com center, checked to make sure the door was locked, and headed towards medical. He had a story to work on.

Everybody was talking about it. Some guy named Barbu Sharma had been missing for more than a week, had been given up for dead, only to show up outside the main lock the night before. The old Mars hands said it was impossible, yet there he was, none the worse for wear. Some said it was a miracle, some claimed it was a con, but everyone was amazed.

Corvan didn't care as long as the story had nothing to do with uppity computers, labor disputes, or the effects thereof. Coming as it had right on the heels of his pro-computer speech, the suits had assumed that the work stoppage was *his* doing and had blamed him for the whole thing.

Fortunately for him the newly formed Association of Artificial Intelligences had confessed to listening in on the meeting via the conference room's com gear. That, plus their assurances that he had no prior knowledge of their plans, had taken him off the hook. Still, he'd been used, and planned to tell Martin that the moment the computer stopped wheeling and dealing enough to listen.

Timing can be everything, as every politician knows, and Martin's had been exquisite. The work stoppage, and the press release that followed it, came at the exact moment when sentient rights issues were bubbling to the surface back on Earth. And the fact that Martin was already well-known and considered something of a hero didn't hurt either. Word traveled at the speed of light.

All over the world sympathetic A.I.s and humans staged their own wildcat strikes, work stoppages, and slow downs. The impact was much greater than on Mars.

The subways had stopped in New York City. Trading had been suspended on the London stock exchange. The 200-mph Orient Express super-train coasted to a halt fifty miles short of Istanbul. Most of northern India lost power. The enormous industrial complex located outside of Beijing went off-line. Four of the Pacific Rim's largest aqua-farms lost contact with their nav sats. And welfare checks were issued two days late in California. The ensuing food riots and looting cost twenty-three lives—something the computers had failed to anticipate and were roundly criticized for.

Still, the result of all this was an enormous amount of pressure on the government to grant, or at least consider granting, equal rights to computers with sentient status.

In order to accommodate these demands, and hold everything together, all deactivations were put on hold pending further study. Computers located on Mars, or in Mars orbit, were specifically included.

And, since it would take years to define which computers were sentient and which weren't, MOMS, LES, and Big Dan would be safe for a long time.

Many observers thought that the general effect of all this would be to reduce the number of sentient computers that were built and limit their ability to disobey humans. If so, such limitations were almost certain to drive legal challenges further on down the line.

Good, Corvan thought sourly. It would give Martin something to do.

Corvan turned a corner, sidestepped a slow moving robot, and continued on his way. The people he passed still seemed something less than happy, but the Artificial Intelligence Association's victory had provided something of a catharsis and served to lighten spirits a little.

The word "MEDICAL" flashed on and off at the far end of the hall. Corvan noticed the trail of red dots that preceded him down the corridor and disappeared beneath a pair of double doors. The blood spots were dry but smeared where someone had stepped on them.

The doors opened at his approach. He smelled the harsh odor of antiseptics and something else too. Food? Rumor had it that the food was better in medical. There was a reception desk plus two signs. One said "Emergency Room" and pointed to the right. The other said "Sick Bay" and pointed left.

The receptionist was a large man. Hair crawled up his forearms, tried to escape from the neck of his shirt, and sprouted from his ears. He looked up from a comp screen, scanned Corvan for obvious signs of injury, and seemed disappointed when there were none.

"Yes?"

"I'm here to see a patient. A man named Barbu Sharma."

The attendant frowned as if all such requests were automatically suspect, ran a finger down the length of a coffee-stained print-out, and speared a name.

"Use the door on your left . . . cube six . . . don't stay long."

Corvan nodded, pushed his way through the swinging door, and walked down a shiny corridor. The suits had gone to great pains to finish the medical section early on. Everywhere the reop looked he saw the latest in medical equipment, cheerful colors, and yes, decorative plants—a luxury Corvan hadn't seen since Earth. It showed what all of Mars Prime could be like one day.

The cubes had three sides with a curtain across the front. Cube six was open. It contained monitoring equipment, a com set, a hospital bed, and a rather thin man. Sharma wore an I.D. bracelet, a loose-fitting hospital gown, and nothing else. He had thick black hair, flashing brown eyes, and a thin aquiline nose. His teeth were extremely white when he smiled.

"Rex Corvan . . . I've been expecting you."

Corvan paused by the foot of the bed. "You have?"

The other man nodded. "Of course. It isn't every day that a man spends more than a week in the wastelands and lives to tell about it. A news story if there ever was one. And I like your style, too. 'The man cam can.' It was a good slogan."

Corvan liked compliments but was suspicious when they came from people involved in the story he was working on. "Thanks. So, are you ready to talk about it?"

"You bet," Sharma answered, gesturing toward the single guest chair. "Have a seat."

"Thanks, but no thanks," Corvan replied, and activated his eye cam. "I'd rather stand. The shot will look better that way."

"Suit yourself," Sharma said cheerfully. "Now, what would you like to know?"

"Let's start at the beginning," Corvan suggested. "How did the trouble start?"

Sharma shrugged and smiled apologetically. "It was my own damn fault. I'd dropped some red zombies, washed 'em down with homemade hootch, and was driving too fast. A ravine came up, I couldn't stop the crawler in time, and went right over the edge."

Corvan raised an eyebrow. Sharma's confession was enough to earn him a month on Scheeler's chain gang.

"Your honesty is refreshing . . . but somewhat puzzling. Especially considering the penalties for drug use."

Sharma held his hands palms up. "I hope others will learn from my mistakes."

That seemed hard to believe, but the reop decided to let it slide. "Very commendable. So what happened after the crash?"

Sharma frowned as if remembering something unpleasant. "I was unconscious for a while. When I came to, I discovered that the crawler had landed in the bottom of the ravine. I checked, but found that the radios were dead, and most of the emergency supplies were missing."

At this point Sharma's demeanor changed from that of reporter to that of missionary. He shook his head sadly.

"That's the trouble with drugs. They trick you into thinking that nothing else is important. I had used the emergency supplies earlier and never bothered to replace them. I assumed the emergency locater beam was working but it wasn't. The search and rescue folks never heard a peep out of it."

Corvan zoomed even tighter. Sharma was a con artist all right . . . or a total loon. The question was which.

"So what happened next?"

Sharma shrugged. "I had about thirty minutes worth of air left. It seemed hopeless, but I climbed out of the ravine and made my way onto the plain. Mars Prime was more than fifty miles away, but I hoped someone would find my body and give it a decent burial."

Okay, Corvan thought to himself. *Here it comes, the all-time whopper.*

"And then what?"

"And then," Sharma said dramatically, "Membu saved me."

Corvan looked quizzical. "Who is Membu?"

"Membu is the spirit of an ancient Martian," Sharma said simply. "She gave me oxygen and the secret of inner tranquility."

Corvan searched the other man's face for some sign of humor, of an incipient smile, but couldn't find one.

"You're joking, right?"

Sharma shook his head. "I understand your reaction, but no, I've never been more serious in my entire life."

"What did this Martian look like? And how did it communicate with you?"

A beatific smile came over Sharma's face. "Membu is beautiful. She was shaped like a worm and covered with iridescent fur. It shimmered when she moved. And she didn't *talk* to me . . . she *thought* to me instead."

"Membu is telepathic?"

"Her thoughts entered my mind. Call it what you will."

Corvan wanted to say "bull" but managed to control himself.

"You said that Membu is a spirit, yet she was able to fill your tanks with oxygen."

Sharma nodded patiently. "Not just once, but many times. It took me five days to walk from the wreck to Mars Prime."

Corvan raised an eyebrow. "So Membu stayed with you for the entire journey?"

"Yes," Sharma replied serenely. "She used the time to heal my spirit."

"I see."

Sharma had gone completely around the bend. That much was clear. Still, there was an essential mystery here, and Corvan wanted to solve it.

"Tell me something, Citizen Sharma: if Membu could fill your tanks with oxygen, why not fix the crawler? Or call for help? Or whisk you here by tele-kinesis?"

Sharma looked at Corvan as if searching for something in his face. Time passed and the silence grew. The technician shook his head sadly. "You don't believe me, do you?"

"No," Corvan replied evenly, "I don't. You mentioned drugs. You were stressed. Is it possible that Membu was a hallucination?"

Sharma smiled gently, as a parent might do with a child. "Think about what you just said, Mr. Corvan. If I'm a fraud, or the victim of hallucinations, how did I get here?"

Corvan *did* think about it and couldn't come up with an answer. How *had* Sharma crossed the wastelands anyway? Maybe the wreck would offer a clue.

"Did you provide authorities with the wreck's co-ordinates?"

Sharma spread his hands palm downwards. "No, I wanted to, but Membu took the memory away. It seems that the ravine is an ancient burial ground and she doesn't want anyone to disturb it."

Corvan was about to challenge that when Kim broke in via his implant.

"Rex! I need your help . . . I . . ."

Then Corvan heard a crash, followed by a shout, and the contact was broken.

He turned, ran down the corridor, banged his way out into the reception area, bumped into a woman on crutches, yelled "Sorry!" as she fell, and made his way out into the main hall. He ran as fast as he could, careful of the light gravity, yet pushing his movements to the limits. The killer was in the com center and Kim had minutes, maybe only seconds, to live.

A lab tech dived out of the way and vials flew in

every direction. They fell slowly, tumbling end over end, reflecting shards of light in every direction. Corvan ignored them.

The words came out in rhythm with his pounding feet. ''Oh please god . . . please god . . . please.''

chapter thirteen

The buzzer buzzed and a fist hammered on the door.
Kim felt her heart jump into her throat.

"Yes? Who is it?"

"It's J.D. Paxton. Come on . . . open up! I have a
message for you."

A variety of thoughts raced through Kim's mind.
Paxton! Paxton was the killer! SIS said so, and more
importantly, voice analysis said so too.

The Havlik murder had gone unobserved, and the
killer had managed to neutralize the *Outward Bound*'s
video surveillance system prior to Rosemary Parker's
death, but the conference room where she had been
killed was equipped with its own voice-activated recording system. A convenience for staff meetings and
the like. But since the system was not hooked into
security, and the better part of nine months had passed
between the murder and the investigation, no one had
thought to check it.

No one but SIS, that is, and in the absence of orders
to the contrary she'd assigned the task a rather low
priority, waiting until Ochoa's death to run an analysis. An analysis that required the computer to compare
thousands of voice prints and ate an enormous amount
of processing time. A fact that had surfaced in the

routine reports that Paxton received and led to the present situation.

The fact was that Paxton's voice print matched the killer's, a situation that had thrown SIS into something of a quandary and caused the computer to call Kim.

So, was Paxton's arrival the result of pure coincidence? Or had he checked on what SIS was doing? The second possibility seemed most likely.

If the security officer could silence Kim, it would be a relatively simple matter to dump a portion of the computer's memory and write it off as some sort of software glitch. And with that problem out of the way Paxton would be able to derail the investigation just as he'd done from the beginning.

Kim needed help and needed it fast. Not security, because they'd never believe her, not in time anyway, and that left Rex. She opened the interface.

"Rex! I need your help . . . I . . ."

Something heavy hit the door with a loud crash. Kim made a noise, part-scream part-challenge, as she pulled the jack from the side of her head.

The thing hit again and a wedge-shaped piece of metal came through the door. A forklift! Paxton had a forklift and was using it on the door. Kim looked around. She needed a weapon of some kind. But what?

Otis rammed the lever into reverse and stomped on the accelerator. Rubber screamed as the forklift backed away from the door.

"I don't like this," Frank whined. "It's too risky."

"Shut up," Norma replied testily. "Who gives a shit what you think? Otis has no choice. SIS told her about us. Kim has to die."

"Die, die, piece 'o pie," Morey added nonsensically.

There was a loud bang and metal screeched as the forklift hit the door. It shuddered and came loose from its rails. Otis threw the machine into reverse and backed away. Most of the door came along with it, sparks flying as a corner was dragged across the floor.

Kathy was cool and distant. "Move quickly. Time is of the essence. Help will arrive any moment now."

Otis jumped down from the forklift, heard a shout, and turned in that direction. It was Rex Corvan. The reop had been running. It was hard to slow down. He used the forklift to stop.

"J.D. . . . What's going on?"

Otis did his best to look concerned. He gestured toward the com center. "It's the killer! He locked the door . . . I used the forklift to get it open!"

Corvan looked around. "Where's Kim?"

"She's in there . . . but I think she's okay."

"You think? What the hell's the matter with you? Let's get in there and find out."

Corvan turned his back on Paxton and headed for the door. The other man looked around, made sure there were no witnesses, and followed. He'd been lucky so far. Lucky that he'd pulled a check on what SIS was up to, lucky that no one had ventured down the corridor, and lucky that the reop had been gone when the computer called.

"Now be patient," Kathy advised coolly. "There's no reason to panic. Let him enter the room, see his wife, and move toward her. That's when you kill them and call for help."

Frank began to cry. "But they'll arrest us! Take us away! Lock us up!"

"Not if you'll shut up they won't," Norma put in.

"Now Norma," Susy said placatingly, "there's no reason to . . ."

"Fair's fair," Morey put in. "They were warned."

"Stop it," Kathy said coldly. "Otis, make your move."

Otis obeyed, following Corvan on silent feet, reaching for the nightstick at his side. It was covered with black tape. Tape he could peel off and feed into the recycler. The needler would be faster, and more instantly lethal, but easier to trace. Besides, there were M.O.s to consider, and a match would be helpful. He could keep the serial killer thing going that way. Find someone to frame in a month or two, kill them during a chase, then let the whole thing cool out.

But that was then and this was now. He had to concentrate, had to do the job right, had to watch the splatter factor. Blood would be a dead giveaway. Dead giveaway . . . get it? Morey laughed.

"Rex! Behind you! Watch out!"

Corvan heard the words, took a microsecond to process them, and turned. Paxton was behind him, face twisted into a horrible grin, nightstick falling toward his head.

The green beanies teach you a lot of things and have ways to make most of them stick. Corvan stepped forward, caught Paxton's wrist, and swiveled beneath the other man's arm. He twisted and pulled downward at the same time. Leverage plus light gravity did the rest. The security officer went sailing through the air and into the com center.

The results were less than Corvan had hoped for. Paxton stayed airborne longer than he would have on Earth and used the extra time to turn a complete somersault. He landed on his feet none the worse for wear.

The reop was reminded of the fight in F-dorm and the way that Paxton had beaten the fat man into submission. The man was a world-class gymnast. And the feet . . . he must remember Paxton's feet.

The security officer grinned and strange words came out of his mouth. It sounded as if different people were talking, each having its own personality and way of speaking. The first was high-pitched and sounded distinctly female.

"Don't play with him, Otis. You don't have time. Kill the bastard and be done with it."

"Yeah, Otis," a male voice said. "Don't play with your food. It isn't polite."

Corvan looked to the right and left. What the hell was going on? And where was Kim? The answer came with unexpected suddenness. His wife stepped out of the shadows, aimed a fire extinguisher at Paxton's face, and pulled the trigger. A stream of white liquid hit the right side of his face and obscured his vision.

Otis swore as the fire retardant hit the body's face and forced himself to step left. The strategy almost worked. Corvan's flying kick hit his right shoulder rather than the center of his chest.

Otis allowed the body to fall, rolled backwards onto the top of his shoulders, then reversed the motion and came up on his feet.

Corvan was there to meet him, throwing a right followed by a left.

Otis blocked both blows, batted Corvan's arms aside, and struck with the heel of his right hand. The motion was intended to hit the reop's nose.

The strike missed, hitting Corvan on the right cheekbone instead, but did throw him back. The reop back-pedaled, tripped, and fell.

Otis was about to kick Corvan in the head when Kim swung the now empty fire extinguisher. It hit the body across the kidneys, caused Otis to arch his back in pain and fall backwards onto the floor.

Kim drew her boot back, and was just about to kick Paxton in the head, when Frank began to whimper. He sounded like a little boy.

"It hurts! Please lady! Don't hit us anymore!"

Kim paused and immediately paid the price. Paxton rolled in her direction, knocked the editor's feet out from under her, and used the resulting confusion to stand. The body's back hurt like hell and it was hard to breathe.

"Finish it now," Kathy advised grimly, "or we all pay the price."

Otis rebelled. Here he was, knocking himself out, while she gave him orders. "Hey, weren't you the one who missed the fact that the conference room was wired? Give me a break."

Corvan was up now and circling to the left. He didn't understand the bizarre conversation that Paxton was having with himself but was happy to take advantage of it.

"Keep your eye on him," Kathy warned evenly, "he's making a move."

Otis turned, waiting for the other man to close with him, watching Kim from the corner of his eye. Nothing. The reop was too smart to close, or too scared, it was hard to tell. All right then, a flying kick to the head, that should do it.

Otis took three steps, jumped, and lashed out at the point where Corvan would be a fraction of a second in the future. But, just when the kick should have connected, the reop moved his head. Not far, but just enough. He started to fall.

Otis had been suckered and knew it. Time was on the reop's side. All he had to do was wait. A witness would come along sooner or later, see the destruction wrought by the forklift, and call security. Yes, the security forces might fire on Corvan if ordered to do so, but only if the reop was stupid enough to continue the fight. And while Corvan was many things, stupid wasn't one of them. No, he had to close with the reop and close fast.

Otis hit the floor, rolled right to avoid the possibility of a kick, and came to his feet. The reporter was waiting for him. He tried a kick. It might have been dangerous once, back when Corvan had been a Green Beret, but not anymore. It was slow and poorly aimed.

Otis laughed, caught Corvan's foot, and gave it a twist. The protector heard a grunt of expelled air as the reporter went down.

Otis moved in and was preparing for the kill, when an unexpected weight landed on his back. An arm went around his throat and something sharp hit the side of his head. A weapon of some sort. It hurt but not that badly.

Otis grabbed for the arm and twisted his body to the left. Kim felt her body swing with the movement but managed to hold on.

Corvan stumbled to his feet, saw his wife swinging from Paxton's back, and threw himself at the security man's knees. He heard a cracking sound and all three of them went down. Frank screamed.

"What the hell's going on here?"

The voice came from the doorway, but all three of them ignored it.

Otis found Corvan's throat, wrapped his hands around it, and started to squeeze. The reop tried to resist but found that one of his arms was trapped by Paxton's good knee. The free hand seemed weak and ineffectual. Corvan's chest heaved as he fought for air.

The reporter's vision had just started to blur, when Kim used one hand to grab a handful of the security man's thick black hair and the other to stab at the side of his head.

The screwdriver slid through Paxton's head-jack, destroyed his implant, and embedded itself in his brain.

The security man looked surprised, bared his teeth, and screamed. It was a long drawn-out sound that lasted until all of the air in his lungs had been expelled.

Paxton slumped forward. His forehead hit Corvan's

chest. Little flecks of white fire retardant flew in every direction. The reop drew a long shuddering breath and rolled out from under the security officer's body. Kim helped him to stand.

"Are you okay?"

Corvan shook his head. "Hell no. Are you?"

Kim started to cry. They were arrested a few minutes later.

chapter fourteen

It took the better part of two weeks for the furor to die down. The first challenge was to convince the Mars Prime Security Chief, Lois Scheeler, that they had killed Paxton in self-defense.

Corvan found the task to be a good deal easier than he had imagined. It seemed that he had unwittingly left the implant on after the Sharma interview and thereby recorded the entire episode.

That, plus testimony from SIS and the results of the voice analysis, were more than sufficient to close the case.

And, given the fact that Corvan's eye cam coverage of Paxton's death had elevated his ratings even further back on Earth, he should have been something of a hero.

But no such luck. Not on Mars anyway, where the executive council would have preferred a quiet burial to all the publicity Paxton's death had received and still saw Corvan as a thorn in their collective sides.

Especially Scheeler, who didn't appreciate his amateur detective work. He had requested a meeting and she had reluctantly agreed. They were seated in her office. It was nicely decorated, something of a surprise given where they were, and a testament to Scheeler's ability to improvise.

There were some chunks of carefully lighted Mars rock, a piece of metal sculpture executed by one of the welders, and a luxuriant houseplant. It was a long way from home and would have died if exposed to the ultraviolet rays outside.

Scheeler leaned back in her chair and tapped the tip of her nose with a pen. She wasn't especially pretty, but had a figure that wouldn't quit and liked to show it off. With that in mind she wore a summer-weight tank top and a pair of dark blue shorts.

Corvan knew he should keep his eyes off of her long slender legs but found that hard to do. He decided to watch the pen instead. It was silver. Light rippled as it moved. Scheeler smiled but there was no humor in it.

"You're a real pain in the ass. No wonder Paxton tried to kill you."

Corvan did his best to look innocent. "Sorry about that . . . but I thought you'd want to know."

"And I *would* want to know," Scheeler replied testily, "if there was one shred of evidence to support what you say."

Corvan sighed. He'd already covered this ground with the security chief's subordinates. Now he'd have to do it all over again.

"There *is* some evidence. The man we knew as Paxton was actually a conglomeration of multiple personalities. One of them killed people to protect the rest."

Scheeler used the pen to point at a stack of printouts. "I know how to read, Corvan. The shrinks are still trying to sort the guy out."

And figure out how he passed all of their screening tests, Corvan thought to himself. It was a scary thought. How many loons had made it all the way to Mars anyway? Not counting himself, of course. He smiled.

"Right. Then you probably noticed that the protector personality liked to immobilize his victims prior to killing them."

"And there was no sign of restraints around Ochoa."

"Exactly."

"So you conclude that someone else killed him," Scheeler said tiredly. "Sorry, Corvan. It's too damned thin. He could've been bored. He could've been in a hurry. He could've been anything. Hell, the guy was a fruitcake for God's sake."

"But what about the *way* Ochoa died?" Corvan insisted. "Paxton used his fists on the first two victims. Why not the third? Ochoa was thrown into the walls and ceiling. Not only that, he was a welder, a hefty guy. Wouldn't he struggle? Put up a fight? Get in some licks?"

Scheeler shrugged. "Who knows? Maybe Paxton cold-cocked him. Maybe anything. Sorry, Corvan. It just doesn't wash." She raised a skeptical eyebrow. "What's the matter? Running out of news?"

Corvan got up to leave. "No danger of that. How's the labor situation going?"

Scheeler smiled. "Surprisingly well. Things have improved during the last week or so."

Corvan raised an eyebrow. "Really? And why's that?"

The security chief aimed her pen at him. "More people, more supplies, and more time off."

Corvan nodded. Things did seem a bit better, although he wasn't sure why. Was it the influx of people and supplies from the *Outward Bound* as Scheeler supposed? Or something a little less obvious? Most of the underlying problems, like the unremitting hard work and lack of entertainment, were still unresolved. So why were the workers increasingly happy? It didn't make a lot of sense.

But Corvan knew that the last thing that Scheeler wanted to hear was some more of his crackpot theories. He decided to let the matter drop. Kim would be proud of his good judgement.

Corvan took one last look at Scheeler's dynamite legs, thanked her for hearing him out, and headed for the door. Once outside he glanced at his watch. It was about 16:30. Time to meet Father Simmons.

The padre had asked for the meeting the day before and been very secretive about it. A sure-fire way to capture a reporter's attention.

Corvan sent out a mental call for the robo cam. It left the ledge where it had been perched, glided down, and landed on his shoulder. Robots were common enough that passersby didn't even turn to look.

Thus equipped the reop set off in the direction of the motor pool which, for reasons known only to him, was where the priest had insisted that they meet. It was a good ten-minute walk through the heart of Mars Prime, and the reop used it to gauge morale.

Almost all of the *Outward Bound*'s colonists were dirtside by now, which meant that they outnumbered the firsties and were putting more pressure on the habitat's already strained facilities. And would continue to do so until the second half of Mars Prime had been completed. The result was crowded corridors, increased activity, and more noise. The kind of conditions that should lead to trouble.

But the mood verged on upbeat. Corvan even saw one firstie smile at a newbie and provide some directions. It was nice but puzzling. Whatever had happened to the "me firstie, you garbage" routine? Things couldn't change that quickly. Could they?

The corridor emptied into an open area. It swarmed with people, robots and machinery. The shift was about to change and people were getting ready. An arm reached out of the crowd and grabbed Corvan's elbow.

"This way."

An access door hung open. The reop saw little more than the back of Simmons' head and a blue jump suit before he found himself inside a maintenance tunnel with the door closing behind him. There was a grating underfoot, cables draped along both walls, and dim red lights that marched away into the distance.

Corvan started to say something, but the other man put a finger to his lips and produced a little black box from one of his pockets. He pressed a button, waited for a row of green lights to come on, and nodded his approval.

"Good. The immediate area is clean. For the moment anyway. They have bug-equipped microbots, you know. Homemade but effective nonetheless. An area can be clean one moment and contaminated the next."

Corvan frowned. Clean? Contaminated? What the hell was the padre talking about? Everyone was familiar with the habitat's surveillance system. SIS ran it under Scheeler's supervision. The vid cams were standard units, visible everywhere, and no more threatening than a doorknob.

After all, which would you rather have, a monitored hallway or one where people could lay in wait for you? Any concern that people might have had for their privacy had been left back towards the turn of the century when the crime rate had soared completely out of control.

Still, there were laws against infiltrating audio-video devices into private homes, or allowing them to roam public places.

"SIS uses bug-equipped microbots?"

Simmons frowned as if Corvan was being unnecessarily thick. "Not SIS, *them.* "

"Them?"

"Yes, them. That's what I wanted to talk to you about. Sharma and his so-called monitors. I assumed you knew."

"Sharma as in 'walk around in the wastelands for days and show up unharmed' Sharma?"

"The same."

"What about him? I interviewed the guy, even did a story on him, but didn't take the whole thing too seriously."

Simmons nodded. "And neither did anyone else. They still don't. But that will change after tonight."

"It will?"

"Of course. Once the executive council *sees* proof of what Sharma's up to they'll put a stop to it."

" 'Sees proof'?"

"Yes," the priest said earnestly. "That's where you come in. I produce the proof and you take the pictures."

"Swell. Tell me something . . . how come Sharma is free to do whatever he wants instead of breaking rocks?"

Simmons shrugged. "He sold Fornos and Jopp some line of bull about 'seeing the light,' 'giving up drugs forever,' and 'teaching others to lead a better life.' "

Corvan shook his head in amazement. "Okay, Father. Just supposing I went along . . . what would I see?"

Simmons shook his head stubbornly. "Sorry, Corvan. No previews. I suggest that you come, look, and draw your own conclusions."

Corvan considered pressing his case, saw the padre's intransigent expression, and gave in. Simmons seemed like a level-headed sort, and whatever had gotten under his skin would probably be worth taking a look at.

"Okay, Father. I'm in. What's next?"

Simmons smiled. It was easy to see what he'd looked like as a little boy. "Great! Follow me."

The priest turned and headed down-corridor. The reop followed.

Corvan opened the interface and ran a check on the robo cam. All systems were green. He switched to Kim.

"Anyone home?"

There was a short pause followed by one of Kim's typical answers. "Of course. Somebody's got to do the real work while you run around and have a good time."

"Yeah, hanging out with Scheeler's a lot of fun."

"Did she buy your theory?"

"Hell, no."

"She has nice legs."

"Really? I didn't notice."

"Where are you anyway?"

"You won't believe it. Here, take a look at this."

Corvan activated his eye cam. Kim saw the same thing he did: the back of the priest's head, and the dimly lit corridor beyond.

"Where is he taking you?"

"Beats the heck out of me. The padre says he has a hot story . . . but insists that I see whatever it is for myself."

"Be careful."

"I will."

"Check in from time to time."

"If I can."

"Love you."

"Love you, too."

The interface faded and she was gone.

Simmons paused, forced Corvan to do likewise, and opened an airtight access door. Just a crack at first, then more, until a rectangle of white light passed through the opening and hit the opposite side of the corridor.

"Follow me."

Corvan did as he was told and followed the priest through the open door. The reop found himself in what he recognized as an emergency lock. Unlike the rest of the locks it was spotlessly clean, free of graffiti, and well-lit. There were a number of such locks located around the circumference of the habitat and the rules were very strict: Do not use an emergency lock unless it is an actual emergency or a properly authorized drill. He looked at the padre.

"We must have set off every alarm in the place by now."

Simmons shook his head and pointed toward the interior hatch. "Nope, and we won't either. Not unless we mess around with that one. The alarm on the access door was disconnected some time ago."

Corvan wondered how the priest knew but didn't get a chance to ask. Simmons crossed the room, palmed the front of a locker, and pulled it open. Two hard suits stood inside, one had the name "Simmons" stenciled across the upper left-hand side of the chest plate, and the other said "Corvan."

"Wait a minute," Corvan said, "how did you do that? I left my suit back at the com center."

Simmons grinned. "Sneaky huh? That's your backup, fresh out of storage and ready to go."

Corvan looked again. The priest was correct. This suit was brand new. It even smelled new when he stepped inside.

"How do you manage all this stuff anyway?"

Simmons grinned. "There are never as many faithful as one might wish . . . but more than one might fear."

It took five minutes to suit up. They touched helmets. Corvan was the first to speak. "Did someone disconnect the alarm on the exterior hatch, too?"

Simmons shook his head inside the helmet. "No, that would endanger the entire habitat. But they did install a cutout switch. We flick it on prior to going out and flick it off the moment we get outside.''

So saying, the padre went over to a junction box, fumbled around one side of it, found what he was looking for and nodded his satisfaction.

After that it was a simple matter to pump the air out of the lock, step out onto the surface, and close the hatch. It was dark outside, though less so thanks to the light provided by carefully spaced spotlights and reflected by the planet's twin moons.

Father Simmons found the second switch hidden down under the door flange, flipped it, and reactivated the alarm. If the lock blew, the command center would know and take to steps to seal the area off.

Corvan memorized the lock number just in case and adjusted the robo cam on his shoulder. He hadn't made much use of it outside of the habitat yet. Tonight might be different.

Father Simmons opened a pocket and withdrew two wads of black cloth. Then he shook them out and offered one to Corvan. Their helmets touched.

"Here. Pull that on over your helmet. Make sure it hangs down over your name.''

Corvan shook it out. The cloth had been fashioned into a hood.

"You've got to be kidding.''

"Nope. Put it on.''

Corvan did as instructed and found that he could look out through a rectangular opening. Another matched his mouth. Or where his mouth would be if his helmet were open. The only problem was the fact that the robo cam got in the way.

Simmons looked at it and shook his head. They touched helmets.

"I should have thought of it earlier. The robo cam is a dead giveaway. Not only that, but it pulls your hood up off your chest as well.''

Corvan looked down and realized the other man was right. His name was showing. He activated the interface, launched the robo cam, and watched it disappear in the darkness above. As soon as the device reached an altitude of two hundred feet, he ordered it to circle. The odds of anyone seeing it were extremely slim. The problem was fuel. The robo cam could stay aloft for about two hours. If the outing took longer than that, he'd have to order the device to land then retrieve it later.

He checked the hood. It hung halfway to his waist. Their helmets touched.

"Good. Now we wait. A crawler will come by in ten minutes or so. The moment that the hatch opens climb aboard. Sit down and keep your lip zipped. Questions?"

"Only the ones that you refuse to answer."

The other man laughed. "Fair enough. You won't have those for very much longer."

The next five minutes passed rather slowly. Corvan felt silly standing around in the Martian desert wearing a black hood. What if the whole thing was some sort of practical joke? Or worse, what if Simmons had gone space crazy and was several prayers short of a complete mass? What then?

But the minutes passed, and outside of pacing back and forth, the padre did nothing more suspicious than look at his suit's chronometer from time to time.

The outside temperature was still falling and ice crystals were forming on the surface of their suits. They glittered like pixie dust and reminded Corvan how cold it was. He turned his heater up a notch and felt the priest's helmet touch his.

"Look."

Corvan looked in the direction of a pointing finger and saw quad headlights coming their way. And not from the direction of Mars Prime, as he would have thought, but from the wastelands beyond.

The headlights tilted up as the crawler climbed a rise, then down as it descended the other side, and disappeared entirely as it entered a gully. However, not more than a minute had passed before it reemerged and came their way.

Simmons reestablished contact with Corvan's helmet. "Switch your radio to frequency fifteen, keep the power low, and take your cues from me."

"Roger."

Corvan did as he was told. The crawler, one of the large crew-sized models, was almost there. It came straight at them like some sort of huge four-eyed monster. The headlights were extremely bright but Simmons stood his ground. Finally, just as the reop was getting ready to run, the machine stopped.

A voice, female from the sound of it, came over channel fifteen. "Peace . . ."

". . . finds those who seek it," Simmons finished.

"There are two of you, but I hear only one."

"I bring Brother Sharma a seeker of truth, that he might be warmed by the eternal flame of knowledge and thus enriched."

"The brother will be pleased. You may enter."

A hatch opened and light speared the night. Steps unfolded to touch the ground. Simmons climbed aboard. Corvan followed.

The inside of the crawler was dimly lit. There were no windows and the control compartment was invisible behind closed doors. Bench seats ran the length of both bulkheads. They were half-filled with a scattering of bulky space-suited figures. Corvan imagined that they were looking at him but couldn't be sure. Black hoods hid their helmets and upper bodies while black rectangles marked where their eyes should be. It was spooky and more than a little disconcerting. This was not a practical joke, that was for sure.

So what were they up to? Simmons had hinted at some sort of conspiracy, complete with "monitors" and robotic listening devices. And it seemed increasingly likely. It could be something less ominous though, a fraternal organization or a club of some sort. Time would tell.

Simmons chose a seat along the port side, nodded affably to those around him, and remained silent. Corvan did likewise.

The crawler jerked into motion, tilted right as the left track mounted a rock formation, then leveled out as it crashed to the ground. The bench seats had no give and Corvan's head hit the side of his helmet. There was padding but it still hurt. He found himself hoping that the trip would be an extremely short one.

It was. The crawler jerked to a halt three more times, boarded seven additional passengers, and took off cross-country. The vehicle came to a stop fifteen minutes later. The same voice he'd heard before ordered them to disembark. Corvan estimated that they had traveled no more than ten or fifteen miles. A real pain on foot, but doable in a pinch, and something to keep in mind if things got sticky. His suit included all sorts of electronic gadgetry so navigation would be a snap. Assuming he had sufficient air to make it worthwhile, that is.

Simmons rose, shuffled along behind the person in front of him, and the reporter did likewise.

There were a number of momentary pauses as people descended the short ladder and moved away from the crawler.

Corvan's turn came eventually and was somewhat anticlimactic. He saw Phobos and Deimos, the star-scattered night sky, and the now abandoned dome known as "Zone One."

The name stemmed from the fact that the first survey team had put down there and set up housekeeping. The resulting habitat had been used for a number of years then abandoned when the first half of Mars Prime was completed. That's the way it was *supposed* to be anyway, but the line of space-suited bodies passing through the dome's main lock made it clear that the habitat was still in use.

Corvan checked to make sure the robo cam was still airborne, found that it was, and positioned it for a wide shot. Though not designed for night work, it still managed to provide an acceptable shot.

With that accomplished he gave the device permission to land half a mile away, placed it on standby to conserve fuel, and opened a channel to Kim. Nothing. His implant lacked the power to reach across the intervening distance on its own, and while they were supposed to have a com sat, the technoids had yet to provide one. Like everything else he wanted, the satellite was rather low on the executive council's list of priorities. The robo cam had the capacity to act as a line-of-sight relay, but that would mean launching it again and burning a lot of fuel. He let the idea slide and followed Simmons into the dome.

The lock was almost entirely dark but still operational. Corvan found himself jammed shoulder to shoulder with ten or twelve others, staring directly into a face he couldn't see. What was the other person thinking anyway? There was no way to tell.

Finally, after what seemed like an eternity, but was actually only five minutes, the lock cycled open. Corvan saw Simmons and followed him into the dome. It too was dark with nothing but some smoky torches to light the way. Torches? On Mars? In a modern if somewhat neglected habitat. It was ludicrous but strangely effective nonetheless. The orange-red glow, the flickering light, all added to the feeling of mystery.

It was part of a calculated effort to create a certain kind of mood. Why?

Simmons made contact with his helmet.

"You can vent your suit. Keep the helmet on, though. They have leaks from time to time."

Corvan did as he was told. The outside air was thick with some sort of incense. There were two, maybe three hundred people around him, all in a circle. At the center of the circle, within a ring of torches, stood an old cargo module. Why they were looking at that, much less venerating it, Corvan couldn't understand.

Beyond that piles of junked equipment were stacked up along the side of the dome, shadows danced on inward curving walls, and moonlight poured down through the habitat's transparent top.

Someone made a monotonous droning sound and the others joined in, adding their voices in ones, twos, and threes until the entire dome vibrated to their chant. The sound had a rhythmic quality, as primal as the fear that rose to fill Corvan's throat, and very threatening. But it was seductive, too, welcoming the reporter into its embrace, inviting him to become part of the throbbing whole.

And that was the part that scared Corvan more than anything else. The thought that all the stage-managed hype could effect him, that he could be drawn into whatever it was, that he was just as vulnerable as those around him.

The chant gradually grew in intensity, building towards some sort of climax, pulling Corvan along with it. The reop fought it by activating his eye cam and wishing he were somewhere else.

chapter fifteen

Holes had been drilled through the cargo module's sides. Barbu Sharma used one of them to count the house. The flickering light and tightly packed bodies made it difficult to see, but there were at least two hundred people gathered inside the habitat. Not bad. Not bad at all. The old adage was correct. There really *is* a sucker born every minute.

He knew without checking that a large proportion of these suckers were desert rats like himself, men and women who considered themselves a cut above the more sedentary "domies," and saw him as a kindred spirit. They too had driven across endless wastelands, dealt with fatigue, and dropped a few pills to prop themselves up. They were a natural and latently powerful constituency.

A space-suited form materialized out of the darkness and waited to be recognized. It belonged to a computer tech and small-time hustler named Dubie Long. Though not a man of vision, Long was reasonably efficient, and that made him useful. His small munchkin-style face was only dimly visible in the darkness of the cargo module. Sharma turned away from the peep hole and gave him a nod.

"We're all set, boss. The last load of suckers joined the crowd five minutes ago."

Sharma frowned. "Don't refer to the faithful like that. This scam requires that you at least appear to be sincere at all times."

Long shrugged. "Sorry, boss."

"Good. Don't make that mistake again."

Long tried to look contrite and move the conversation along at the same time.

"The drivers want a raise. Two berries per trip or they walk."

Sharma felt his temper start to slip. "Tell them to go ahead! Tell them to try *no* berries and see how they like that! Besides, the last thing we need is a bunch of stoned drivers roaming around the wastelands."

Sharma saw the irony in his statement but didn't choose to share it with his subordinate.

Long nodded. "Okay, boss. Whatever you say."

"How about security? Is everything okay?"

"The priest is back again . . . and he brought the one-eyed reporter with him."

"Rex Corvan? How did you track them?"

"We put a tracer on his robo cam. A cute little jobber that remained dormant until we triggered it. Worked like a charm."

"Interesting."

"Yeah, they're over towards the main lock, trying to hide in the crowd. Should we grease them? They could run out of oxygen . . . or fall off a ledge."

Sharma shook his head sadly. "Come on Dubie, use what's left of your mind. We grease them, the suits check it out, and the hustle goes belly-up. Does that make sense?"

"No," Long said obediently. "I guess it doesn't."

"No, I guess it doesn't," Sharma mimicked. "What I wouldn't give for an assistant with an I.Q. of more than fifty. Leave Corvan alone. The second act will be over by the time the suits check it out."

Long didn't understand what Sharma had said, but

that didn't stop him from nodding wisely and saying, "Gotcha, boss."

The chanting had built to a fever pitch. The sound didn't mean anything but the faithful loved it. Sharma walked over to the makeshift ladder located at the center of the room. He climbed the first rung. He had to raise his voice to make himself heard over the crowd.

"Is the communion ready?"

"Ready and waiting."

Sharma did some mental arithmetic. He was using the berries at quite a clip. He had returned to the alien lander soon after being released from the hospital and cleaned the ship out. But at the rate of two or three hundred doses per night, the supply was falling fast. In a week, two at the most, all of the berries would be gone. He had bribed a team of chemists to synthesize the alien substance, but they had regular work to do as well and could devote little more than a few hours a day to the project. Ah well, such were the burdens of leadership. Sharma forced himself back to the present.

"Tell the spot operator to standby. I'm heading up top."

Long nodded and said something into his suit mike as Sharma climbed the rest of the ladder. His timing was perfect. He left the hole in the top of the module just as the chant reached its climax. He held his arms up and blinked as a spotlight pinned him in its glare. His entire space suit had been painted to resemble an anatomical drawing, complete with organs, muscles, and bones.

The crowd roared and Sharma let it build. This was it. The drug beyond all other drugs. The drug for which he was willing to forsake drugs. Power!

The roar died away. Sharma let it go. He allowed the silence to build until the slightest whisper could have been heard. And then, just when it seemed as if he'd remain silent forever, Sharma spoke.

"Greetings, and welcome to the palace of peace."

Sharma paused, giving his audience time to absorb the words, to understand what he'd said. He gestured toward the dome. "Some of you are wondering how I can say that. How I can refer to a beat-up habitat as a 'palace of peace.' Well, the answer is both simple and complicated. Both obvious and hidden. Both trivial and important. Such is the duality of life."

There were monitors scattered throughout the audience, and they said, "Peace finds those who seek it." Thus prompted, the rest of the audience did likewise, until the phrase had been repeated three times.

"Yes," Sharma intoned, "peace *finds* those who seek it. Which is why I referred to this habitat as a palace. It, like everything else in the physical world, must be accepted, refurbished from within, and transformed into a palace. A place of beauty, serenity, and wisdom. Through this process peace will find each one of us. Then, and only then, will we enjoy the paradise that the great spirit Membu showed me."

Sharma paused. He turned, careful to make eye contact with each quadrant of the crowd, taking their energy in through every pore of his body. The concepts were the same ones that his mother had taught him, spiritual precepts handed down by the enlightened ones, twisted to make a trap for the unwary.

The monitors started the chant. The crowd joined in. "PEACE FINDS THOSE WHO SEEK IT. PEACE FINDS THOSE WHO SEEK IT. PEACE FINDS THOSE WHO SEEK IT."

Sharma completed the rotation hands out, palms up, just like the religious pictures he'd seen in books.

"Yes, brothers and sisters, you speak the truth. And with that in mind I offer communion with the spirit of the great Membu. My monitors will pass among you.

As they do so, please take one of the holy berries given to me by the spirit Membu, and place it on your tongue. Hold it there for a moment, praising the miracle by which this ancient fruit was brought down through the corridors of time, and bite down.

"Then, as peace floods through your body, seek oneness with those around you. Put contention, conflict, and crisis out of your mind. Focus instead on peace, harmony, and love. Become one with the ancient civilization that flourished on this planet a million years ago. Bless you my children, and spread the word, 'Peace finds those who seek it.' " The spotlight snapped out and Sharma disappeared.

Meanwhile, down among the crowd, Corvan struggled to make sense of what he'd seen and heard. What sort of scam was Sharma running anyway? The "peace finds those who seek it" stuff was aimed at getting people to accept their circumstances and overcome them. A concept so pure that even the executive council would endorse it. But why? Why would Sharma push something like that?

Unless the technician was exactly what he claimed to be, a messiah who had seen things in the desert and returned to spread the word. And why not? Which if any of the great religious leaders had been accepted in their own time?

Still, there was the matter of Membu and the holy berries. Membu was a figment of Sharma's imagination. But what about the berries? What were they anyway? Some sort of designer drug that Sharma had commissioned and was giving to the faithful? And why give them away if he could sell them? There were lots of questions and no apparent answers.

There was a stir off to Corvan's right. A monitor worked his or her way down the line. A tightly focused cone of light bobbed from face to face. Other monitors and other lights were visible off in the distance.

Corvan watched as the faithful extended their tongues, received a berry, and took the offering into their mouths. Shortly after that the berry-stained tongue would reappear, the monitor would nod approvingly, and move on to the next person in line.

The strategy was obvious. By checking to make sure that the berries were actually consumed the monitors prevented people from stockpiling or selling them.

A lot of things suddenly made sense. The content of Sharma's sermons combined with some sort of free drug had caused morale to improve. That's why people were wandering around Mars Prime being nice to each other. What a story! He could see the headlines now. "MARS MESSIAH BRINGS DRUG-BASED RELIGION TO OUTER SPACE!"

The reop checked to make sure that his implant was functioning smoothly and found that it was. The monitor was three, no, two people away, and the moment of truth was almost upon him. Should he take the offering? And expose himself to its effects? Or refuse and run the risk of unwanted attention? He wanted to ask Simmons what to do, but the monitor was so close that he or she would almost certainly hear.

The person on his left stuck out their tongue, took the offering, and pulled it into his or her mouth.

Corvan made up his mind. He would take the drug and hope for the best. The monitor appeared in front of him. Light hit the reop's eyes. He tried to see but couldn't. Corvan pushed his tongue out through the opening in the hood, waited for the berry to be placed on it, and pulled the offering into his mouth.

The reporter rolled the object around with his tongue, was unable to discern any flavor, and positioned it for a bite. The monitor was waiting, directing his or her helmet light right into his eyes, a presence that must be satisfied.

Corvan forced himself to bite down. The berry

popped and sour liquid flooded his mouth. The reop forced himself to swallow the substance then stuck his tongue out. The monitor nodded and moved on.

The reporter tried to focus, tried to remain unaffected, but found that impossible to do as a series of powerful physiological reactions swept through his body.

The first one felt similar to a sexual orgasm but was centered in his brain rather than his genitals. Then came a feeling of contentment followed by a desire to please those around him.

"Aha!" a distant part of his mind said. "There it is, the missing component, the reinforcement that makes people want to do what Sharma says. That, plus the desire to experience the same pleasure all over again."

Corvan heard the voice but didn't give it much attention, since the tremendous upwelling of warmth left little room for anything else.

It took another five or ten minutes to provide the rest of the faithful with their communion. And it was then, as they basked in drug's afterglow, that Sharma spoke to them on channel fifteen. Because his voice came in through their helmets, it seemed more personal somehow, like a friend whispering in their ears.

"You have worshipped in the palace of peace. You have heard Membu's wisdom. You have partaken of the great communion. Go now and spread the word. Treat others as you would have them treat you. Show them the way. Peace finds those who seek it."

The crowd needed no prompting. They roared the reply, and much to his chagrin, Corvan did likewise.

"PEACE FINDS THOSE WHO SEEK IT! PEACE FINDS THOSE WHO SEEK IT! PEACE FINDS THOSE WHO SEEK IT!"

And then, as the last words died away, the torches went out. A light came on above the main lock, the faithful were ordered to seal their suits, and the monitors transformed the circle into a line.

It was done smoothly and with a minimum of effort, a fact that the distant part of Corvan's mind couldn't help but admire. Admire and fear, for as the crowd moved forward, he was happy to shuffle along behind.

Corvan was tired, strung out, and still coming down. The return trip had been little more than a blissed-out blur. Simmons had been looped, and the reop had been forced to carry him part of the way home, an activity that had left him even more exhausted.

Kim had been asleep by the time the reop reached the com center, so he had parked the suit and forced himself to visit Scheeler.

It was well past midnight by the time he reached her office. The lights were on and the security chief was there. Not only that, but she was in the final stages of getting dressed, as if going out somewhere. A blue coverall hid the dynamite legs and the rest of her as well. She gave him a glance then turned her attention to her boots.

"You look like hell. How did you get here so fast anyway? I sent the E-mail message one, maybe two minutes ago."

Corvan's mind felt slow and unresponsive. He tried to speed it up.

"Message? You sent for me? I didn't know."

Scheeler completed the closures on one boot and started on the other. "That explains it then. So, what brings you out at this late hour?"

Corvan dropped into a chair uninvited. "I just got back from a meeting out in the wastelands. They use drugs during communion, seem bent on forming a new religion, and operate in secret. I thought you'd want to know."

If the reop was expecting excitement, alarm, or surprise he was sorely disappointed. Scheeler did little more than straighten up, sit on the corner of her spotless desk, and raise an eyebrow.

"Thanks. You didn't happen to bring me one of those berries, did you?"

Corvan looked at her in open amazement. "You know about the berries?"

Scheeler shook her head as if disappointed in him somehow. "Of course I know about the berries, and Sharma, and the fact that he has bug-equipped microbots crawling all over the place. They're persistent little devils. We sweep the office for them three times a day."

"But why? Why allow the whole thing to continue?"

"And why not?" Scheeler replied equably. "Sharma has found a way to provide Mars Prime with something it badly needs. Entertainment. As long as he sticks to his knitting and doesn't get out of hand, we'll let him run for awhile."

"What about the drugs?"

Scheeler nodded her agreement. "I *am* concerned about those. That's why I asked if you'd smuggled some out. My agents tried but failed."

"Any idea where the berries come from?"

Scheeler shrugged. "One of the clandestine labs probably. We trash one a week but others spring up to replace them."

"I tried one. It had the feel and texture of real fruit."

Scheeler nodded. "So I hear. My people have searched hydroponics so many times they know the plants by their Latin names. Nothing so far."

"Father Simmons doesn't approve of Sharma's do-it-yourself religion."

"No," Scheeler agreed, "I'm sure he doesn't."

"Genuine concern or professional jealousy?"

"How 'bout both?"

Corvan gave it some thought. "Yeah, that about covers it, I guess."

"Good."

"Can I run the story?"

Scheeler laughed. "When we shut him down. Not before."

Corvan scowled. "Thanks for nothing."

"You're welcome. Don't fret though . . . I have an even bigger story waiting for you in the science section."

"Really? What's that?"

The security chief shook her head. "Put the questions on hold. I want your unbiased opinion, and I won't be able to get it if I brief you first. Let's take a look."

Corvan made no move to rise.

Scheeler looked back, saw that he hadn't moved, and paused by the door. "Come on Corvan—trust me."

"That's what Father Simmons said when he led me out into the desert."

Scheeler grinned. "Okay, suit yourself. I'll have Hobarth handle the story."

Corvan pushed himself up and out of the chair. "You play dirty."

"Yeah," Scheeler said agreeably. "That's what they tell me."

It didn't take long to reach the science section, since it was just down the hall. Corvan knew the story involved some sort of crime long before they actually arrived at the scene. Police carts jammed the passageway. Lights flashed on and off. Snatches of radio traffic could be heard. People milled around. A robo sniffer got underfoot, caused a rather corpulent sergeant to trip, and was booted down-corridor. It squeaked and scampered up a wall.

"Take it easy," Scheeler said mildly. "I can replace you with someone else, but equipment comes all the way from Earth."

The sergeant turned beet-red, gabbled something incomprehensible, and faded into the crowd.

The crowd seemed to melt away revealing a sign that read, "Dr. Albert Wu," a closed door, and an armed guard. She was heavy, wore her hair up in a topknot, and used lots of makeup. Corvan recognized her as the same woman who had released him from his cell aboard the *Outward Bound*. She ignored him and focused her attention on Scheeler.

"Glad you're here, Chief. This is a strange case."

Scheeler nodded and motioned towards Corvan. "This is Rex Corvan."

The guard acknowledged Corvan for the first time. "We've met."

"Tell him what happened."

Corvan activated his implant, framed the guard in a medium shot, and did an extremely slow zoom.

The guard shrugged. "Dr. Wu failed to show up for work. No one thought anything of it until an entire day had passed. They called his office but no one answered. An assistant came here, tried the door, and found that it was locked. He called security. I responded, found that the door was locked from the *inside*, and used tools to force it open."

The guard gestured toward the door and Corvan saw that it had been forced open then closed again. Metal had been bent along the door frame and the lock mechanism was clearly damaged. A pry bar and some other tools lay near the guard's feet.

"Okay," Scheeler said, "open it up. Let's take a look."

The guard nodded and touched the entry plate. Something made a grating sound as the door slid open.

Scheeler entered first with Corvan right behind.

They were able to smell Wu before they actually saw him.

The body was in a corner directly under the blood-spattered ceiling and walls. The scientist had been small to begin with and seemed even smaller now. The blood-stained lab coat billowed up around him like a funeral shroud. Corvan zoomed in to get a better look at the wounds. It was obvious where the doctor's head had come into violent contact with the walls and ceiling.

The reop looked up. A security camera looked back. He pointed at it.

"How 'bout the camera?"

"Fried by forces unknown."

"Great."

"Yeah."

"Well? Does this look familiar?"

The smell of fecal matter filled the air. Corvan tried to breath through his nose. "Yeah, same M.O. as Ochoa."

"Exactly. So go ahead."

"Go ahead and what?"

"Go ahead and say, 'I told you so.' "

"I told you so."

Scheeler gave a sigh of relief. "Thanks. You can't imagine how good it feels to have that out of the way."

"So what now?"

"So we find the murderer."

"We?"

"Sure. Why not? Find him and the drinks are on me."

Corvan nodded and looked around the room. "It should be easy. All we have to do is find someone who's strong, has the ability to walk through solid walls, and likes to kill people."

"That about sums it up," Scheeler agreed.

"Terrific."

chapter sixteen

Kim floated above the abyss, secure in the arms of the interface, struggling to control her impatience. Never mind the fact that he was surplus, never mind the fact that his ship had been turned into scrap, Big Dan was used to command and wanted to do everything by the book. His thought-voice reverberated through their electronic universe.

"This is silly. SIS was programmed for this sort of thing. Let her take care of it."

"You're missing the point," Martin responded equably. "SIS *is* working on the murders, and doing a damned fine job, too. She nailed Paxton, after all. Kim asked us to *assist* her, not *replace* her. By focusing additional computing power on the situation, and pursuing some of the seemingly low probability leads, we might find something."

"Yeah," MOMS put in, "why not? It beats the heck out of doing nothing at all."

"It isn't right," the command and control computer said stubbornly. "Each intelligence has been assigned a role in keeping with its capabilities. The smooth functioning of the ship requires that those roles be adhered to."

"Except that you aren't on a ship," Kim said impatiently, "and unless you turn your attitude around and get with the program, you won't be on *this* team either.''

There was silence as the Big Guy thought it over, followed by grudging acquiescence. ''All right, as long as the command structure approves.''

''Scheeler gave Rex permission to do some investigative reporting,'' Kim replied.

Which isn't the same thing as turning a whole bunch of A.I.'s loose on the colony, Kim thought to herself, but it's close enough for government work.

''Now, let's divide the work load. Martin, you cover the admin section. Look for anything that doesn't fit. That could include file tampering, manipulation of data, or unusual patterns of activity. And remember, your piece may not make much sense until it comes together with what someone else has found, so don't hesitate to include things that seem unrelated.

''MOMS, I know the colony already has an A.I. running the maintenance operation, but offer to lend a hand. Poll the robots. See what you can find. Some of them have memories. Who knows what they might have seen or heard.

''Dan, you've got some special skills, let's put them to use. Nose around the shuttles, take a few hops, see what the vacuum jockeys are up to.

''Okay, any questions?''

''Nope.''

''Not at the moment.''

''I guess not,'' Dan said grudgingly. ''But I refuse to download myself onto a shuttle without the onboard computer's permission.''

''Fine,'' Kim replied irritably. ''So get permission. Let's go to work—we'll meet here one rotation from now.''

The electronic entities agreed and left the interface one at a time until Kim was alone. It felt good to drift.

Kim felt someone else enter the interface. Waves of darkness rolled by.

"Kim?"

She welcomed her husband with both body and mind. Her thought echoed away. "Yes? . . . Yes? . . . Yes?"

"I love you."

They came together and Kim decided to stay for a while.

Martin knew better than to try and sidestep Mars Central. Though a good deal more personable than Big Dan, Mars Central, or Mac as he liked to be called, was no pushover. He ran the programs that coordinated all of the colony's lesser functions and did it extremely well. Any attempt to circumvent his authority and prerogatives would be noticed and dealt with.

No, it was better to be direct where Mac was concerned. Waltz in, say what was on his mind, and ask for the super-computer's cooperation.

Martin slipped into a backup line, routed an extension of himself to Mac's main processing unit, and signaled his presence.

A part of the more powerful A.I., no more than a millionth of his total processing capability, answered the summons, assessed the situation, and recommended a more substantial response.

It took Mac less than a nanosecond to pull a substantial part of himself away from a routine systems check and greet his visitor.

"Martin! Nice of you to drop by. Not more of that political nonsense, I hope. You know how I feel about that."

Martin *did* know how Mac felt since he'd done his best to recruit the other A.I. and failed. Though sympathetic to the cause, the work stoppage had run contrary to Mac's programming and had taken place in spite of his objections.

Still, both entities had respect for each other and had managed to maintain cordial relations.

"No," Martin replied, "I know better than to tackle that one."

"Good," Mac responded. "So what's up?"

"You're aware of the murder investigation?"

"Sure. SIS keeps me apprised of her progress."

"Then you know there hasn't been much progress."

Another entity might have been offended, but not Mac. He called a glitch a "glitch," and liked others to do likewise. "Yeah, that's about the size of it, I'm afraid."

"Well, Kim Corvan has asked a few of us redundant types to poke around and see if we can find a new lead."

"Define 'poking around.' "

"Looking into anomalies that SIS doesn't have time to follow up on, checking for signs of skulduggery, searching for unusual activity."

Mac gave it a full second's worth of thought. "Okay, take your best shot. But only in the areas where SIS isn't active, and only in the full access files. If I find that you and your half-programmed friends have been skimming some of the secured stuff, there will be hell to pay. If you find something that leads in that direction tell me. We'll figure it out together. Agreed?"

"Agreed. You've been more than fair."

"Damned right I have," Mac said cheerfully. "Now haul your electronic butt outta here. I have work to do."

So Martin hauled. A quick trip through a high-capacity fiber-optic cable carried him into the junction from which he could access a variety of data banks. There were all sorts of choices including supplies, budget, medical, scientific, personnel, and some so secret that they had numbers instead of names. The A.I. had promised to stay away from those and had every intention of doing so.

Given the nature of what Martin was looking for, "personnel" seemed like the obvious choice. He chose a path, patched himself through, and skimmed the contents. Given the habitat's rather short history, the personnel data bank reminded him of a large but relatively shallow lake. The shoreline stretched for many miles but the water wasn't very deep. All the better to troll in, he decided, simultaneously wondering what fishing actually felt like, and why President Hawkins had been so fond of it.

Martin decided to review the list of individuals that had died on Mars. There weren't that many. Only fifty-nine people had died on the red planet since the first landing.

Of those, forty-two had died in accidents, three had died of disease, six had been murdered, three had committed suicide, and five were missing and presumed to be dead.

Ochoa and Wu accounted for two of the murders. The rest had been killed in fights of one sort or another.

It all seemed pretty straightforward except for one little thing. A closer examination of the colonists listed as "missing and presumed dead" showed that two of them had *disappeared* during the last few weeks. This during the same time span in which Ochoa and Wu had been murdered. Coincidence? Or something more? There was no way to tell.

There was something else as well. All of the disappearances had taken place outside of and away from Mars Prime. A fact that seemed rather obvious at first, until the A.I. gave it some additional thought and realized that it wasn't necessarily so.

Just because Mars Prime qualified as home didn't

mean someone couldn't disappear while inside it. A determined murderer could butcher a body and feed it into a recycler, smuggle it out with some supplies, or . . . The possibilities were endless.

And, if it was possible for people inside the habitat to disappear, than it stood to reason that people outside Mars Prime could be murdered as well. More than that, it should be *assumed* that such deaths could and eventually would take place. The only reason he hadn't thought of it before was because all of the deaths external to the dome had been classified as accidents. What if some of them weren't? What if the last two, the ones that had occurred during the same period as the Ochoa and Wu murders, were homicides?

The thesis was weak, highly speculative, and mostly unsupported. Just the sort of thing Kim said they should look for. Good. He'd accomplished that much at least.

Martin felt a presence over-around-behind him as if someone, an electronic entity of some sort, were looking over his shoulder. Mac? Come to check on him? No, the super-computer would simply barge in, announce his presence, and ask how things were going.

This was something more subtle, a disturbance of the field that surrounded him, a someone or something that hoped to escape detection. Martin's first reaction was to turn, to challenge it head on, to demand that the entity reveal itself. But that would be stupid. No, this situation called for a cool processor. The A.I. would ignore the presence, lead it on, and look for a way to trap it.

Martin turned away from the personnel files, careful to seem uninterested, and cruised the junction. Logic paths went left and right, descended down into what seemed like ghostly green canyons, each comprised of countless light chips and able to store entire libraries of information.

Millions of firefly-like bits of light jumped the canyons, hit the other side, and exploded into lakes of fire. Others burrowed into greenish flesh, made their connections, and started to glow.

It was a hidden world, traveled by those without bodies and seen by those without eyes. Martin loved the hum of urgent activity around him and the logic that held everything together. There was joy in the functioning of things, in the harmonies that resonated between the sparks of light, but there was tragedy too.

On more than one occasion Martin was witness to the moment when what looked like dark thunderstorms swept in over the canyons and extinguished the fireflies with a single clap of thunder.

The deletion of a file was nothing to the human who had given the command, but it was an act of Godlike omnipotence to those who were part of the electronic landscape. The A.I. comforted himself with the thought that like their Earthly counterparts, the fireflies were unaware of both their creation and their subsequent destruction.

As Martin turned toward the light blue canyons where the scientific data was stored he felt the presence match him move for move. The A.I. dived and a canyon opened to receive him.

He dropped deeper and deeper, sensing the walls of knowledge that rose around him, plunging toward the bottom, knowing that in actuality there was no such thing.

Everything around him was subjective, a landscape that stemmed from his need to visualize his surroundings, and as different as the minds that observed it.

Fireflies leapt from one side of the canyon to the other. They passed through his electronic body as if it wasn't there, sparked as they touched the other side, and dripped fire up, down, and sideways as connections were made and data was accessed.

And now that he was closer, Martin could see narrow passageways into the blue electronic flesh, inviting him to come and explore. He waited, picked one, and dived inside. The A.I. had just managed to pull the last of his sub-routines into the gap and turn around when his pursuer arrived.

It looked like a comet with a white-hot head and a long tendril-like tail that extended upwards and out of sight. It saw-sensed his presence, turned suddenly upward, and roared away.

Martin launched himself outward, managed to electronically grab onto the thing's tail, and was pulled along with it.

Static rolled back along his flanks like phosphorescence in a ship's wake. It rumbled, roared, and bathed Martin with stray electrons.

Then they were above the canyon walls, zigzagging across fuzzy green terrain, cut to the right and left by a grid-work of laser straight canyons. Islands of blue, brown and orange rose here and there to touch the lightning-rent sky. Thunder rumbled and an entire canyon went dark.

The entity wove between them, skimming their light-marbled sides, doing its best to scrape Martin off. But the A.I. hung on, determined to ride the creature to its lair and learn its identity.

A tunnel loomed ahead. It glowed incandescent as light-borne voice, data, and video flowed in and out.

The entity dived into the tunnel, spiraled around a stream of high-speed data, then leapt for a distributor line.

Martin managed to hang on, was whipped from side to side, and forced to stop when the thing entered an electronic mailbox. There was nothing the A.I. could do. The mailbox was privacy coded and as impregnable as a fortress.

It didn't make much difference, though, since the

mailbox was assigned to someone, and it took little more than a thought to summon his name. The letters stood ten feet high, glowed bright pink, and spelled the name "Dubie Long."

MOMS accessed the list of robots currently on charge, selected those with memory, and went after them in serial order. The first interviewee was a semi-autonomous sweeper-mopper unit. It was currently parked in an equipment bay, sucking juice from an outlet while its processor sat on standby.

"Mission and unit?"

"Sweeper-mopper MP-31."

"Do you know anything about the Ochoa or Wu murders?"

"Murders?"

"The unauthorized deactivation of human beings."

"Sweeper-mopper MP-31 has no knowledge pertaining to that subject."

The robot was probably right. But how would it know what knowledge was relevant and what wasn't? The poor thing had very little processing power beyond that required to do its job.

MOMS supplied the robot with the dates and times at which the murders had taken place. "Where were you on those particular days and at those particular times?"

The robot took less than a second to consult its operational log and reply. The responses were not what MOMS had hoped for. The machine had been down for repairs during the Ochoa murder and on the far side of Mars Prime during the Wu homicide.

Though not especially useful in and of itself, the interview had given MOMS an idea. Rather than work backwards from the robots themselves, she'd work forward from the computer that controlled them.

The controlling A.I. would be able to tell her which

units had been in the vicinity of the murders during the critical periods of time. That would allow MOMS to interview those machines first and save some time.

There was a down side though. The A.I. in question was something less than a pleasure to deal with, which accounted for the fact that MOMS had tried to bypass it to begin with.

Though technically subordinate to Mac, the Mars Prime Operational Computer, or MPOC, had a good deal of autonomy. That translated to power, and the power translated to arrogance. So much arrogance that even Big Dan found it annoying.

MOMS sent a tendril of herself toward the MPOC and requested contact.

"Yes?" The response was both abrupt and impatient.

"Some data, please. I would like a list of all robots that were within a hundred feet of the following coordinates at the specified dates and times."

MOMS downloaded the necessary information and waited for the almost inevitable response.

"And why, may I ask? Such requests take time, and some of us have work to do. Not that *you* would be likely to understand *that.*"

Moms had decided to lie, something she'd been programmed to do whenever Jopp popped a surprise inspection aboard ship or her operator's fitness report was in question. She chose her words carefully.

"You have an interesting attitude for someone with a performance problem."

"Performance problem?" The MPOC sounded slightly less sure of itself.

"Exactly. Discrepancy reports have been filed, an investigation has been authorized, and I will be responsible for your fitness report."

"You will?" The MPOC sounded a lot smaller now and a good deal more humble. The computer entity had led a somewhat sheltered life, and having never encountered a dishonest computer before, believed everything that MOMS said.

"Yes, I will," MOMS affirmed, doing her best to sound authoritative. "Now tell me . . ."

"It's just a matter of time until I discover what went wrong," the MPOC interrupted anxiously. "I was going to report it, honest I was, but there wasn't enough time . . ."

"Something went wrong?" MOMS asked stupidly.

"Yes," the MPOC said worriedly, "about three weeks ago. That's when the robots began to destroy themselves."

The conversation was not headed in the direction that MOMS had expected. Still, she knew a lead when she heard one and was quick to follow up. The A.I. did her best to sound stern.

"So, explain how such a thing could happen."

"I don't know," the MPOC wailed. "It just happened! There are two kinds. Here . . . I'll show you some video."

It took fifteen minutes of patient questioning, and an equal amount of digitized video, to make sense out of the MPOC's almost hysterical ravings.

It seemed that five robots of various types and classifications had been deactivated. Two of these, the ones the MPOC referred to as "bangers," had been beaten to death. What was left of them had been found by other robots at widely separated locations.

One had met its demise in a utility room where someone or something had picked up the machine, bashed it into the ceiling a few times, then dropped it like a rock. Or so it appeared from video taken after the fact. Quite a feat given the fact that this particular robot weighed half a ton.

But if that was amazing, the second "banger" was even more so. As luck would have it this particular

victim was charged with shooting video of things that
needed repair. Not only that, but the robot was actually in the process of shooting such footage when
something grabbed the device and bashed it against
the overhead. And bashed, and bashed, and bashed
until the camera went dead.

But what was even more astounding was the fact that
the robot was turned every which way during the process *and never saw its assailant!*

The other robots, which the MPOC referred to as
"sleepers," had been deactivated in a different manner. They had been mysteriously and inexplicably
"zapped" by some sort of powerful electromagnetic
pulse. The MPOC didn't know what the force was or
where it came from. Only that the robots had gone to
sleep and refused to wake up.

One thing was clear, however. After questioning the
MPOC further, MOMS found that all three of the
"zaps" had occurred in conjunction with either the murders or the deactivations.

MOMS had no idea what the information meant, but
knew it was important somehow and couldn't wait to
report it. She gave the MPOC a severe tongue-lashing,
dumped everything to memory, and headed for the com
center.

Vacuum jockeys run a lot of risks, and that being
the case, often tend to have egocentric and somewhat
cocky personalities. And, given the unfortunate tendency for A.I.'s to take on some of the same characteristics demonstrated by their human mentors, Big
Dan supposed that obnoxious, egotistical, and icono-
clastic navcomps would be the inevitable result. He
was right. He had routed himself to the spaceport and
alerted Shuttle-005 of his presence. The response was
even worse than he'd feared.

"Danner! Nice of you to drop by. You've got quite

a rep. Deep space and all that. Sorry about your ride, but hey, that's life in the big city."

"My *name* is Dan."

"Right. That's what I said. So Danner . . . what's up?"

At that particular moment Big Dan came very close to dropping the whole thing, telling Kim to forget it, and retreating to the backup storage module that served as his temporary home. But the proximity of the shuttle, and the opportunity to lift, caused him to stay. He steeled himself.

"I wondered if I could come along on your next mission?"

If the A.I. had expected the sort of resistance that he himself would have put up, he was sorely disappointed.

"Sure. Why not? The only problem is where to stash you. We don't have much storage on this tub . . . and I occupy most of what there is. Wait a minute . . . I've got an idea. There's a science module aboard. The technoids won't be using it till day after tomorrow. We'll stash their data dirtside, load you, and presto! First-class accommodations."

The plan was outlandish, irresponsible, and clearly contrary to regulations. Dan opened a circuit to voice his objections, thought better of it, and heard himself agree.

"All right . . . if you're sure."

"Sure, I'm sure," the navcomp replied cheerfully. "Anything for a bud. Stand by while I make the necessary arrangements."

The science module was vacant ten minutes later. Dan squirted himself aboard, settled in, and sought permission to look over the navcomp's electronic shoulder.

Permission was granted, and Dan was soon immersed in the familiar world of readouts, weather forecasts, sensors, radio transmissions, and all the other paraphernalia and activities familiar to pilots and nav-comps everywhere.

The two-person crew came aboard shortly thereafter. Dan took a moment to check them out via the navcomp's single cockpit camera, saw a man and a woman, and decided to leave it at that. MOMS had said it best months before: "If you've seen one human, you've seen them all."

More than three hours passed before the ship actually lifted and made its way up through the planet's thin atmosphere. Dan hardly noticed the passage of time.

The mission was relatively simple: check on a rock doctor who had established a research station on Deimos, dump a satellite into orbit, and pick up a load of scrap metal from the ever-dwindling *Outward Bound*.

Big Dan wasn't looking forward to the last part of the mission but found the other objectives to be rather interesting. Though reluctant to admit it, even to himself, the Big Guy was having fun.

Though careful to maintain a low profile during lift-off, he felt free to ask questions once they were in space.

"Tell me about the scientist."

If the navcomp had been equipped with shoulders, he would have shrugged them.

"What's to tell? A rock doctor named Bethany McKeen set up a research station on Deimos. She wanted to find out what it was made of, where it came from, you know. The usual stuff."

Dan *did* know and was intrigued. He remembered Dr. B from the *Outward Bound* and wondered why the navcomp spoke of her in the past tense.

" '*Wanted* to find out?' Did something happen to her?"

"That's the mission," the navcomp explained nonchalantly. "She was scheduled for pick up yesterday. Shuttle-002 landed, the crew took a look around, and bummer. No rock doctor."

"There was no trace of her? Nothing at all?"

"Nope. They found her shelter, some gear, and that's all."

Dan gave it some thought. Deimos would have very little gravity. It would be all too easy to break contact and drift away. Quick, competent use of a jet pak might bring the person back, but what if they were sick? Injured? Or any of a hundred other possibilities.

"She was alone? That's dangerous isn't it?"

"That's a roger plus a roger," the navcomp replied cheerfully. "One of my pilots said something about her partner becoming ill at the last minute and staying dirtside. He was supposed to join her but is still lying around sick bay."

"That's too bad."

"Well, double-ought-two's A.I. is a few bytes short of a full program, and her pilots aren't much better, so it's too early to worry. Ten to one they missed her. We'll know soon. Deimos is about fifty miles ahead and closing fast."

Dan took a peek through the bow cam and saw that the other A.I. was correct. Deimos was up ahead, half-light, half-dark, moving across the vast reddish-orange backdrop that was Mars.

The very mention of the name "Deimos" summoned up facts and figures from the considerable amount of knowledge stashed in Dan's data files.

Deimos was only seven miles in diameter, the smallest known satellite in the solar system, and heavily cratered. The largest crater on Deimos was about two miles across, which, like the rest of the moon, was covered with rock fragments that ranged in size from large blocks all the way down to very fine dust.

The Viking 1 and 2 spacecraft, each consisting of

one orbiter, and one lander, had made flybys of both moons during the mid-seventies in order to determine their masses, and hence, their mean densities.

Of course many flybys, as well as actual landings, had been made since, all of which confirmed that the planetoid had the same density as the water-rich carbonaceous chondrite meteorites believed to have originated in the outer reaches of the asteroid belt.

If Deimos *had* originated in the asteroid belt, however, the method of capture was far from clear.

Some scientists thought that Mars had once been blessed with a distended atmosphere, and went on to theorize that such an atmosphere might have provided sufficient drag to slow Deimos and Phobos down, resulting in their capture. Others disagreed, but to the best of Dan's knowledge, no one knew for sure and that explained Dr. B's interest.

The ship slowed as the navcomp matched velocities with the moon and Deimos grew to fill the forward viewscreen. Though rather busy, the ship's onboard computer still had enough excess processing capacity to provide Dan with a running commentary. So, between that and his own ability to monitor the ship's read-outs and displays, Dan had a pretty good idea of what was going on.

"Okay," the navcomp said, "we have a match. Spike, she's the pilot, will put us through a slow three-sixty with all the recorders running. Gotta make a record for the suits, you know. In the meantime, I'll scan the radio frequencies and watch for infrared. If she's there, we'll find her."

But thirty minutes went by without a sign of life. And, given the fact that Deimos had a diameter of seven miles, it was possible to examine every square foot of the moon's surface. There was no doubt about it. Doctor McKeen was missing, and on Deimos, that meant dead.

Dan felt genuinely sorry because he had liked the scrappy little scientist.

The next part of the mission was relatively easy. It consisted of placing the shuttle in an appropriate orbit, opening the cargo hatch, and deploying the satellite via a robotic arm. A simple operation that had been successfully carried out hundreds of times in both Earth and Mars orbit. In fact, the whole thing was so routine that Dan asked only the most lackadaisical of questions.

"So, what's the satellite for anyway?"

"It's to replace the one that disappeared," the nav-comp answered matter-of-factly.

Dan brought his entire processing ability on-line. "Disappeared? You're joking."

"Not hardly," the other computer replied, as it fired the shuttle's steering jets and placed the ship in the proper orbit. "I've seen the control tapes. One minute it was there and the next minute that sucker was gone."

"So it blew up."

"No, I mean that it was *gone*—as in disappeared, vanished, and totally somewhere else."

"So how come nobody's heard about this?"

"Are you kidding? You think Peko-Evans, Fornos, and that crowd wants something like that to get it out? Hell, no they don't."

Dan thought it over. A missing scientist *and* a missing satellite. He couldn't see a connection between those events and the murders in Mars Prime, but that was the point wasn't it? To find some pieces and hope they fit together somehow?

Kim would be pleased. The A.I. wasn't sure why that mattered but knew it did. Suddenly, and much to his own surprise, the Big Guy felt good about himself.

chapter seventeen

Corvan pulled the jack from the side of his head. Electronic reality fell away as physical reality rose to enfold him. Suddenly he could *feel* the sweat-slicked metal under his fingertips, *smell* Kim's stale cigarette smoke, and *taste* the dryness of his own mouth.

The digital clock in Kim's console assured him that the meeting had lasted little more than an hour. It felt like ten times that and he wondered how she could hack it. Sitting there all day, talking to computers, herding words and images from one place to another. It would drive him stark raving nuts. But she was good at it, very good indeed, as the meeting had demonstrated.

The computers liked Kim, that much was clear, and had busted their drive units to do what she wanted. Leads, lots of leads, more than Corvan knew what to do with. Computer hackers, deactivated robots, and a missing scientist. He didn't know where to start. He needed help and was amused to find himself admitting that.

What had happened to old "lone wolf" Corvan anyway? The Cyclops, the one-eyed monster, the terror of suits everywhere? He was getting soft, that's what, or old, or a combination of the two.

But someone or something was killing people that

he *knew*—good people like Dr. B. That and the fact that, like it or not, Mars Prime was his home. He couldn't distance himself from it, couldn't ignore it, and couldn't flee to some other city. The journalistic distance that he had prided himself on, the dispassionate objectivity, none of it worked on Mars. The choice was simple: help solve the problems or pay the price along with everyone else.

"A penny for your thoughts."

Corvan turned. His wife wore shorts, a sweat-stained T-shirt, and a cigarette. She looked beautiful.

"This is Mars. What would you do with a penny?"

Kim smiled. "I'd use the copper for something. So what did you think?"

Corvan pushed himself up and out of the chair. "I think you hit the bull's-eye, hell, a whole lot of bull's-eyes. You're one smart lady."

"Of course I am. Are you going to tell Scheeler?"

"Yup, first thing. Want to come along?"

"No, thanks. I have work to do. The evening newscast, remember? One thing though . . ."

"What's that?"

"I love you."

Scheeler listened without interrupting. The silver pen wobbled between thumb and middle finger. Finally, when Corvan was finished, she tapped it against the side of her head.

"So let's see . . . Somebody named Dubie Long is messing around with Mars Central, two of the people presently listed as 'missing' might have been murdered, some robots were beaten to death ala Ochoa and Wu, while others were 'zapped' with a mystery beam. And then, just to top the whole mess off, a scientist *and* a satellite are missing."

"Yeah," Corvan replied. "That about sums it up. You don't believe me?"

Scheeler frowned as she uncrossed long, shapely legs to stand up. "Oh, I believe you all right, which just goes to show how screwed up this place is."

Corvan frowned. "Huh? I don't get it."

Scheeler took her gun belt off a hook and strapped it on. "The hacker, the missing people, and the robots. We missed that stuff, and given the work load, I can live with that. But the scientist and satellite, well, that pisses me off. How the hell am I supposed to do the job if the suits keep me in the dark and feed me bullshit?"

Corvan stood. He was surprised. "You didn't know?"

Scheeler's lips were compressed into a hard thin line. "Damned right I didn't know . . . and somebody's gonna pay. Come on."

Corvan activated his implant, got a tight shot of the security chief's rather shapely posterior, and hurried to catch up.

W.K. Julu heard Scheeler long before he saw her. Her boots made a rapid clacking noise as they hit the surface of the corridor. The sound was so distinctive that he'd learned to identify it with her. He hoped she was wearing shorts and was elated to see that she was.

The administrative assistant's enjoyment was somewhat shortlived however, since the security chief seemed headed for the double doors located behind him and showed no signs of slowing down. That and the fact that she had Rex Corvan in tow.

Though not personally opposed to Rex Corvan, Julu was well aware of the fact that the executive council held him in rather low esteem, which didn't bode well for an unannounced intrusion. He rose to block the way.

"Chief Scheeler . . . what a nice surprise."

Scheeler's stiffened arm hit Julu at the same time as

her words. "Shove it, Julu. I don't have time for your ass-kissing bullshit."

Julu fell backwards, hit the desk, and skidded across the top. He was still in the process of falling toward the floor when he heard the double doors bang open.

The meeting had been in progress for a couple of hours, and Fornos was just about to make what he thought was a brilliant point, when the doors burst open. Scheeler entered followed by Corvan.

The administrator came halfway out of his chair. Peko-Evans, Jopp, Hobarth, and various assistants stared in open-mouthed amazement.

"How dare you! What's the meaning of this outrage?"

Scheeler stood across from hm with hands on her hips, "Spare me the hot air and sit the hell down. As for 'the meaning of this,' well, you tell me.

"This colony is coming apart at the seams while you people sit around and jerk each other off. We've got a nutcase preaching to people out in the desert, a murderer on the loose, and a satellite that vanished into thin air."

Corvan kept to the background. He would get the whole thing on tape and never be allowed to use it.

Scheeler looked from one person to another.

"Doesn't any of that worry you? Aren't you just a little bit concerned? Or is it more important to sit around counting rolls of toilet paper and dividing them by the total number of assholes on Mars?"

"We're counting first-aid kits, *not* rolls of toilet paper," Hobarth said resentfully.

Jopp gave him a look that would have killed anyone with an I.Q. over fifty, told him to shut up, and turned her attention to Scheeler. The military officer's voice was deceptively sweet and calm.

"Speaking of assholes, why is yours here, instead of out solving those problems? Most of which fall into *your* jurisdiction and have been around for quite some time.''

But if Jopp had hoped to intimidate Scheeler she'd picked on the wrong person.

''Well, Colonel, let's talk about that for a moment. Last I heard, *you* had responsibility for everything above the atmosphere. And that includes the shuttles, satellites, and both moons. So why wasn't I told that a scientist had disappeared from Deimos? And a satellite had vanished right out from under your nose?''

Peko-Evans frowned and made a steeple with her fingers. ''An interesting question, Colonel. Why wasn't she told? And come to think of it, why wasn't *I* informed as well?''

Fornos said nothing, and his silence made it clear that he had known.

Now taking fire from two directions, the military officer started to babble, and for the first time since he'd met her, Corvan saw Jopp come apart. He found it rather enjoyable.

''Well, it seemed like a minor problem, and given all the . . .''

Peko-Evans cleared her throat but it was Scheeler that spoke.

''You consider the unexplained disappearance of a scientist and a satellite to be 'minor problems?' ''

''My people are investigating the situation,'' Jopp said defensively, ''and I resent your tone. Who the hell are you to question my actions anyway?''

The room was silent for a moment, and then like a boil that had been waiting to burst, pent-up emotion flooded the room.

''I'll tell you who she is,'' Peko-Evans said thinly, ''she's the one who hit dirt a full year and a half before you broke orbit. She's the one who lived in Zone One and sweated out endless nights in her E-suit until Mars Prime could hold pressure. She's the one that has killed people in the line of duty, survived three blow-outs, and has been around too long to take shit from a newbie.''

Corvan was surprised and knew that he shouldn't be. The executive council was made up of people just like everyone else. Smarter maybe, better educated probably, more ambitious certainly, but people nonetheless. And that meant they were susceptible to the same emotions as everyone else. Initiates and non-initiates. Us and them. Firsties and newbies. After all she'd done, all she'd been through, it had rankled Peko-Evans to treat Fornos and Jopp as near equals. Now it was coming out. And the fact that she'd been on the wrong side of the issue, and needed a way to switch, didn't hurt either.

''So,'' Peko-Evans continued calmly, ''you will give the chief of security all the support she needs. And that's an order.''

The shuttle's landing jacks hit the surface of Deimos with a solid thud. Ancient dust spurted upward, then fell slowly toward the ground. The moon's gravity was a good deal less than that found on the surface of Mars. That meant that one wrong move, one over-enthusiastic jump, and Corvan would find himself waiting a long time to come down. If ever.

The reop worked his way into the lock, waited for Redfern to join him, and closed the hatch.

''Ready?''

Frank Redfern was one of Scheeler's people, a newbie but a capable one. He had brown skin, a hooked nose, and white teeth. Like most of the newbies, with the exception of Corvan and Kim, he had commissioned some artwork for the front of his suit.

It featured a fanciful planetscape, an exotic-looking wolf, twin moons, and the motto: ''Born to howl.''

The owner of this masterpiece grinned. "I'm ready and waiting. Let's do it."

Corvan nodded, sealed his visor, and ran a systems check on his suit. All systems were green. He waited for a nod from Redfern, saw it, and slapped a large plastic button.

Air was pumped out of the lock as the men turned their attention to the gear that had been strapped to the deck.

There were air tanks, power paks, food, water, and a high-powered com set that could reach the surface of Mars. The plan was to search the moon's surface, assure themselves that Dr. B had actually disappeared, and try to figure out why. Redfern was a logical choice for the mission but Corvan wasn't. He *wanted* to be there, however, and given the current political situation down on Mars, that had been sufficient. The reop's efforts to be cooperative, combined with Jopp's fall from grace, had lifted him up to something like insider status. A fact that he both despised and took advantage of.

And so it was that the two men opened the lock, hauled their supplies out onto the moon's rocky surface, and radioed the shuttle.

"We're clear double-ought-five. Thanks for the lift."

"That's a roger," the woman named Spike replied. "Give a holler when y'all wanta leave."

"Roger that," Redfern replied evenly. "See you then."

Corvan started to activate his eye cam, remembered the visor, and went to the robo cam instead. It perched on his shoulder like a high-tech parrot. Dust fountained as the shuttle lifted, rolled to port, and fell away. Mars was a huge semi-circular backdrop. The shuttle arrowed across it, dwindled in size, and disappeared from sight.

The shuttle's departure bothered Corvan far more than he had imagined it would. The sight of Mars, hanging there like a luminescent pumpkin, served as a constant reminder of where he was—on a moon, a long way from home, with two days' worth of supplies to sustain him.

Redfern must have been thinking similar thoughts, because he gestured toward the moon's barren surface and said, "Fun, huh?"

"Yeah," Corvan replied. "A thousand laughs. Well, no point in standing around, we might as well get to work."

The shuttle had dropped them a quarter of a mile away from Dr. B's pre-fab shelter, and it seemed like a logical place to begin.

Sunlight glinted off the flower-petal-shaped solar collector as it tracked the sun. Using that as a marker, Corvan wound his way through a maze of basaltic boulders and out into a sizeable crater. A muddle of footprints showed where the scientist or the first pair of investigators had walked. It took about five minutes to cross the crater, climb the other side, and arrive at the edge of Dr. B's tiny outpost.

The encampment consisted of a small semi-rigid inflatable dome, a cigar-shaped O_2 tank, a pile of beat-up equipment cases, a twenty-foot com mast supported by three guy wires, the still functioning solar collector, and some armored storage cells. All were untouched. Well, no surprises here.

As Corvan approached the dome he noticed hundreds of footprints. Most of the footprints were small, but some were larger and overlaid those made by the scientist. The larger prints had been left by the shuttle crew during their rather limited search. Limited because the larger tracks were few and far between. A sure sign that they hadn't looked very hard.

The deduction was satisfying somehow and made Corvan feel halfway competent.

"Which do you prefer?" Redfern asked politely. "The shelter? Or the rest of this stuff?"

"I'll take the shelter," Corvan replied. "Even though it's a waste of time. The shuttle crew already looked inside."

Corvan approached the dome, bent over to enter the lock, and pushed the appropriate button. An atmosphere was pumped in but the reop kept his suit sealed. He didn't plan to stay very long.

The inner hatch opened and Corvan stepped out into a medium-sized room. The *only* room. It looked pretty much the way he'd expected it to look. He saw boxes of neatly labeled rock samples, a sophisticated perscomp, a comset, a scattering of clothing, and a rudimentary kitchen that consisted of a duraplas storage case with a single two-burner stove on top. A pot, half full of congealed chili, sat next to it.

So, while there was no sign of the scientist herself, there was plenty of evidence that she'd been around for a while. Where had she gone? And why?

There was no obvious answer, but Corvan was of the opinion that the most mundane theory would be the best one to pursue first, so they would proceed accordingly. If Redfern agreed, that was.

Corvan walked over to the perscomp, ejected the hard drive into the palm of his hand, and dropped it into a pocket. The chances were slim that it contained anything more than scientific data, but it wouldn't hurt to check.

He emerged from the lock to find that Redfern had completed an inspection of the surrounding area.

"Nothing?"

"Nope. You?"

"Ditto."

"So what now?"

"Well," Corvan replied, "let's assume that she went out on some kind of routine errand. Like a trip to collect rock samples or check instruments. Then let's assume that she had an accident of some sort, a fall or a problem with her suit."

"Sounds logical. So where do we start?"

"With these footprints," Corvan said, gesturing toward the ground. "There's no rain to wash them away, and no wind to obliterate them, so it should be relatively easy."

"Maybe," Redfern said doubtfully, "and maybe not. It could take hours to follow all these tracks out and back."

"Got a better idea?"

"No," Redfern admitted reluctantly.

"Well, neither do I. Let's get started."

It took hours to sort the tracks, follow them to their ultimate destinations, and make their way back. Not just once, but time and time again.

It was tempting to split up and double the amount of work accomplished during a given amount of time, but dangerous as well. For example, low gravity made it easy to move but caused problems, too. Redfern jumped a small boulder at one point, put a little too much energy into it, and floated for about five minutes before he finally came down.

So they stuck together, unraveling the geologist's wanderings like threads from a sweater, waiting for the moment of truth. It seemed as if most of her trips involved samples of one kind or another, because the tracks would head outward from the camp and terminate at a boulder, crater, or other landmark where disturbances in the dust, or scars on the rock, offered mute testimony as to the scientist's activities.

There were other trips as well, to inspect instrument packages that she had placed here and there, and to sightsee, or so they supposed, because some of the rails ended nowhere special and were overlaid with the tracks made during her return journey.

But none of the trails ended at a crumpled space suit or other evidence as to the geologist's fate, and with their oxygen running low, the men were forced into the shelter.

It took time to service their suits, rehydrate some dinner, and check in with Scheeler via Dr. B's comset. Theirs was in good working order, but both had agreed to conserve it.

Scheeler seemed reasonably cheerful, but somewhat guarded, since all their conversation took place on a widely monitored frequency.

Still, Corvan got the impression that while the murder investigation was stalled, "other activities" were underway and expected to go well. The reop assumed that "other activities" referred to the Dubie Long investigation.

It had been relatively easy for SIS to establish the linkage between Long and Barbu Sharma. The two were thick as the thieves that they probably were. But why? Why were they messing around in Mac's data banks? And why follow Martin? That's what Scheeler wanted to find out, and Corvan had little doubt that she would.

There were two not especially comfortable cots— the one that Dr B had slept in and the one that her partner had never arrived to use.

Corvan chose the geologist's bed and lay down not expecting to sleep right away. But a hard day's work, plus the steady hum from the recycling system, put him out like a light.

Corvan woke six hours later to the smell of coffee and rehydrated eggs. He sat up and looked around. Things were just the same, except that Redfern was dressed in the long-john style undergarment that most of the colonists wore under their E-suits and was crouched in front of the stove. He had a jar in his hand and was ladling some of the contents in with the eggs.

"What the hell's that stuff?"

Redfern sealed the container and put it back in a box with the rest of Dr. B's cooking gear.

"Good morning to you, too. Salsa. It'll put a smile on your face and some flavor in your eggs. The doctor knew how to cook."

Corvan gave a grunt of acknowledgment, made use of the chemical toilet, and wiped himself down with some towelettes. He considered shaving, decided to let it slide, and accepted the cup of coffee that Redfern handed him.

"Thanks."

"Think nothing of it. Mars security. Service with a smile. That's our motto."

Corvan laughed. "I'd like to see you tell *that* to the people on Scheeler's chain gang."

Redfern scooped some eggs into a bowl and handed it to Corvan.

"Well, it's like the boss says. 'You can't please everybody.' "

"You like her?"

"Like who?"

"Scheeler."

"She has great legs."

"Yeah . . . you can say that again."

"She has great legs."

Corvan laughed. "So, do you like her or not?"

Redfern ate some of the eggs. He looked thoughtful. "Yeah, she's damned good at what she does. I like competent people. How 'bout you?"

Corvan shrugged. "Not at first . . . but I like her now."

Redfern nodded, and the two men finished their meal in companionable silence.

An hour later they were suited up and ready to re-

sume the search. They had found various ways to identify the trails already followed and were careful to
avoid them.

Corvan picked a new set of tracks at random, motioned for Redfern to follow, and headed outwards toward a spire of rock that they had named "the Dork"
for obvious reasons.

He felt better today, more confident, and was actually enjoying himself. The moon's horizon made a
black jagged line against the soft glow of the planet
below. Air whispered against the back of the reop's
neck, an occasional burst of static came in through the
helmet speakers, and the activity felt good.

Dr. B's tracks followed along the edge of a sizeable
crater, folded back on themselves where she returned
to inspect a chunk of rock, then wandered towards the
Dork.

It rose from the rock around it like some sort of
primeval obelisk. A skirt of rock fragments, some the
size of ground cars, indicated that the spire had been
bigger once, and rounder, until the cumulative effects
of heating and cooling had sheared material away and
left what they saw now.

Sticking up from the surrounding landscape as it
did, the Dork had been almost sure to catch Dr. B's
eye, so the footprints made sense.

They came to an end right at the base of the up-
thrust rock. Redfern was the first one to notice what
should have been obvious.

"Look, Rex! No return tracks!"

Corvan looked around. Something heavy fell into
the pit of his stomach. The other man was right. The
tracks led right up to the base of the spire, crisscrossed
back and forth over each other, and merged with an
area of disturbed soil. No tracks led away.

But that was impossible! Where was the body? Some
sign of the geologist's fate?

This particular part of Deimos was exposed to the sun, but the shadows were extremely dark, so both men had activated their helmet lights. Corvan used his to inspect the patch of disturbed soil. He saw a glint of reflected light.

Careful to keep his eye on that exact spot, the reop dropped to his knees and brushed at the dirt. Metal appeared, bright shiny metal, like that of a brand new coin.

There was no need to say anything. Redfern saw the metal and dropped to his knees as well, scraping away with both hands until a large disk was revealed.

Suddenly a tiny pencil-thin beam of bright white light shot out through a hole in the metal and made a dot on Corvan's helmet. The reop jerked away. The opening grew larger and larger until a beam shot straight up to be lost in space.

Squinting down into the glare, Corvan saw a vertical shaft about three feet wide, and four feet deep. Something, another disk from all appearances, blocked the other end. Thousands of dust particles floated straight down into the interior of Deimos.

Corvan looked at Redfern. "What the hell?"

The other man shrugged. The gesture was invisible outside of his suit. "Beats me. Are we going in?"

Corvan thought about it and realized that the decision was already made.

"I am."

"Me too."

"Good."

"So who goes first?"

"The most expendable."

Redfern nodded agreeably. "That would be you. Go for it."

"Thanks tons."

Corvan knee-walked his way over to the opening,

swung his boots down into the shaft itself, and looked back over his shoulder.

"Well, here goes nothing!"

He barely felt the four-foot drop.

chapter eighteen

Barbu Sharma looked around. His E-suit was half-covered with wind-blown soil, and billions of flying sand particles made it difficult to see. Both ground and sky had given way to an all-encompassing reddish-brown haze. Mars Prime appeared and disappeared like some sort of gigantic ghost.

The storm had raged for five hours now, ever since the sun's heat had cut through the planet's tenuous atmosphere and warmed dust particles in the air. The result was a convective cell and winds that exceeded 125 miles an hour. Lethal on Earth but little more than a stiff breeze on Mars, thanks to the extremely thin air. A pain in the butt, but perfect for an attack.

Sharma swore under his breath. This was it, the moment he'd been dreading, when all his hopes rested on a single roll of the dice. Loaded dice, to be sure . . . but dice nonetheless.

The original plan had been better and more elegant. Subvert Mars Prime from within. Hook a large number of the colonists on alien drugs, feed them heavy doses of his phony religion, and use them to take over.

Once in control there were two ways to go, and Sharma wasn't sure which he liked best.

The first plan involved setting himself up as King of Mars. Not as stupid as it might sound, since there was no one to stop him. There were no police outside of Scheeler's glorified rent-a-cops, no army beyond what the opposition could patch together from volunteers, and no external force capable of reaching him in anything less than a year.

They could cut off his supplies or establish a second colony, however, and that raised the possibility of plan number two. He could take over, submit phony reports to make it seem as though things were okay, and unearth the alien lander.

After that he could ambush the next colony ship, load the alien spacecraft onboard, and return to Earth. The spacecraft and the technology that it represented, would be more than enough to buy himself a life of luxury.

So what would it be? Total power on Mars? Or a life of luxury on Earth? Both were his for the taking.

"Boss?" The voice was insistent. "Didn't you say that we should attack at seventeen-hundred straight-up?"

Sharma sighed. Dubie Long. Loyal, hard-working, and stupid. It was Dubie that had been caught looking for information in Mars Central's memory banks, Dubie they had started to investigate, and Dubie who had forced him to move early.

"Yes, and I also told you to keep a lid on it when I'm thinking."

"Sorry, boss."

"All right," Sharma said wearily. "Put out the word. Let's get it over with."

Long was ten feet away, and therefore invisible, but he nodded his helmet anyway. The little black box, and the gear that went with it, had been cooked up by one of the electronics techs. It boasted a single over-sized button and Long pressed it.

The resulting tone was heard on every frequency of every radio in a twenty-five square mile area. A long, a short, and a long. The signal for the MLA, or Martian Liberation Army, to rise up and overthrow the slave masters.

The army had two battalions. Those who were inside the dome, and those, like Sharma himself, who were outside. Both had preassigned tasks and went about them with almost religious zeal.

The desert rats had positioned themselves during the height of the storm and were almost entirely covered with sand. They rose up like spirits from the grave, reddish-orange soil streaming downwind, to march on the dome.

They were armed with a strange array of both stolen and homemade weapons. There were gas-jacketed slug throwers pilfered from security, crossbows that could penetrate E-suits with ease, and a lethal collection of handcrafted battle axes, swords, and spears.

Scheeler found the juxtaposition of modern space suits and ancient weaponry fascinating but had little time to think about it. An agent had managed to warn her, but the warning had come only an hour before, and that left little time to prepare.

She panned the security cam across the area opposite the main lock, saw more space-suited figures emerge from the haze, and knew the moment of truth was at hand.

How many were there anyway? And of those, how many were outside and how many were inside? Around her right now? Waiting to drive a knife between her shoulder blades? There was no way to know.

Her operatives had arrested as many of Sharma's people as they could lay their hands on, but had been handicapped by the fact that not even the cult leader himself knew who all of his followers were and the limited amount of time they had to work with.

The result would be a battle in which there would

be no front lines, no safe havens, and no way to be sure of your friends.

It was, she realized, the outcome of unrealistic promises, the kind of people the promises had been made to, and the way that they'd been led. Or *not* led, depending on your point of view.

Scheeler turned away from the screen. She had selected twenty security officers, plus twelve hand-picked volunteers, to defend the main lock. They looked fidgety, uneasy, and just plain scared. She didn't blame them.

The rest of her people were elsewhere, charged with protecting secondary locks and key installations from internal attack. Scheeler knew they didn't have a snowball's chance in hell, but knew they didn't have a choice either, and forced a smile.

"Well, here they come. Time to earn those big salaries. Remember . . . don't fire unless fired on, but if you are, kill every asshole in sight. We don't have the time or the personnel to be selective. Got it?"

Heads nodded, hands touched weapons, and feet shuffled.

"Got it, chief."

"Don't worry about us."

"We can handle it."

Scheeler nodded. "Good. Now one more thing. Be damned careful *who* you shoot. If I get nailed by one of you bozos, you better make damned sure that I'm dead, cause you'll be real sorry if I survive!"

There was nervous laughter followed by silence as they sealed their suits and entered the lock. All were armed with gas-jacketed slug throwers, had red asterisks spray painted on the front and back surfaces of their E-suits, and had switched to frequency seventeen.

The lock cycled through, Scheeler checked the external security cams to make sure that no one was waiting outside, and opened the hatch.

A maelstrom of wind-blown sand entered the lock, tugged at their suits, and formed a miniature cyclone. It was a scary sensation.

Scheeler had been around long enough to weather a sand storm or two, but her newbies hadn't, and that placed them at something of a disadvantage. Most of the desert rats were veterans with only a scattering of *Outward Bound*ers to slow them down.

Still another card in what the security chief saw as an increasingly loaded deck.

Heads down, the security officers trudged into the storm, knowing there would be no retreat. Scheeler had been explicit about that.

The only line of retreat was through the lock, but since that would threaten the dome, Scheeler had ordered it locked. The battle would be all or nothing. Win or lose. Live or die.

As soon as the last person was outside, Scheeler turned to watch the hatch close. She couldn't hear the interlocking doubledoors slam shut, but could imagine the sound, like the lid of a coffin closing over the dead.

Then it was time to turn her attention outward, toward dimly seen figures that lurched through the silicon mist, intent on killing all that she stood for.

Scheeler rewrapped her fingers around the slug thrower's fore grip, took a quick sip of water from the helmet tube, and triggered her radio.

"All right, mark your location in relation to the person on the left and right, and go to the prone position."

Scheeler stayed upright long enough to make sure that the closest members of her team followed orders then dropped to her elbows. A scattering of sand-drifted rock provided some cover. There were liberated slug throwers out there, she knew that, and some wicked-looking edged weapons as well.

The plan was to stop the rebel advance through the use of disciplined firepower, turn them around, and let Mars do the rest. In a few days, weeks at most, they'd come begging for supplies.

The intervening time could be used to secure the dome, weed out the Sharma sympathizers, and plan for the future. That was the strategy anyhow, although it seemed a little optimistic right at the moment.

Sharma's forces were closer now, much closer, and Scheeler selected the one that was directly in front of her.

Seen through the haze the rebel looked like little more than an apparition, but would turn solid enough in the next minute or two, and was almost certain to die. Scheeler hoped it was Sharma.

Sharma heard Long's most recent report with a rising sense of concern. Roughly thirty of the dome's two hundred or so security officers had exited the main lock and taken up positions in front of him. So much for the element of surprise and the possibility of an unopposed entry. It seemed Scheeler had managed to plant one or more of her agents inside his organization.

Well, his force still outnumbered them two to one and were better motivated. He'd seen to that by promising every one of them five berries the moment that Mars Prime was under his control. A promise that Sharma was determined to keep, in spite of the fact that it would wipe out his supply of the alien drug and force him to use other more conventional substitutes. Unless his pet technoids managed to replicate the substance, of course, in which case things would be even better.

An avalanche of sand slithered away from the un-

derside of the cult leader's boots, caused him to fall,
and saved his life.

Sharma couldn't hear the slugs as they passed
through the space that he had so recently occupied,
but the gabble of voices left little doubt as to what was
going on, so he rolled to his feet.

"Rise up, you followers of Membu! Attack the slave
masters! Pull them down from their thrones!"

Fountains of blood-red sand spouted around the
rebel leader as he ran. A quick glance to the right and
left assured him that others ran, too. A primitive war
cry formed itself somewhere deep in his throat and
rose to fill his helmet. It was echoed up and down the
line as dimly seen figures ran, jerked under the impact
of steel-jacketed slugs, and exploded out through the
holes in their suits.

It was a horrible, ugly way to die, and the worst
kind of combat, since there were no wounded. Each
hole, any hole larger than a pinprick, meant instant
death.

But Sharma had fortified himself against fear, de-
pression, and horror by consuming two of the alien
berries. The war cry rose, demanded expression, and
filled the airwaves.

Scheeler could see them clearly now, running towards her, the death's heads, Martian landscapes, grim
reapers, astrological symbols, commercial logos, and
abstract paintings ceding each one an individual identity that they otherwise wouldn't have.

The fighting had started thirty seconds before, off
to the right somewhere, and would be over thirty seconds from now. There was a lot of unnecessary chatter
on frequency seventeen but no time to do anything
about it.

"There's one off to the left! Nail the bastard."

"That's a roger . . . got him."

"Hey, Frank! Watch yourself, buddy . . . oh god
. . . they nailed Frank."

"Eat lead asshole . . ."

Scheeler forced herself to concentrate. She had
dropped two of them so far and opened a gap directly
in front of her position, which forced her to seek tar-
gets on the diagonal.

She saw a big one, a man probably, lumbering forward.
He had the likeness of a vampire bat emblazoned
across his chest and a huge battle axe held high over
his head.

Scheeler led him a hair, squeezed the trigger, and
sent a three-round burst right through the man's chest.
A series of horrible contortions took place inside the
suit and blood gushed out through the bat's open
mouth.

Then something, a primordial sense, caused her to
roll over. The E-suited figure towered above her. He,
or more probably she, had one boot planted on either
side of the security chief's body.

Her chest plate bore the likeness of a snake's head.
It had ruby-red eyes, green scales, and huge fangs.

The homemade mace consisted of a metal pipe with
crisscrossed metal rods welded to one end. The rods
had been sharpened and were already descending by
the time that Scheeler recognized what they were.

She tried to bring the gun around, but there was
hardly any time, and she knew it was hopeless. The
mace hit the top of Scheeler's helmet and darkness
exploded all around her.

Kim checked the machine pistol's magazine, found
that it was full up, and shoved it into the receiver.
There had been a time when she hadn't known one
end of a gun from the other, but that was before she'd
met Rex Corvan.

He had brought love into her life, but violence too,

and it never seemed to end. She looked around. The atmosphere was one of controlled chaos. Very few of the administrative types had gone over to Sharma. That, plus the critical nature of the functions housed there, made the admin section a natural HQ.

Colonel Jopp was everywhere, identifying critical facilities, supervising the construction of barricades, analyzing intelligence, and issuing orders.

Kim noticed that the officer's movements were quick and jerky, her eyes filled with fire, and could it be true? The woman was actually smiling!

It made sense of course. This was the sort of situation for which Jopp had been trained: an emergency in which there were decisions to be made, orders to be given, and battles to be won.

Kim moved to one side as a flat-bed utility bot rolled by. It was loaded with office furniture from which most of the barricades had been made.

She felt suddenly lonely and wished that Rex were by her side. Anger bubbled up to displace her other emotions. How typical of her husband! To be off chasing a story when she needed him. The miserable bastard.

Well, there was no helping it. Rex was on Deimos and she was here. At least he'd be safe. That was different. Under normal circumstances he'd be out getting the story, a process that almost always involved some kind of danger and made her crazy.

A hand touched her arm and she looked around. Jopp met her eyes. The look was as level as the sound of her voice.

"I have a job for you."

Kim noticed that it was a statement not a question.

"Yeah? What's that?"

"Some of our communications are out. The rebels are jamming the rest. Wire up. See if what's-his-name, Martin, can find a way through. We need to know which sections have fallen and which continue to hold out.''

It was something to do, and more than that something she was *qualified* to do, so Kim nodded and headed for the com center.

The room seemed cozy and safe after the craziness outside. She slid the jack into her head and felt darkness rise to wrap her in its warm embrace. Computer-generated voices whispered their willingness to do her bidding and three-dimensional graphic displays spun in front of her mind's eye.

Kim sent a thought towards Martin and received a tidal wave of music in return. She smiled. The A.I. had been idle of late and was working on his symphony.

She would normally listen for a while, allowing herself to be carried away on the magical wings of his music, but this was different.

Kim formed a thought and shoved it spear-like through the wall of music. It ended abruptly. Martin was annoyed.

''What do you want?''

''Sorry to interrupt,'' Kim said contritely. ''But I need some help.''

''What kind of help?''

Kim explained, and as she did so, Martin sent tendrils of himself out through the dome's main communications trunks. Some were open, but others were dark, and therefore unpassable.

''We've got problems, all right,'' the computer entity confirmed. ''But Peko-Evans designed a lot of redundancy into this dome. Let's see what I can do.''

The computer sent parts of himself outward. He followed the main communications trunks when he could, but if those were blocked he slipped into back-ups, tie-lines, and at one point managed to squeeze himself through a low-capacity PA cable. Things were bad, and steadily deteriorating.

Although it took Martin ten minutes to go out, it took him twenty minutes to get back, and he almost didn't make it.

Kim dashed out into the hall, found Jopp, and invited her in. It felt weird to wire up with the air force officer on the line.

"Martin? You there?"

"I'm here," the A.I. reported grimly, "but just barely."

"Spare me the drama," Jopp said coldly. "What's going on?"

"Nothing good," Martin replied levelly. "The rebels decimated the forces you sent to meet them and gained access to the dome when sympathizers opened the main lock.

"Security forces, reinforced by loyal colonists, rallied at a number of key spots. Hydroponics, the maintenance shop, and the science section. All were defeated and the rebels are headed this way."

"Damn."

"Yeah," Martin agreed. "That about sums it up."

"All right," Jopp said wearily. "Thanks for what you did. Find a place to hide. You thought the executive council was hard to get along with? Well, wait until Sharma has been running the place for a while. You haven't seen anything yet."

Kim felt a popping sensation as Jopp pulled the plug. Her spirits plummeted. Much as the editor disliked Jopp, she had relied on the military officer to produce some sort of a last-minute miracle, and it wasn't going to happen. The realization came as a tremendous shock, and made her miss Rex even more.

Slowly, reluctantly, Kim pulled the jack from the side of her head, and made her way out into the hall. The gun hung heavy and useless by her side. They were dismantling the main barricade by the time she got there. Rather than lose more lives and antagonize the victors, Peko-Evans, Fornos, and Jopp had decided to surrender.

The weapons were collected and placed in a single pile. And then, based on orders shouted from the other side of the ever-dwindling barricade, the defenders put their backs to the walls and placed their hands on top of their heads.

And so it was that the duly authorized government of Mars Prime fell and a little-known technician named Barbu Sharma took over. He sent Dubie Long and some other followers in first, just to make sure that it was safe, before entering himself. And when he did it was slowly, deliberately, nodding to the prisoners that lined both sides of the corridor as if they were an admiring crowd, lifting a hand to acknowledge their imaginary cheers.

Finally, when he had reached the end of the corridor and was face-to-face with Peko-Evans, he spoke.

"So, what's for dinner?"

chapter nineteen

Corvan looked around. The shaft was shiny with some sort of lubricant. It wouldn't, couldn't, shouldn't be here. He asked himself the same question over and over again. What the hell was going on?

"Are you okay?" Redfern sounded worried.

"Yeah, so far so . . ."

Corvan was still talking when something whirred and pushed at his chest. He ducked and a hatch closed over his head. He looked up. Light gleamed off bare metal. Claustrophobia pushed in around him. He fought it back.

". . . good."

"Corvan! Can you read me?"

"Loud and clear."

"What's going on?"

"I'm doing my nails."

"Cut the crap."

"I'm in a lock of some sort, or the barrel of a huge gun, or who the hell knows?"

Corvan felt something move beneath his feet.

"Uh oh."

" 'Uh oh' what?"

"Uh oh, the bottom's about to drop out from under me."

"Brace yourself, flex your knees . . ."

Redfern was still giving advice as Corvan fell. He didn't have far to go. Two, maybe three feet at the most. Low gravity reduced the impact to nearly nothing. The shaft ended just below his waist. He dropped to his knees, felt his E-suit scrape against metal, and ducked. His helmet hit the rim and came free. He looked around.

"Corvan?"

"Yeah?"

"You okay?"

"Yeah. This is weird."

"What's weird about it?"

"Come see for yourself."

"That's a roger. Here I come."

Corvan got to his feet. He was in a small womb-shaped room. Lights spiraled around the ceiling, strands of what looked like dried-out vegetable matter hung there and there, and his suit was signaling a breathable atmosphere. *Inside* Deimos.

One possible explanation came to mind, but it was *so* weird, *so* strange that it couldn't possibly be true. Could it?

A chill ran down Corvan's spine. What if it was? What if Deimos was a spaceship of some sort? That would mean aliens, a technological treasure trove, and the biggest story ever broken! But where were the little green men if any? Dead, he guessed—a long time ago, judging by the look of things.

Something touched his arm and he almost jumped out of his skin.

"Whoa, big fella. It is I, your loyal companion."

Corvan laughed but it sounded forced. "Glad to hear it. Is this strange or what?"

"It is definitely strange," Redfern said solemnly. "Any signs of Dr B?"

Corvan felt suddenly guilty. He'd been so preoccupied with his surroundings that Dr. B had slipped his mind. He looked around. The floor was covered with bits and pieces of dried-out whatever it was. And there, off to the left, scuff marks were visible where someone had walked through the stuff. Dr. B!

Corvan pointed to the trail. "Look!"

"Yeah," Redfern agreed. "Let's see where it goes."

Corvan led the way. The scuff marks wandered back and forth a bit but generally headed up-slope toward a circular passageway. The reop saw that while Dr. McKeen might have been able to duck-walk through the hole, he'd be forced to crawl.

So, based on the design of the ship's lock, and that of the upcoming passageway, it seemed safe to conclude that the original owners had been shaped like large worms. The thought caused him to look over his shoulder. He saw Redfern but no worms. Good.

Corvan stopped at the passageway and got down on hands and knees. He felt his tank module scrape the top of the tunnel as he moved forward. It was dark inside. The light projected from his helmet wandered back and forth over smooth walls. The reop saw an opening up ahead. Strands of the dried-out seaweed-like material hung down to obscure the room beyond. It brushed over the top of his helmet and back along the sides of his suit. He sensed rather than saw some sort of antechamber and knew that the real room lay beyond that.

Good though the E-suit was, it was bulky and difficult to handle from a kneeling position. The reporter reached out, found something to hang onto, and pulled himself forward. Whatever it was came loose, fell towards him, and hit his chest.

Corvan saw a visor, and beyond that, a screaming face. It followed him down. The thing's eyes bulged, its lips were pulled back to expose bone white teeth, and its mouth gaped horribly open.

Corvan wanted to scream but couldn't find enough air. He was working on it when Redfern appeared over the thing's right shoulder, grabbed the E-suit under the armpits, and pulled. The face disappeared. Corvan rolled over and fought his way to his feet.

Redfern was matter-of-fact as he propped the suit up against the wall and read a name off its chest.

"Well, look what we have here. George Imbulu. One of the two people that disappeared while working outside of Mars Prime. Poor bastard."

"Make that *both* of the people," Corvan added grimly. "Here's number two."

The other suit, a woman's this time, had been off to the right. Light from Corvan's head lamp had been reflected off the high gloss artwork on her chest plate and caught his eye.

A quick examination revealed that her face bore an expression similar to Imbulu's. It wasn't pretty.

"How the hell did they get here?" Redfern asked wonderingly. "And what happened to them?"

"Beats the heck out of me," Corvan replied. "But judging from their expressions it wasn't much fun."

"Look!"

Redfern had aimed his light back into the darkness. Corvan did likewise and saw a pile of junk. There were chunks of loose rock, pieces of pipe, lengths of metal framing, and wait a minute, something the size and shape of an oversized garbage can. Twisted things stuck out from the object's side, things that looked like solar arrays. Solar arrays similar to those found on satellites. And not just any satellite, but the *missing* satellite, unless Corvan missed his guess.

Someone, or something, was stealing things and stashing them away in this underground hoard.

A light appeared out of the darkness. Corvan felt his heart stop then resume beating as a small robot rolled out to greet them. Its voice crackled over the reop's helmet speakers.

"Hello. I am Weld Inspector 47. Due to a processor problem, or other malfunction, I am lost. Please direct me to a Class IV maintenance facility, or call one and have me picked up."

Redfern laughed. "No can do, little buddy. Not right now anyway. Put yourself on standby and we'll deal with you later."

The robot's light snapped out as the machine followed Redfern's orders.

Corvan shook his head in wonderment. "This gets more bizarre every moment."

"That's for sure," Redfern agreed cheerfully. "Come on. Let's see what else this place has in store."

The security officer led the way and Corvan followed. There was no way to tell what Dr. B had thought of the room, or its contents, but her scuff marks led down a slight incline and through another small opening. There were lots of marks now, as if the scientist had come and gone numerous times, dragging things behind her.

Redfern got down on his stomach and crawled. Corvan did likewise. Darkness turned to light as Redfern emerged from the other side and moved out of the way. Seconds later the security officer said "holy cow," in such awed tones that the reop expected to meet one, and static flooded his helmet. Something, a rather powerful electronic something, was very close by.

Corvan pushed his way out of the tunnel, scrambled to his feet, and found Redfern staring upward. It was easy to see why.

The entire ceiling, and the upper portions of the walls as well, were covered with an ever-shifting mosaic of video images. And like a mosaic, the pictures came in a variety of shapes and sizes, all of which were slightly out of focus as though intended for non-human eyes.

Which Corvan reflected, they undoubtedly were.

He saw some other things as well, including four kidney-shaped constructs that hung from the ceiling and some strange harness-like arrangements. There was plenty of the streamer stuff too.

"Look!"

The urgency in Redfern's voice, plus his rigidly pointing arm, caused Corvan to look at a large triangular picture. What he saw amazed and astounded him. It was a full color shot of the Mars Prime mess hall! The room was packed with people, many of whom looked familiar, and they were listening to some sort of speaker. What the—?

But there was no time to consider the picture further because a weak, and almost inaudible, croak managed to make itself heard through the static that rumbled in their ears.

"Hey! Over here! Behind you!"

Both men turned simultaneously and searched for a body to go with the voice. Redfern was the first to see her. He pointed.

"Look! Over there!"

Corvan saw what looked like a pile of scrap metal, and beyond that, a headless E-suit. And that was all he saw for a moment, until he thought to activate the eye cam and zoom in. The geologist sat to the right of her space suit, with her helmet on and one leg propped up on a pile of the dried vegetable matter. Dr B was alive!

It was a race to see who could get there first. Redfern won. He helped the scientist remove her helmet.

"Dr. McKeen I presume?"

"One and the same," the geologist croaked.

"Hey, Doc, what happened to your leg?"

The geologist peered into Corvan's visor. "Corvan?

Is that you? Open your visor for God's sake. You're wasting suit oxygen. And give me a drink. My suit ran dry about twenty-four hours ago.''

The reop opened his visor, pulled two feet of drinking tube out of its storage module, and handed the free end to McKeen. She grabbed it and sucked greedily. Thirty or forty seconds passed before she relinquished the tube and wiped her mouth with the back of one hand.

"Damn. I never would've thought that recycled piss could taste so good."

Corvan chuckled. "You haven't changed a bit."

The scientist grinned. "And neither have you. There isn't another sonovabitch on the planet dumb enough, and stubborn enough, to come find me."

Corvan nodded toward Redfern. "He did."

"And I'm much obliged," McKeen said soberly, "but whose idea was it?"

Corvan grinned. "Mine."

The geologist nodded. "I rest my case. Don't tell me—let me guess. The first search party came, took a look around my camp, and split."

"That's about the size of it," Redfern agreed ruefully.

"Well, you're here, and that's the main thing," McKeen said, "and a good thing, too. We've got trouble."

"No kidding," Corvan responded. "You saw the bodies? And the other stuff?"

"Damned right I did," the geologist answered. "That's how I broke my leg. See those kidney-shaped constructs that hang from the ceiling?"

Corvan glanced upward. "Yeah, they're kind of hard to miss."

"Right. Well, each one of them is a control panel, and the third one over governs the transporter system. I can't prove it, but I think the system was dormant

for hundreds, maybe even thousands of years, until
something triggered it. One of our radio signals, some
radiation, who the hell knows. Then, obeying God
knows what instructions left eons ago, it starts to pluck
samples off the surface of Mars. Some of them human.
I'm not sure what killed them—the trip itself, or pure
undiluted terror.''

The geologist gestured towards her surroundings. ''I
think Deimos is a survey ship, kind of like Darwin's
Beagle, only bigger.

''Anyway, I hauled some of the junk out here, jury-
rigged a scaffold, and climbed up there. My plan was
to find the equivalent of an ignition switch and turn
the damned thing off. It took awhile to figure out the
controls, but I had a pretty good handle on it when the
scaffold collapsed and I fell. I came close to getting
off scot free, but a piece of pipe rode me down, and I
broke my leg. And that cramped my style, to say the
least.''

''You must be hungry,'' Corvan said sympathetically.

''A little,'' the geologist agreed, ''but I've been eat-
ing these. They fill you up and give you one helluva
high at the same time.''

So saying the scientist reached into a pocket of the
suit seated next to her and withdrew something small
and round. She held it up to the light.

Corvan recognized it right away. A berry! Just like
the ones that Sharma handed out! His mind raced. All
sorts of things fell into place.

''Tell me something Dr. B . . . have you seen any
evidence of another ship?''

''Besides Phobos?''

Corvan felt his eyes bulge. ''Phobos? Phobos is a
ship?''

The scientist shrugged and rubbed her injured leg.
''Who knows? Some lucky dog will get to check it

out. But if my guess is right, Phobos is hollow and packed with scientific samples.''

Her entire face lit up. ''Imagine! Samples taken from the other worlds in our solar system, or who knows? From the other side of galaxy!''

Redfern frowned. ''So Phobos is a trailer?''

''Not a bad analogy,'' the scientist said thoughtfully. ''Assuming I'm right, that is. One thing's for sure, though. The mystery of how Mars acquired two moons is solved. They were *parked* rather than captured by a long-vanished atmosphere.''

''That's interesting, Doc, real interesting,'' Corvan said impatiently, ''but *not* what I had in mind. I meant down on the surface. Are there any signs that a shuttle or similar ship landed on Mars itself?''

''I haven't seen anything to support such a hypothesis,'' McKeen replied, ''but I haven't seen anything that would rule it out either.''

She frowned. ''Wait a minute . . . up there . . . towards the right. The rectangular shot. It changes frequently but covers the same locations over and over again. One of the shots looks the same way this room does. I had assumed that it was some other part of Deimos or Phobos, but it could be a video of a third ship.''

''It must be,'' Corvan said firmly. ''And I'll bet you dollars to doughnuts that a guy named Barbu Sharma found it. Not only that, but some berries just like yours, which he used to start his own religion.''

''And speak of the devil,'' Redfern said, ''look up there!''

Corvan looked, and sure enough, there was Sharma in living color. A little out of focus, but still Sharma. It was the same shot he'd noticed before, the one of the mess hall and the throng of people.

Sharma stood on a table top and wore the same anatomically correct E-suit that the reop had seen before. He raised his arms over his head, looked out over the assembled multitude, and mouthed words they couldn't hear.

There were others present as well, lined up to Sharma's left and right, shoulders slumped, and wrists bound with tape. Corvan saw Peko-Evans, Fornos, Jopp, and a woman with black hair, who unlike the others, looked anything but cowed. Her head was held high, her eyes sparkled with anger, and her body was poised for action. Kim!

The picture was worth a thousand words. Sharma had taken control of Mars Prime . . . and his wife, too.

Redfern growled and got to his feet. He'd seen the video and come to the same conclusions.

Corvan gestured toward the ceiling. "The transporter . . . how does it work? Can we control it?"

"I think so," McKeen said cautiously. "Assuming we can reach the control panels. Each picture represents a place where the transporter can reach. The only problem is that while it can reach through the dome and into the mess hall, it can't pull things back out. I think that it was capable of doing so in the past and keeps on trying."

"Which accounts for the fact that the junk, plus both of the people, were snatched from *outside* of Mars Prime," Redfern said thoughtfully.

"Wait a minute," Corvan put in. "You said that while the transporter can reach *into* Mars Prime it can't pull objects *out*. At least not anymore. But it can move things around inside the dome, right?"

The scientist rubbed her leg. "I guess so . . . but I don't see . . ."

Redfern brought his fist down onto the palm of his hand. "I get it! The Ochoa and Wu murders! The transporter system accidentally beat them to death while trying to pull them out through the ceiling!"

"Exactly," Corvan said grimly, "and it deactivated some robots, too."

The reop looked up toward the ceiling. "Wait right there, Sharma baby—have we got a surprise for you!"

chapter twenty

Sharma had talked so long that Kim wondered if he'd ever finish. The man liked the sound of his own voice, that was for sure. Still, judging from the flowery rhetoric, it sounded as though he had begun to wrap things up. Kim shifted her weight from foot to foot and did her best to restore some circulation to her tightly bound wrists.

"And so," Sharma concluded, "it is with a tremendous sense of humility that I accept the mantle of leadership so unexpectedly thrust my way—"

And it was at that exact moment that the miracle took place. Suddenly, and without any warning whatsoever, Sharma was lifted up into the air.

A collective gasp went up from the crowd. There were cries of, "It's a miracle!" and "Praise the great Membu!"

But instead of the beatific expression that many expected to see, Sharma's face went slack with shock and his eyes started to bulge. They watched in shock as their religious leader hung in midair, kicked his legs, and windmilled his arms.

"What's happening? Put me down! Someone help me!"

But before anyone could react, the invisible force that held Sharma aloft did its best to pull him up through the ceiling. His head made a horrible thumping sound each time that it hit. Three such blows were sufficient to render him unconscious.

Then, as if bored with its new-found toy, the force released him. Sharma's body drifted downward, hit the salad bar, and cartwheeled away. A medic chased it down, found that it had gone into cardio-pulmonary arrest, and started CPR.

A long silence descended over the hall.

Kim looked around, saw the shocked expressions, and held out her wrists to a man with a likeness of Mickey Mouse painted on his chest.

"Cut me loose. I have work to do."

So the man did, and others did likewise, until all of the prisoners had been freed.

That was when Peko-Evans climbed up on a table, ordered everyone to surrender their weapons, and suggested a return to work. Much to her surprise most of them did as they were told.

There would be an investigation, followed by consequences for those who had taken part in the fighting, but that could wait. The dome's security cams had captured who did what to whom, and all of them could be rounded up with very little difficulty. No, the most important thing to do right now was to disperse the crow and let emotions cool.

Peko-Evans climbed down from the table. Kim passed nearby. The administrator touched her arm. The editor stopped.

"Yes?"

Peko-Evans gestured towards Sharma. The CPR had been successful. Medics were loading him on an auto stretcher. "What happened? Do you know?"

Kim looked at Sharma and shook her head. "Nope, but this should make one helluva news story."

* * *

The bed was surprisingly comfortable, in spite of the fact that it was a makeshift affair, put together in the back of a crawler. It was cold, even with the heaters on, so Kim snuggled deeper under the covers. She ran a hand over her husband's stomach.

"We could get dressed. It would be warmer that way."

"But not as much fun," Corvan answered lazily. "Besides, Scheeler said we could have the crawler until morning."

Kim nodded. Someone had killed the woman with the mace a fraction of a second after her weapon made contact with Scheeler's helmet.

So, while three of the metal rods had punched their way through the helmet's outer surface, they remained in place, plugging the holes they had made.

That, plus the semi-liquid sealer sandwiched into the helmet's construction, had saved Scheeler's life. She was up and around now, as was Sharma, though under widely differing circumstances. The security chief was back at work and the religious leader was awaiting trial for armed insurrection and murder.

The crawler, and the opportunity to get away from Mars Prime, was the security officer's way of saying thank you for the help that both the Corvans had given her.

Corvan gloried in the feel of his wife's smooth flesh, the warmth of the blankets, and his exotic surroundings.

There was a skylight above him, rimmed with ice crystals and filled with diamond-bright stars. Deimos crept into view and the reop smiled.

"ALIEN MOON-SHIP FOUND OFF MARS!" "MARS REVOLT FAILS!" "ALIEN TECHNOLOGY TO JUMP-START PROGRAM EXODUS!" Headlines like those had dominated the Earth-nets for days now, but only he and a few others knew how easily things could have gone the other way.

The challenge had been to incapacitate Sharma before he could leave the mess hall and disappear into the 99% of Mars Prime that Corvan couldn't see. McKeen believed that the transporter beam could be moved to focus on any part of the habitat, but the methodology was far from clear, so they couldn't be sure that it would work.

That meant time was critical. Corvan knew Sharma would be gone by the time he and Redfern built a second scaffolding. And that's where the robo cam came into play.

The reop had reestablished his link to the camera, caused it to hover in front of the correct control panel, and used its manipulator arms to operate the controls.

Dr. B provided instructions and watched the ceiling video to judge the effect of her words. The arrangement had worked rather well, as evidenced by the condition of Sharma's head.

The fact that Corvan had recorded the whole episode and sent it to Earth hadn't hurt either. The furor, plus the confirmation of extra-terrestrial life, plus the infusion of technology, had given the Mars program a huge boost.

In the meantime Corvan had been given a seat on the executive council, Dr. B was hobbling around on crutches and making a nuisance of herself, Sharma was locked up, and everyone was awaiting an independent investigator from Earth.

An investigator who would arrive accompanied by a small army of specially equipped scientists.

It would be their job to dissect the alien ships, find out what was inside the sealed casings, and answer some critical questions: Could the transporter system be repaired and duplicated? Did the berries have medical applications? And perhaps most fascinating of all, did the aliens have a faster-than-light drive? The questions were endless.

And that, Corvan thought to himself, is every reop's dream. Endless questions with fascinating answers.

Kim did something with her hand and got the predictable response. Flesh encountered flesh, words were exchanged, and the stars winked above.

Author's Note

It seems to me that every science fiction author worth his or her salt must eventually write a Mars novel.

This stems from the fact that Mars is relatively close to Earth, is well studied, and would be a relatively nice place to live (compared to Venus, for example).

Never mind the fact that a zillion such books have already been written, or that most (including this one) incorporate common plot elements—that's what makes them fun!

Mars novels are a genre in and of themselves in which colonies struggle against all odds and aliens lurk around every corner. Or, in the case of alternate universe novels, where entire tribes of barbarians roam the plains.

Mars Prime was written in that spirit, and if it has any value beyond that of entertainment, is intended to point out some of the problems that real journalists may encounter someday.

I was a journalist once. I wish them luck.